THE MEMORY HOUSE

A Love Story in Two Acts

JENETTA JAMES

Quills & Quartos
PUBLISHING

Edited by Christina Boyd and Lisa Sieck

Cover by Cloud Cat Design

ISBN : 978-1-951033-49-1 (ebook) and 978-1-951033-99-6 (paperback)

THE DOOR

The promise was made upon her head,
in the golden hour.
Like light on lawn and sunset red,
and in her hand a flower.

That flower called her from the garden,
Gave strength her hands, and feet to step.
And in its fervour, sought no pardon,
But treasured, loved, her soul to le'p.

For she had seen the curtain sway,
in the years before.
Th'unseeing stale moved away,
Gone chains, gone dim cruel law.

Her faith in it had stood the test,
had grasped, had clung, had fed with
     cheer.
Back turned on succour and on rest,
her heart, a mighty beast to rear.

Thus she had seen, but would she know,
the day, the hour, the moment come?
The beginning of the end of woe,
the cue to face th'embazoned sun.

Tis dark within the memory house,
but the promise sears without.
That door which stands ajar must close,
The gnarled and deadened wood, repose.

For, the promise was made upon her head,
in the golden hour.
She saw the glimpse, heard what was said,
and never feared love's power.

— ETHEL TURNER EVERETT
(1858)

PROLOGUE

There was no light, so she felt her way. She could not risk a candle. A fresh one—far too bright; a gutted one—wild, unreliable. And it would have left a smell, the memory of a burning. A trail for any person to find. No. She could manage without and still do all that must be done.

Trembling hands moved along polished walnut, Chantilly lace, a rounded glass with yesterday's water. Indistinct shapes and sharp edges alike, cloaked in a moonless black. Furnishings loomed tall and indistinct. The air smelt of rose water, but it was not sweet. It put her in mind of fruit that had gone bad: softened, sickened, died. Lucky that she knew her way, for the quicker the night was over, then the morn would come. She moved. Her leather-shod feet slipped suddenly on the thick pile of the carpet, and she gasped. A whimper, almost inaudible. But terror was creeping into her heart like smoke under a door. Straightening herself, she inhaled deeply, calming herself by force of will. Old resolutions rallied and her mind sharpened. Be steady, be quick, be gone.

In the distance, a door opened; voices rumbled.

She strode across the room and crouched down, soundlessly. Nimble fingers worked at the lock, which had always been tricky, eccentric. It had a knack. The tiny clicks sounded like roars, like engines firing up, but that was unavoidable. And she knew that she exaggerated it, for fear made monsters of all. The lock turned. As the box opened, it creaked. Swiftly, she loaded the contents into the bag at her side. It would be heavy, but she was strong. Nearly there, almost complete. She pictured herself gliding through the streets like a phantom. The risks she knew, and the sacrifices too. But it was worth it. For friendship, for loyalty, for love.

Somewhere, a dog barked.

She held her breath to listen, but nothing came. A bead of sweat began on her back. It snaked down her. Her cloak was itchy against her neck. And too hot as well. Although the fire in the grate had burned down, the heat had not gone. A deep orange glow winked across the room, the scent of wood smoke. She stood jerkily, pulling up the bag. It dug into her shoulder, unbalanced her.

About to depart, a thought came. She had not locked the box. It would be the work of a moment, over in a trice. The sort of task which there was no merit in leaving undone. It would not do for this room to appear disarranged, invaded. What questions would then be asked? Why cause more strife when there was trouble enough? So, like a cat, she crept back and knelt on the floor to attend to it. Her hand was perspiring, wet, slippery as a fish. Close, lock, turn.

Footsteps on the stair, a cough, and then closer.

As the door opened, she gagged on her own breath. A welling horror seized her. Movement was impossible, escape unthinkable. She knew her only chance was the darkness. Silence gave way to heavy breathing. It was not hers. Breaking through the air like an axe hacking. Nobody knew she was here—or they should not. She had taken such care not to be seen, not to confide. Kept herself closed like a cupboard. Like a locket with a secret inside. But by some mischance, some error of plot, here she was, snared. It could not be. Her wretched mind raced, memory tripping over hopes, plans, things which may have been. Her body coiled, ready to burst.

A clatter of porcelain; an object fell, breaking, scattering. Inside her, a scream rose, and her heart thudded. She turned, to see a flash of terrible movement. She let out a cry, but it was not as loud as her own pain, could not be. Her head exploded. She moved savagely, crawling along the carpet, coughing, choking. She tried to stand. Suddenly, there were all colours, spiralling, sparking, even white. And sound too, a great deafening cacophony. Noise that moved the very floor under her feet, juddered the bones of her being. Her mouth was full of hot wetness and her body, fighting, began to break. It fell. Thereafter, everything was black.

The last word that she heard was 'whore'.

I

KITTY

MARCH 1859

WHEN LIFE GREW VEXING, MISS KITTY CATHCART IMAGINED her world from the air. Her eyes would flutter closed, and she, lady of fashion, object of glances, keeper of secrets, would be elevated. Suddenly, she would look down upon her life and see it differently. As though it were far off, flickering, vanishingly small.

So it was, one Tuesday evening, at the beginning of the Season.

Kitty was a vision in blush silk, duck egg piping at the seams, delicate lace around creamy shoulders. Hers was a fine gown, the best. Tiny waist, expansive skirt. Her blonde hair had been coiled to her head, like spun gold. She was a shape that might have been blown in glass: fine, extravagant, masterful. People looked at her, of course. Stray eyes would glide and linger. She was accustomed to such attentions. That day, Kensington chattered with cold and crocuses peeked into the frozen air. The grand houses of Veronica Gardens stood white and then grey against the darkening sky. When they were built, men had called them brash, excessive. Then, they had grown used to them. Palaces to house rich men were part and parcel of the modern world, after all. It was now the middle of the century and Kitty was twenty-three. She straightened the ribbons of her bonnet to the sound of her father's heavy step thudding down the stairs. Servants began to stir, to open doors, to ready cloaks.

And in her imaginings, she soared, escaped, broke free. It was a game that she played with herself. She and her father would appear like balls, marbles, pinpricks even. Rolling out of their grand home, down the steps, and into the waiting carriage. Doors clicked closed but from the air, one could hardly hear. Wheels ached into life, dredging water, straw, muck. The polished roof getting smaller and smaller, the boy on the back too. She could feel far away from herself, a spectator to her own life. The house, 50 Veronica Gardens, together with the little church standing opposite, became like a speck on a great blank canvas. And before long, Kitty could not see herself at all. From a distance, she might be gone.

Inevitably, such whimsy could not continue.

Sir Roland settled himself on his seat in the carriage, muttering and smarting at some fancied offence of a business associate. Kitty had not been listening. She raised her eyebrows in silence, for she knew the narrative well enough. Her father's tale was a tale of generation. Of empire. Name and fortune built brick by hard-won brick. It was a story of wealth heaped on riches, piled on plenty, and still he found no succour in it. The carriage quivered as Rivers mounted his seat above them; he cracked his whip and they were off.

Barrelling through the streets in unlit luxury, they regarded one another. The sight of her father's form, finely attired, swaying, reminded Kitty of the previous year's Season. Of course, it had not all been disagreeable. Being in town rather than in Yorkshire had enabled her to pursue her plan, to make progress, and that was a blessing indeed. But against that, she had only narrowly escaped being forced into matrimony with any number of candidates championed by Sir Roland, not one of them pleasing to her. Their dealings with her father, she could not vouch for. They were, as her maid, Violet Springer, had remarked in an unguarded moment, 'like rats in a bag.' Kitty smiled, for she knew it was true.

Sir Roland shook his fist as he spoke.

"Well, if he thinks I shall stand idly by and be swindled, he is in for a shock. E'god! Brindle is a fool and a scoundrel."

Sir Roland's nostrils flared at this pronouncement, and Kitty stifled her smile. Mr Brindle, a mainstay of the monologue that passed for conversation in the Cathcart household, was a former business associate of Sir Roland. They had met as young men in trade, Sir Roland as a manufacturer of engines and Brindle as a youthful and brilliant engineer. After a period of symbiosis, their two personalities had clashed, and for some years now, they had been locked in a costly conflict conducted by way of their lawyers. Mr Brindle was discussed often and at length. Frock-coated agents came and went from Veronica Gardens when Sir Roland was in town and even visited Longhaven, glancing at Kitty's form as she drifted past their tired eyes.

In the carriage, Kitty took a deep breath. The thought of another Brindle lecture made her ache. She made a bid to forestall him.

"How goes your new factory, Papa?"

Sir Roland looked alarmed by the question.

"It is in profit, Kitty, and that is the material point."

He stopped short, and she stopped too. Kitty had that gift of always being able to converse with her fellow man, always being able to tease out a tale. But not with her father. They were as closed off from one another as two people ever were. A gloom descended over her, and she looked away.

"Smile, girl. E'god. You have enough to smile about."

Kitty, who had been watching the street whittling by out of the window, turned her face to Sir Roland and did as he bade.

"Aye, Papa. I am blessed, indeed, with a loving family whose company this evening I am much anticipating."

He smirked. He was as unmoved by his daughter's beauty as he was tired of her cheek.

"Loving family indeed. You are blessed with youth and riches and good looks. You will do well to use them to your advantage, and mine. Your wilfulness and fixed opinions, you can keep to yourself."

"I do not know what you mean, sir."

"You inherit it from your mother. Well, this evening I wish to see my only child smiling and laughing gracefully. You will behave, Kitty. If you are asked to play, you will employ your talents and damned well play. When you are spoken to, you will listen. And when you speak, you shall display the conversational charms I have paid for in heavy coin, and nothing more."

"I love to play, Papa. I would not dream of declining. Although my skill does not compare to Philomena's. As for listening, I have listened to you all my life, have I not? Most conscientiously."

"Hmm. Good. We need to find you a husband. You are nearly four and twenty. This charade of your resistance has gone on long enough. With my money and your mother's lineage, you are a fine prospect. It is your duty to me to play your role. You will do your part of the performance, Kitty, or there will be consequences."

Kitty straightened her back against the velvet cushion of the carriage bench. She recalled, as she knew he did, the events of the previous year. How she had conspired never to be out of the company of her cousins. How she had evaded a dozen rich men with leering eyes and bursting girths standing beside her father. Danced with men of little fortune or none. Befriended the unimportant. The same the year before.

"I thought we were to Aunt Margaret's this evening, Papa, for a quiet musical evening with family and some friends. That is what she said when she called last week to invite us, I am sure. If I thought I were attending a reception with the Prince of Wales, then I would have dressed the part. And I would be looking forward to it less."

Sir Roland exhaled loudly and fumbled with his pocket watch.

"If I could get you under the nose of the Prince of Wales, I damned well would." A mirthless amusement danced across his face, and Kitty blanched. "Your aunt Margaret has invited more people than you think. Neighbours, odd young men known to George. Neither use nor decoration, most of them. My solicitor, Haworth, of all men, who is also retained by your aunt is expected. There shall be other guests, far more important. In particular, you shall meet Lord Trefusis. He is a gentleman whom you would do

9

well to impress. He is a man of standing, a man of means. Unmarried."

She felt rather than saw his eyes fix upon her like pins.

"Widowed?"

"Yes, but that should concern you naught. His marriage was childless. I understand his estate in Cornwall to be vast and grand. Beautiful, if one cares for such things."

Kitty shuddered.

"And far away from Longhaven and from London. But maybe that is why it appeals to you, Papa?"

"Maybe it is."

Their bodies jolted as the carriage came to a halt outside the home of Mrs Margaret Christie. Neither wishing to linger with the other, Sir Roland and his daughter quit the questionable comforts of the carriage and proceeded up the wrought iron framed steps and into the home of her only living relations. Immediately, the atmosphere in Kitty's mind changed for the better. She entered the familiar entrance hall as though it were her own. Cloaks were removed, greetings exchanged, and heels clicked along tiled corridors until the door to the drawing room was opened before them, and they joined the hubbub of the party.

Kitty's eyes alighted on the friendly form of her cousin George Christie in conversation with a lady. They spoke animatedly, hands waving, and Kitty wondered what they could be saying. George was so flustered around ladies, so naive as to his own attractions. Her other cousin and George's sister, Philomena, was playing the piano gently from the corner of the room. Guests collected around the instrument, without appearing to see her. She nodded to her cousin and almost imperceptibly, their eyes met. Kitty continued to scan the room. Friends, neighbours, associates, a couple of new faces. She recalled her father's mention of Lord Trefusis but wilfully forgot it.

The lady of the house, observing her niece from across the room, advanced upon her, smiling broadly and clutching a tiny fan. Beside her was a sensible looking man of middling years, whom Kitty had never seen before.

"My dear Kitty. How well you look this evening."

Her aunt stroked her gloved arm.

"Aunt Margaret."

They bobbed curtseys to one another and inclined their heads in greeting. The man smiled politely and looked about him as if poised on the edge of speech.

"Mr Haworth, I believe you are acquainted with my brother, Sir Roland Cathcart. May I present my niece, Miss Catherine Cathcart. Kitty, this is Mr Haworth, who is our solicitor of many years and our friend. Kitty is the image of her late lamented mama, my sister, and quite the jewel of the family, are you not, my dear?"

Aunt Margaret twitched her fan, apparently ignoring her own daughter (very pretty and, more significantly, intelligent and agreeable) on the other side of the room. Kitty, who was used to her aunt's well-meant silliness, smiled and greeted the gentleman who responded with perfect manners and no unruly or unwelcome glances.

"I could not claim such a thing, Aunt. It is a pleasure to meet you, Mr Haworth. Do you reside in town?"

"Yes, I do, Miss Cathcart. Mrs Haworth and I live in Battersea. My office is in Fleet Street. I am somewhat of a visitor to this very gracious part of London but a jolly thankful one. It is an honour to be included. That is not a cordiality extended often to a humble solicitor—"

"Is it not? Well, maybe it should be, sir. I believe that you are retained by my father, as well as my aunt, so I suspect you have more than earned your invitation this evening." She looked at him, keenly, and for a thinly sliced moment, they understood one another perfectly.

"I have had the honour of serving Sir Roland for many years, yes. It is, how shall I say, a continuing education."

His eyes, which Kitty had noticed hid a subtle kind of twinkle, flashed up as George, handsome and well-dressed, strode confidently towards them, accompanied by another.

"Cousin Kitty." He bowed, laughing slightly, and squeezed Kitty's hand as a brother might do. "I see you have been introduced to Haworth. Let me present to you his protégé, and my friend, Mr Faraday."

Kitty glanced to the tall figure beside her cousin and made the polite and charming greeting that she made to every new person who crossed her path. Her eyes rested on the square line of his shoulder beneath his frock coat and, as he rose from his bow, the flash of his blue eyes assailed her, unexpectedly. He was not like George's other friends.

She turned to Mr Haworth.

"Have you been introduced to my cousin, Mr Christie, sir? George Christie is, I like to tell people, my most favoured male cousin. He knows, of course, that it is no compliment, for he is in a constituency of one. It is, you see, just we three. George, his sister, Philomena, whom you see at the pianoforte, and me. Mrs Christie, who is their mama, was the only sister of my late mama..."

Kitty fingered the cool edges of her cameo.

"And so, Mr Haworth, Mr...Faraday, we are small in number, but we are formidable in combination, are we not, Cousin?"

She looked to George, who nodded and began singing the praises of cousin and sister alike. Mr Faraday, Kitty observed, said nothing and moved not an inch. He looked at her, with no obvious feeling, as though he were observing a change in the weather. It was a new sensation. Kitty liked to be admired, but she could not abide being considered. She realised with a start that George was addressing her, but she had not been paying attention.

"Kitty, dear? I said Faraday here was up at Cambridge with me. Classics, subject of kings, eh, Faraday? Feels like a lifetime ago now, mind you." George continued to natter of acquaintances past, of heady conversations with young men over buttered crumpets, of punting expeditions, and the free-flowing wine of the college table. Kitty chanced a glance at his friend's face. She saw something there that she could not place. Was it anger or resentment? Hardness certainly—and an unwillingness to be drawn.

"Couldn't believe it when I saw him standing there with old Haworth in our drawing room. Last man I expected to see in my own house. You could have knocked me down. Jolly glad though. It's been far too long, what?" George looked to his friend whose expression softened. He smiled in agreement.

"Indeed, it has, Christie. I recalled the name, of course, but I did not realise it would be you. Mr Haworth simply informed me that we were to the home of Mrs Christie who is a long-standing client of the firm. I had no idea that it was to be a reunion."

"Firm?" Kitty's eyes darted between Mr Haworth and Mr Faraday. She noted the expensive appearance of the latter's frock coat and his tall, proud bearing. If he had been a friend of George's up at Cambridge and now found himself in work at a firm of solicitors, then she speculated that thereby hung a tale. Kitty enjoyed tales.

Mr Faraday himself answered her. "Haworth & Gates, solicitors, Miss Cathcart. I have the honour of being articled to Mr Haworth." With that he looked at her. His gaze did not waver. "Many of my friends from Cambridge are young men of property, rich in family connexions. Alas, I have not that advantage and so, there you have it. I must shift for myself. I trust that you do not disapprove, Miss Cathcart?"

The question startled her; it was so direct and unbending. It was not a polite question to put to a young lady in company, yet he did so without appearing to do wrong. She had met men such as Mr Faraday before. Educated young men who wore their learning like a weapon and regarded her sex and privileges with disdain. How they would be surprised if they knew the truth about her! Kitty wanted to say something clever and sting him back, but she was momentarily stopped. She had not been disapproving; she had been wondering. Contrition swept over her, combined with irritation at having been misunderstood.

"No, of course not."

Kitty turned away to her aunt Margaret who had, just at that moment, spoken to her and begun to fiddle with the lace of her sleeve. She prattled and her little hands waved about before her niece's eyes. For her own part, Kitty strained to hear the conversation that passed between her cousin and Mr Faraday.

"My cousin is not one to disapprove of anyone. She is as generous of judgment as she is of spirit. She will exchange words with any person, high or low, and she shall always spare them a laugh and a good wish. It is her way. She sparkles and flares and does not have an unkind word for any person. There is one condition though."

"And what is that?" Faraday asked the question. Kitty startled, out of sight.

"Adoration. Kitty must be adored by all who know her. If you don't adore her, I'm afraid that she does not know how to deal with you."

Dash George for speaking of her so openly and so slanderously. And to an outsider too! Mr Faraday did not answer.

Sir Roland had separated from Kitty the moment they entered the saloon, and in her joy at seeing her family, she had paid scant attention to his whereabouts. He had a way of moving about quietly and of suddenly being present when one least expected it. Such a moment then took place as he approached his only child in the company of another gentleman—younger maybe than he, older, certainly, than Kitty. She knew from the set of her father's expression that he was making for her.

"Kitty, my dear," he said, the words seeming to stick in his throat, "may I introduce Lord Trefusis. Trefusis, this is my daughter, Catherine, heiress to the Cathcart empire, you might say."

"Miss Catherine." He bowed with an effort and Kitty noted that his collar was somewhat dusty.

"My lord"—she curtseyed low—"it is a pleasure to make your acquaintance."

As she rose, her eyes alighted, not on Lord Trefusis, but on another. Over his shoulder, some way across the room, there was Mr Faraday. Like charcoal drawn on oils, out of place. He turned slightly, from his conversation with George and another gentleman and Kitty caught his eye. Rapidly, she returned her attention to her father's friend.

"I hear, my lord, that you are a native of Cornwall. Is that not the case? I have heard such wonders of the place. People say that it is quite another country."

"It is, Miss Catherine, it is. But I must say that the pleasures of town are not to be underestimated. Particularly with acquaintances such as yours to be made, eh? Were I guaranteed such company in London each evening, heaven knows, I should never return to the countryside." He smiled, appearing to expect some manner of response to this speech.

Kitty was not to be left speechless.

"Gosh, you flatter me, my lord. In any case, I should guard against the false pleasures of town if I were you. It is exciting, to be sure, and there are so many people to meet and places to go. However much I enjoy London, I find that it is the country where I feel most at home. My father's estate is in Yorkshire, and I could well forgo the attractions of the city for its advantages."

"My daughter has a gift for being at home in town and the countryside, my lord. She can make herself comfortable in any place. It is one of her most excellent skills."

"Do you take pleasure in the theatre, Miss Cathcart?" He did not wait for her to answer. "For if you do, I propose that you and your honoured father accompany me to Drury Lane this very week. It would be just the thing to enthral you, eh?"

"I thank you, my lord, for the invitation. I shall have to check with my father and my aunt—"

"I can't imagine that either of them would object, Miss Cathcart, although I know that Sir Roland is not a lover of the theatre himself. I'll wager that he will be in support of this particular visit." He nudged her with a stiff elbow. "As for Mrs Christie, does she command your own movements as well as her own?"

"No, my lord. But she takes a great interest in me, I am pleased to say. And when we are in town, I am much in her company, and that of my cousins." Kitty looked around the room. *Where is George? Where is Philomena?*

"Well, I daresay that they may come along as well. I am not a man to deny the pleasures of others. All who wish to may attend. Come one, come all. Let us be a large party. But I must ask the honour of sitting beside you, Miss Cathcart. I must ask that—"

"Did somebody say the theatre?" George's cheery voice sang out from behind Kitty, like a bird in the morning. She was glad indeed. What a brick he could be. She forgave him his earlier trespass and wished for nothing more than to kiss his cherubic face.

"I say, I do love the theatre."

Lord Trefusis blinked and paused before announcing that Mr

Christie must join the party. His lordship was then accosted by another gentleman and the unhappy exchange was at an end. Kitty released a breath, knowing that she should be well protected in the company of her cousin.

No doubt he believed her out of earshot when he turned to Mr Faraday and remarked: "Poor, Kitty. She cannot run forever. My uncle shall have her married to wealth and lineage if it is his last act. It is the great determination of his life." But Kitty had heard and blanched. She turned to her cousin and raised an eyebrow in challenge.

"You should not listen to gossip, Mr Faraday. It is a pale shadow of truth. And in any event, it is no real entertainment." She tapped her finger lightly on George's arm, and an idea came to her. "I believe we should have some dancing."

She turned and moved towards the pianoforte.

"Philomena, may we have a reel?"

And that was how it was. Kitty commanded the furniture be moved back and the company take partners, and all began to dance. She knew her aunt would not mind and, indeed, that lady smiled proudly on the whole proceeding. Kitty danced with George twice and with others. A neighbour who grasped her arm for longer than was polite. And a boy who had once asked for her hand but had had to settle for friendship. It being impossible to politely refuse, she danced with Lord Trefusis, but he became somewhat breathless, and it was a relief when the set concluded. Then she danced with George again. They passed one another arm to arm and grasped hands, weaving about like two strings of yarn.

"Don't take umbrage, old thing. I trust Faraday. No need to worry that he will pass things on." George's tone was contrite.

"Say no more about it, dear. I am sure you are right." They moved back and then together. "And anyway, he can pass on what he chooses."

George squeezed her hand and gave her a wink. She laughed, gaiety coursing through her, lightening her mood. Mr Faraday, she observed, kept to the edge of the room. She rather hoped he might ask her to dance, but rather surprisingly, he did not. Instead, his expressionless face appeared and reappeared as she danced with other men.

Kitty forced herself to look away from the inscrutable Mr Faraday and found her eyes resting upon her neglected cousin. At the end of the dance, she declined several requests in favour of sitting beside Philomena on the narrow piano bench.

"May I turn your pages?"

"I don't have pages, Kitty dear. When it comes to reels, memory is the thing."

Philomena spared her cousin a smile before turning back to the keyboard.

"Do you need anything? A shawl."

"Certainly not. I am dreadfully warm with that fire and all this thumping about."

"Do you need me to play while you rest?"

"No."

"There is no need to be quite so definite on the subject. My pride shall be wounded."

Philomena completed the stanza before answering. "Your pride is quite capable of withstanding my plain speaking, is it not?"

"I suppose it is. Know thyself and all that." There was a pause. "Is your hair different?" Kitty tried to study it without appearing to do so.

"Smithers did it. Aided and abetted by Mother. Who will be disappointed by the way—that I have played all evening rather than set about husband-catching."

Kitty laughed lightly. "Shall I go and placate her?"

"No. Sit beside me. We can gossip and call it musical collaboration. How is that?" Philomena shifted slightly on the bench, making room for her cousin and the two ladies giggled in conspiracy.

"Perfect."

Kitty ignored the stony face of her father glowering at her from across the room.

LATER, THE COLD NIGHT AIR BIT AGAINST KITTY'S SKIN AS SHE

alighted the carriage in Veronica Gardens. At once exhausted and invigorated, she sped up the stone steps to the great front door of number 50. It opened like a trap. Sir Roland, she heard muttering behind her. She did not turn her head as he spoke. Homecomings were always difficult.

Inside, butter yellow candlelight flickered against the walls of the hall and shadows crept on the wide staircase. Assembled were Havers, the butler, and footman Albert. Kitty shot them expansive smiles each. Both men hovering, eyes darting, calculating, wondering. Havers stepped forward and assisted Kitty with the removal of her cloak.

"Thank you, Havers."

He nodded in the darkness and Kitty noted the careful, almost reverent, manner he held her garment.

The hall clock struck the hour and a brassy clanging thrummed through the yawning chasm of the house. Sir Roland passed his top hat to Albert and looked to Kitty, opening his mouth to speak. She turned sharply towards the wide staircase.

"I'm terribly fatigued, Papa." She yawned and stroked her cameo again. "I think I shall to bed. I've had such an agreeable evening. Goodnight, Papa."

She ascended the stairs without looking back.

As Kitty stepped into her chambers, Violet shut the door behind her with a heavy, certain clunk. Kitty discarded her gloves on the bed.

"You need not have waited up so late, Violet."

Kitty looked about her to the dimly lit familiarity of the place. In the grate, the fire burned a sort of titian gold. The rich-textured curtains puddled on the carpeted floor beneath the windows. She felt an urge to sweep them back and consider the street and the little church (*her* church as she thought of it) with its tiny yard of weathered gravestones and early spring flowers. She longed for the cold air of the night on her face, for movement, for the outdoors.

"It is no trouble, Miss Cathcart. I like to hang your gown directly you take it off. Have you had a pleasant evening, miss?" enquired Violet, her fingers busy unfastening her mistress's bodice.

Kitty sighed.

"A little odd. I felt...rather unsettled. But—I cannot quite say, Violet. Pleasant to see my aunt and George and Philomena."

"They are well, I hope?"

"They are the same as ever. Philomena played beautifully and was seldom complimented. Smithers has done something odd to her hair. George chattered and was as agreeable as he always is. My aunt was an excellent hostess. She smiles at all the correct moments, but I cannot say how much she really hears."

Violet straightened to her full height and gently took the gown over Kitty's head. Her eyes paused for a moment on a small stain near the hem that she strained to examine in the flickering light. Some splash of wine from a reckless acquaintance, more than likely. Violet placed the gown on the chaise, no doubt planning to clean and press it at some spare moment.

"And others? Was the party well attended, miss?"

"It was. There were a number of George and Philomena's particular friends. New people too."

The notion of mentioning Mr Faraday played around Kitty's mind. The thought was water; it ran through her fingers before she could measure it. No. Mr Faraday was a man of no significance to her, and she need not give an account of him to Violet.

"My father insisted on introducing me to a Lord Trefusis, and I believe we shall be obliged to attend the theatre with him in the near future."

"Very nice, miss."

"Well, you may not think that if you had met him."

Her gown removed, Kitty sat at her vanity and the two women exchanged smiles in the glass.

"Indeed? Doesn't he have much to recommend him?"

"He has nothing to recommend to me. He is old, but he is not ancient. He is not handsome, but his appearance is by no means damning. In his manner, he is somewhat lascivious, which I do not welcome. I believe I detected a rather odd smell but cannot be certain that it was him."

Their eyes met in the glass again as Violet released the pins from her mistress's long blonde hair and they laughed. Loud, loose, guileless laughter. Released, Kitty's hair tumbled freely about her shoulders.

The fire crackled. A worm of worry coiled in Kitty's mind.

"Gosh. It is as well to laugh on it, but how long can it go on? I am more convinced than ever that the selection of a husband for me by my father is a doomed enterprise. For we both know that between us two, there is not one shred of sympathy. How can he even begin to find the gentleman to secure my future happiness? It is quite hopeless. The Christies do what they can for me, but I do believe that they grow weary of this game of cat and mouse. My aunt has advised me to turn my mind to marriage and try to find the best in Papa's plans."

She looked to Violet who tilted her head in an indication of sympathy. Over her shoulder, the gas light in the street outside shone through a tiny gap in the curtains. Kitty had a sudden far away feeling, as though she were floating on air or running through the streets in her nightgown, bound for another world. In her head, the weather was balmy not bone-chilling cold and no part of her was afraid of the unknown.

"Possibly there is some wisdom in that, miss?" Violet's voice brought her back to reality. "If only Sir Roland could find a gentleman who was agreeable to you as well as satisfactory to him, would that not be acceptable?"

"Maybe, dear Violet."

She cast her maid a sceptical look. A rumble and a bang from below announced that the servants were bolting the front door against the night.

❧ 2 ❧

JOSIE

FEBRUARY 2018

It was not the first time in her life that Josie Minton had sat in the window of a busy café with a black coffee and a copy of *The Lady* open at the 'Situations Vacant' page. Her legs were crossed in a strained tangle under the rickety chair. Outside, a dirty red bus whooshed past and splashed a muddy puddle over the pavement. *Concentrate, Josie.* Against all the forces of inclination and habit, she had left her Kindle beside her bed. She just *had* to sort this out. It could not be put off any longer. With that thought, she crossed her arms and trained her eyes on the page:

> Full time Nanny wanted for 3 girls aged 4, 6 & 10 in Henley with some travel. Horse experience desired.

Please God, no. Josie pictured herself trudging around muddy fields in the driving rain and smelling of soggy equine.

> Nanny/Housekeeper wanted in Chiswick for vegan family with boys aged 3 and 5. French speaker preferred.

Let's not and say we did, as an old boss of hers once said. There were some other positions, scattered across the home counties, all of them hinting at the little quirks and unreasonable dogmas of the families in question. Josie knew that she would probably at least enquire about all of them, because however dreadful they looked on paper, you never quite knew until you spoke to them. Once you have heard a person's voice and listened to how they talk about their kids, you are better placed to know whether they are offering a potentially happy position or a Mandalay-style nightmare, which you will need to find an excuse to leave as soon as possible. Or at least you can hope.

Experienced Nanny wanted for twin girls aged 2 years in South Ken/SW7. Please telephone Cavendish on London 463 2288.

Josie took a sip of her coffee and watched the bustle of the street. It was satisfying to sit back and think of all the lives rushing about, of the imperfect rage of activity that was life in the City. Something about it made her feel alive, as though she was part of something bigger than herself. She did not want to be driving around B roads of the home counties in someone else's four-by-four.

With that thought, she took out her mobile and called the number.

"Hello. Have I reached Mrs Cavendish?"

"Speaking," said a posh, shrill female voice. Josie held the phone slightly away from her ear.

"Erm, hello. My name is Josie Minton, and I have seen your advertisement in *The Lady*." The words she wanted to get out suddenly dissipated. They were sucked up. Mangled. It wasn't the first time that had happened to her either. "I was wondering...well, I was wondering about how I might apply."

"Can you tell me anything about yourself, Miss Minton? Are you currently working as a nanny, for example?"

"Yes, yes, of course, you want to know that. I should have said... I am currently nanny to three little girls in Notting Hill. I have been with them for four years—" Josie stopped short. She knew that she should make it clear that she needed another job because the Petersons were moving abroad rather than they had given her the boot. But they were her friends and it felt wrong to start publishing their circumstances to a perfect stranger. Especially a stranger with a voice like a dagger.

"How old are the girls, Miss Minton?"

"They are three-year-old twins and the elder one is seven."

"So, you cared for the twins from babies then?"

"Yes, I joined the family when Mrs Peterson was expecting." With her mind's eye, Josie saw the twins' faces and was overwhelmed with sadness. She was somewhere far away when she became aware that Mrs Cavendish had started talking again.

"So how many years' experience did you have before this family, Miss Minton?"

"Erm, well, I took my first nannying job in 2008, so I suppose that it has been ten years now." Josie thought of all the time and a heaviness settled in her stomach. There was a brief silence in which she was not sure whether Mrs Cavendish expected her to elaborate. If she did, then she must have given up in disappointment.

"Okay. Well, thank you for calling, Miss Minton. You sound sane so could I ask you to send me a CV and covering letter, please? I'll give you my email address. Would that be all right?" She did not wait for an answer. "I asked in the advertisement to be rung first as I wanted to stop silly young women who have no experience from applying. I didn't want to be deluged. But you sound reasonable and as though you at least have some idea, so I will look forward to reading more about you. I have had a couple of others as well and so thought that I might like to interview in a couple of days' time. I hope that you are not climbing Everest or some such?"

"No, no. I'm not," said Josie, briefly considering the unlikeliness of that idea. "Interview in a couple of days would be fine." A sudden thought seized her. "Where is the job?" She had always been taught to ask questions when being interviewed. It made you seem interested, committed, apparently.

"Veronica Gardens. Do you know it?"

Josie admitted that she did not.

The 'goodbye' that followed before the line went dead was

faster than a flash of light, and somehow Josie could not force herself to call any of the other numbers. She took a deep breath and drained her coffee.

JOSIE OPENED THE BIG BLUE FRONT DOOR OF THE PETERSONS' Notting Hill townhouse and found that it thudded against something unexpected on the inside.

"Hang on, Jo." Annie Peterson's voice was as agitated as ever, and Josie heard her dragging things across the hall floor. "I've just got to get this box out of the way."

She did just that and opened the door. The wide, polished wooden hall was lined with piled up colour-coded boxes with things like 'study' and 'living room' scrawled on them. Josie noticed that one box bore Tom Peterson's handwriting: 'crap that doesn't go anywhere'. Knowing that would send Annie over the edge, she said nothing.

"You've made good progress here," said Josie, hanging her jacket up on the hook beside the front door. She had taken all the clothes that the kids had grown out of to a charity shop herself that morning. Once, the hooks in the hall had been so crammed with summer jackets and winter warmers and hats and umbrellas that she thought they may fall off. Now they just looked naked, empty. It made her feel uncertain, threatened. She turned away and smiled at Annie who was shaking her head. Tom appeared in the kitchen doorway at the end of the hall.

"Hi, Josie. Coffee?"

"Yes, please, if you're making one."

"I'm always making one. Coming right up."

He disappeared at a sauntering pace back into the kitchen, and Josie heard the whizz and gurgle of the coffee machine. She knelt and considered Annie's collection of self-help books which had been lined up against the skirting board.

"Do you want these boxed, Annie?"

"Yes, please. That would be great. Many hands make light work, but you wouldn't think that this morning. My god. All he has done is make coffee and read the newspaper. Anyone would think that we weren't packing up a house we have lived in for ten years and moving to Dubai in, literally, a week. And it's not as if he's looking after the kids instead. They've been watching TV all morning. Thank god for Cbeebies, that's all I can say."

Josie packed the books and laughed a gentle laugh, acknowledging and sympathising, without committing. She had that skill, learned over many years of being a spare part in other people's homes, of diffusing tension. Of being a load bearer for other people's conflicts. She sealed up the box and turned to Annie.

"Definitely. Love Cbeebies, every nanny's best friend. What are you going to do without it in Dubai?"

"What am I going to do without you?" Annie leaned closer and fixed Josie with a serious stare; her best attempt at persuasion had always been to take the direct approach. "You could still come, you know. Our house is massive, and I can tell the agency out there that I don't need the woman they are sending to me. She won't be as good as you, Josie. I know you don't want to be too far from your sister, but you can have holidays home every few months, and there's Skype and—"

"Annie..."

"The kids love you. You know they do. I've had to promise them that we will have a 'Josie room' in the new house..."

The whizz of the coffee machine ceased, the kitchen door opened, and Tom appeared, handing a cup to Josie on the floor.

"Leave her alone, Annie. She's made her decision. If the kids need therapy, then we'll just have to take it on the chin. Anyway, what are you doing down there, Josie? Isn't today your day off? I thought you were going out to what's-her-name's house."

"Lauren? Yes, I am but not till later. You've got a few packing hours to get out of me before then." She winked, hoping to conceal the hollowness, the fear.

Tom's mobile rang, and he retreated into the kitchen, talking loudly about contract terms and share prices and such. Meanwhile, Annie and Josie carried on packing, working harmoniously as they had done for the last four years. Annie was a high-strung neurotic who sorted her novels into alphabetical order by author name, but that wasn't all she was. She was the woman who had hugged Josie when her dad died, came to his funeral when she hadn't even known him, for friendship's sake. She was the woman who never said anything when Josie's sister rang asking her for money but who ring-fenced some of her wages into investments and pensions to protect her from her own generosity. They had sorted each other's washing, borrowed each other's clothes. They had sat together in doctor's waiting rooms when the twins were poorly and on the sofa watching romantic films when they were sleeping. These two women had lived together like two halves of a pair of scissors. Josie watched Annie writing out more detailed instructions for the removal people and smiled. She recalled the severity in Mrs Cavendish's voice on the phone and a chill of worry went through her. Annie stood up from a sea of boxes and began to prattle about logistics. Maddening and mercurial though she was, Josie would be sad to say goodbye.

"What time do you need to leave to get to Lauren's?" asked Annie some hours and many boxes later.

"Not until five thirty-ish. Dinner's at seven but it takes me half an hour on the Tube, and I get there early so I can gossip before other people arrive."

"Gossip?" Annie looked disbelieving. "I bet you help her with the food." She stared over the top of her heavy-rimmed spectacles in an accusing manner.

"Sometimes, but only because I don't want to die of food poisoning!"

That much was true, for Lauren was no chef.

"Well, you had better get going. What are you going to wear?"

"I hadn't really thought about it. I'll probably wear my black dress."

"Oh, not that thing again. Josie, wear something different. Shake it up a bit. Running around after the kids keeps you slim. Show it off. I bought a new Jigsaw dress last week. It would fit you. Try it on."

"Oh, I couldn't. Then it might need washing, and you're just about to emigrate!"

"Never mind that. Bloody, do it."

AND SO, JOSIE FOUND HERSELF KNOCKING ON HER FRIEND Lauren's front door, wearing not only Annie's dress but also (because there would have been a fuss if she had said 'no') a pair of her shoes. Lauren took her coat and they hugged their hellos.

"Wow, sexy dress. Has Old Battle-axe put your wages up?"

"No, it's her dress. And she's not really a battle-axe. She just does a good impression." Annie and Lauren had met a couple of times and clashed slightly as two people who are alike frequently do.

The two friends exchanged gossip and tossed salads and laid the table for dinner. Overhead, Josie could hear Lauren's husband, Simon, attempting to put their two hyperactive children to bed, little feet stomping on carpeted floor and half-completed bedtime stories arrested by bursts of hysterical laughing. Lauren's eyes flicked up to the ceiling.

"Bloody kids. I don't know how you put up with three, day in and day out. It would do me in."

"Well, it's not for much longer. They are off to Dubai on Monday."

"How are your applications going?"

If it were Lauren whose employer and home were disappearing off to the Middle East in less than a week, she would not have put off trying to find another job until today. She would have been all over the 'Situations Vacant' like a rash, distributing her perfectly preened CV liberally. Josie didn't dare tell her organised friend of how tardy she had been and so she fudged it.

"Not too bad. I haven't got anything yet, but I spoke to a woman in South Ken today, and I've got a good feeling about it."

She didn't have a good feeling about it, but Lauren was a girl who thrived on optimism.

"Do you know where in South Ken?"

"Veronica Gardens." Josie swept a pile of chopped tomatoes into the salad bowl. "Doesn't mean anything to me."

"Nor me. But it all sounds very posh..."

The stomping and protesting from upstairs having stopped, they were joined by Lauren's husband who poured gin and tonics. In time, each of them opened the door to the parade of work colleagues and old chums who had been invited. Lauren was one of the few friends from university who Josie kept up with. It was eleven years since they had left Oxford and turned up in the big city with their sale price shoes and lofty aspirations. It felt like longer.

After what had happened, Josie found it easier to cut herself off, but Lauren was not the sort of girl who took 'no' for an answer. That, combined with the fact that she actually really liked her, was how Josie found herself sat at her dining table, sandwiched between a pregnant woman Lauren had met at the NCT and a newly married couple from Simon's work. Opposite her sat Lauren's cousin whose two-month-old baby was asleep upstairs in his travel cot. His mother sat staring without blinking at the plastic baby monitor, which she positioned next to her empty wine glass on the table, her breasts swelling like buoys above the V-neck of her nursing dress.

Lauren did the introductions, dancing around the room, encouraging friendly nods and handshakes. "This is my best friend, Josie" made her blush.

Later in the evening, the nursing mother's husband leaned towards Josie and gawping at the way Annie's Jigsaw dress clung to her body asked: "So, what do you do then, Josie?"

"I'm a nanny."

"A nanny? Good lord. I thought you were up at Oxford with Lauren. Must be a bit of a busman's holiday coming here for the evening." He laughed at his own joke, and to be polite, Josie tried to join in.

"It's fine. As long as you don't ask me to burp your baby or change his nappy, that is."

"How do you get the buggers off to sleep? Can't understand why the little man doesn't just close his eyes of an evening. But we've had all manner of problems. Ginny getting out of bed all through the night. Bloody ridiculous."

"Well, the children I look after are a bit past all that now."

"What did you do when they were babies?"

He moved closer, pouring more wine into Josie's glass. His shirt was tight over his belly, and his breath was sour and boozy.

"I drugged them." His expression faltered, poised between laughter and asking more questions. Josie had heard it all before and wasn't really up for it. In her head, Tom's voice came to her: *"Isn't today your day off?"*

"I think I'll just see if Lauren needs any help in the kitchen."

JOSIE WAS LUCKY TO CATCH THE LAST TUBE, AND IT WAS HALF past midnight by the time she got home to the Petersons. She had, notwithstanding the lecherous dad, the display of pregnant bumps, lactating breasts, and entwined couples, enjoyed the evening. After years of practice and mind-bending self-control, she had learned to take her pleasures in small doses. Walking back from the station, her heels echoed around the sodium lit street, and she began to think of the comforts of 'home' such as it was: getting into her pyjamas and sinking into bed with a cup of tea and a few pages of Ethel Turner Everett on her Kindle. Turning the key in the lock as gingerly as possible, she gently pushed the door open; standing on the mat, she took off Annie's high heels so as not to make noise clonking around in the hall. She need not have bothered as she soon heard a commotion of children crying and Annie calling out instructions to Tom from upstairs. Josie hung up her coat and dashed up to the nursery, hearing before she entered, the unmistakable sound of a child vomiting.

"Welcome home, Josie," said Annie as she looked around the scene in the twin's bedroom, sick everywhere, both children crying.

"I'll just get this dress off. Then I'll strip the bed."

❧ 3 ❧

KITTY

APRIL 1859

THE DAYS AT VERONICA GARDENS PASSED MUCH THE SAME AS
ever they did when Sir Roland and his daughter were in town.
Mornings were a slow and private affair with Kitty about her
toilette, breaking her fast in private, and writing letters. Specu-
lating on matters within and without her control, planning events
as far as she was able, setting aside time for her own endeavours.
Sometimes there were callers: Aunt Margaret alone or with
Philomena, others too. Kitty, as the de facto lady of the house, was
occasionally called upon to assist the housekeeper, Mrs Cooper,
with some matter or other. This was seldom, however, as Mrs
Cooper was a capable woman who continued to regard Kitty as a
beloved child who had lost her mother tragically and prematurely.
If Kitty volunteered assistance, more often than not, she found her
arm squeezed affectionately as the old lady's head would tilt:
"Now, there is no need for that, Miss Cathcart." She did all she
could to avoid bothering *the dear miss* with the business of the
household. Kitty, for her own part, acquiesced in this arrangement
and used the time for her own ends. Sir Roland went about his
business with scant regard for his domestic arrangements. He
attended meetings, met with gentlemen of trade and profession.
He spoke infrequently to Kitty, except to make her aware that

they, together with her aunt and cousins, were to attend the theatre with Lord Trefusis at the end of the week.

So it was, therefore, that Kitty was at her leisure in the drawing room one morning. The sun streamed through the tall windows, and she was finding her blue day gown a trifle hot. Alone, and reading a novel of Mrs Gaskell gifted to her by Philomena, she tucked her slippered feet under her on the chaise and smiled inwardly at the unfolding of the story between the covers. At a moment in the tale when she would have far preferred to have continued reading, she became aware of a carriage drawing up outside. Beyond the silk patterned walls of the drawing room, the front door was opened, and a number of feet began to click about in the tiled hall. Indistinct male voices sounded, but Kitty could not make them out. It was unusual for callers to appear without warning. Kitty put aside her book, brought her feet to the floor, and waited for the visitors to be announced. Growing impatient, she stood and chanced a glance out of the window onto the street. The carriage was a serviceable affair, not a bit grand. She did not know to whom it belonged but gave a silent prayer of thanks that it was unlikely to be Lord Trefusis's conveyance. Kitty paced the room but the hallway beyond was now quite silent, and she was forced to conclude that whoever the visitors were, they were not for her. Assuming that the door had been opened to some business associate of Sir Roland's, and that his study was now thick with talk of dividends and the storage and transportation of metal, Kitty sat back down to her book.

When the bell rang for lunch, Kitty put away her reading and wandered on instinct to the grand, oak-lined dining room. A maid sweeping the bottom step of the staircase bobbed her a curtsey, and the hall clock, polished to a shine that was almost vicious, struck the hour. Her father's droning voice she could hear in the middle distance, but she was well used to that.

As she rounded the corner and entered the room, Kitty experienced a sensation most unfamiliar. She was quite speechless with surprise.

There, standing beside her father, below a portrait of her mother painted some two decades before this moment, was Mr

Faraday, listening in silence as her father held forth. He acknowledged her arrival with a bow and, for a moment, the air in the room heated and expanded, pressed against her skin like an iron. She fought this reaction with a gentle bob in his direction, which she hoped he understood to be polite, nothing more.

Sir Roland broke not a moment in his diatribe, which, Kitty rapidly gathered, was the latest instalment in his dispute with Mr Brindle. His account of the last months' correspondence went on just a little too long, and a look of confusion crossed Mr Faraday's face, although, it did not linger there. Kitty knew quite well that her father was deliberately ignoring her presence. After a time, he desisted. Having sought to introduce the two young people, Sir Roland declared himself astounded that they had already met.

"Mr Faraday attended Mrs Christie's party last week, Papa. He was with Mr Haworth."

"Really?" Sir Roland looked to his guest, questioningly. "I did not see you there, boy. How very odd for Haworth to fetch along his clerk!"

"It was an honour to be invited, sir. Mr Haworth had thought to introduce me to you, I believe, knowing that I was intended for this particular task. However, regrettably, the chance did not arise."

A vision flashed across Kitty's mind of her father stuck like a limpet to Lord Trefusis, and she perfectly understood. Why Mr Faraday did not mention his prior acquaintance, nay friendship, with George was a mystery to her. Surely any talented young man, who wished to get on in the world, would use all the connexions he had?

Sir Roland grunted as he sat in his place at the head of the table. The table had been laid for four, and Kitty observed the places as she took her accustomed place beside her father. They each sat and servants shuffled around them with serving dishes and decanters and potatoes balanced on silver spoons. Sir Roland glowered as Kitty was served first.

"Are we expecting another guest for luncheon, Papa?"

"No. Haworth was here this morning, but he was unable to stay. Shame. He's a good man, Haworth, and a damned fine solicitor." Sir Roland tightened his fist on the table and his eyes narrowed. "Knows this business with Brindle as well as any man. You have a good master there, boy."

He looked to Mr Faraday as he said this, and Kitty wished for the floor to swallow her whole. Upon Mr Faraday's face, she observed, when she chanced him a look, perfect inscrutability at being so addressed.

"Mr Haworth is an excellent master, Sir Roland. I call myself very fortunate. And his knowledge of the case is unsurpassed. I do not believe that the solicitor acting on behalf of Mr Brindle could possibly have the same grasp of the facts and the law."

At this pronouncement, Kitty looked him squarely in the face. Teasing her father? At his own table? What a creature this Faraday man was.

"No indeed." Sir Roland spoke in between and during mouthfuls. "The man's a charlatan. Doesn't know his business, doesn't know the law! I've a mind to report him to the Attorney General. Writes damned, stupid letters."

Having spoken thus, the man of the house fixed his eyes upon his meal, which continued in a somewhat uncomfortable silence, silver scraping on china occasionally. After a period, and unable to bear the absence of conversation a moment longer, Kitty ventured a question.

"Do you work on the case as well, Mr Faraday?"

"I do, Miss Cathcart. I have been given a task that I believe shall take some weeks, at the least. Sir Roland has generously made his own papers available to me for the purpose. I shall be working on them. Here."

"Here?"

She said it too quickly to appear disinterested. Her mind surely bubbled.

Kitty thought of the small study, adjacent to the library, lonely and covered over with dust. It seemed remarkably proximate, and she was momentarily stopped in her habitual ready chatter.

"How very industrious. I shall speak to Mrs Cooper and ensure that you are kept supplied with tea."

"That is solicitous of you, miss. However, I have a great deal to do. I cannot imagine that there shall be time for tea."

THE DOOR TO HER CHAMBER SWEPT OPEN, AND THE USUAL low shuffle of Violet going about her errands began. Kitty shifted in the vast expanse of her bed as the curtains were swiftly drawn, and the morning light burst through the window. She closed her eyes tightly and plunged face forwards into the pillow.

"Good morning, Miss Kitty."

Begrudgingly, she replied: "Hmm."

Kitty yawned loudly and stretched out. She had sat at her desk for half the night, candlelight flickering against the page. Between that and the strange circling confusion in her head, she had slept poorly. The light and sound of the city at night had always kept her from slumber, even as a child. Carriages clattering, voices, footsteps. Men droning out the hour. Even a person who was happy and content would surely be kept from rest.

"It is a glorious morning, miss." Violet busied herself pinning back the heavy curtains and moving Kitty's water jug before turning to her mistress and smiling a broad smile. The sun quite beamed out behind her and Kitty squinted to see.

"You are terribly cheerful this morning."

"Are you not, miss?"

"No, I am afraid not. I slept rather ill, Violet." Kitty pushed herself up and leaned back against the embrace of her pillows. Her memory flitted to the previous night. To the hours of dimly lit toil in this very room.

Violet condoled with laughing eyes at her mistress's lack of sleep and moved about the room with piles of linen. In the street, bright sunshine rained down, bouncing on the roofs of the houses and the little church and reflecting the vivid green of the park like magic. Kitty began to grow accustomed to the light.

"It is your afternoon off today, Violet."

"It is, miss. I shall be walking out at one o'clock. Do I assume that there is a little job for me to do?"

"You do, if you wouldn't mind. Thank you, Violet. Where

would I be without you?" The two ladies regarded one another and laughed. After a pause, Kitty ventured a question. She took care to appear as nonchalant as possible.

"I believe we are to expect Mr Faraday today. He is that young clerk undertaking some work for Papa. Do you know what arrangements have been made for him, Violet?"

"Yes, miss. The small table in the library has been made ready. I had it from Mrs Cooper, and Maisie was in there cleaning this morning. But he's not *expected*, miss. He's already here."

"Already here?" Kitty's eyebrows raised and leaned forward in bed for the first time that morning. "How very eager."

"Ah. Here you are, Mr Faraday."

Kitty swept into her father's library and peered around. It was an enormous room, standing upon almost half of the ground floor of the house, yet it always felt crowded with objects. Unlike the fashionable libraries of many gentlemen, it was not arranged to showcase the owner's education and scholastic achievements. There were books aplenty, but they were not there to impress others—nor would Sir Roland have invited outsiders to peruse them. The room was packed to bursting with files and records; bookcases stood floor to ceiling down each side. At one end of the room, an oval table, polished to a squeak, gleamed; all of its chairs tucked in, unoccupied. Kitty had seen it in action on other occasions: tall, frock-coated gentlemen sitting around smoking and talking of business. Now it was quite empty, as was Sir Roland's desk, which stood in the centre of the room like a throne, his pen poised like a knife on its surface. At the opposite end of the room, stood the conservatory, separated from the library only by a wall of glass and an excess of foliage. For these reasons, the space within was dimmer than it should have been and tinged with a heavy green, which Kitty fancied stuck to those who entered. It had always made her laugh to think of the green-skinned men strutting about within. Presently, Mr Faraday, who had been seated at the viewless desk, which faced the east wall, reserved for secretaries and other underlings, stood and greeted her. A look of confusion crossed his face and was rapidly replaced with sternness.

"Good morning, miss."

"How industrious you are. I was wondering whether you have everything you need?"

"Yes, thank you."

His response was clipped, sharp even.

"Is there anything I can obtain for you?"

"No, Miss Cathcart, I don't believe there is."

"Well, how satisfactory…"

Kitty began pacing about the room, the hem of her wide pale blue skirts quietly sweeping the floor. Her fingers tapped on the small book she held, and her eyelids twitched. Having taken a turn about the room, she stood stock still. It was most disconcerting to see Mr Faraday exhale and stare down at his papers.

"Yes, I am quite well provided for, miss."

"In that case, I shall not bother you."

And with that, she plumped down on the small chaise before the fire and opened her book, as though it were the most normal thing in the world for a young woman of society to keep company with a clerk in one of the least attractive rooms in the house. Mr Faraday sat at his desk with his back to her, his long legs only just accommodated beneath the table. They were like two bookends on a shelf, without any books in between.

"You shall not bother me, Miss Cathcart. But your presence here may bother your father. He may consider it to be…inappropriate."

"He shall not consider it to be anything, because he shall not know." She placed her book beside her on the chaise and leaned towards his back. "My father is away from the house for the day." She smiled a satisfied smile at the back of his head. "In any case, please do not concern yourself with my father's wishes for me. If he is unhappy about where I spend my time, it is I who shall know of it, not you."

He stiffened and took up his pen. Kitty considered him over the top of her book and regretted that he was not more forthcoming. A coldness appeared to exist between them, but she was adamant that it need not remain.

"You are discomforted, sir."

"No, I assure you. I am perfectly contented."

There followed an extended period of chilly silence in which the shuffling of paper, the turning of pages, and the occasional movement of Kitty's skirts were the only sounds. Eventually, she gave up hope of him speaking.

"How did you enjoy meeting with my cousin again?"

He paused his pen over the paper but did not turn around.

"I enjoyed it very much. It has been some years."

"Yes, it must have been. George came down from Cambridge three years ago. Were you and he exact contemporaries?"

"We were."

"And do you miss your studies, Mr Faraday? I should love to have attended a university. My word. To have years in which there is nothing but reading and studying and thinking. What fortune!"

With that, he turned to face her, pen in hand.

"It was good fortune, miss, while it lasted. I cannot say that it prepared me for life though."

"Why not?"

He took in a breath, and his eyes quite flashed. Suddenly, the same heat and tension she felt when she saw him in the dining room the previous day returned, and an uncharacteristic nervousness crept over her.

"I cannot answer that question, Miss Cathcart, without taking up all of your day, and mine. And since I can see that you have many pages left to read"—he nodded to the book beside her—"and I have many hours of work to complete for your father, shall we"— he paused over the words—"postpone this discussion to another time?"

"If you insist. I shall look forward to re-commencing later. But do not think that you shall have me forget. I do not give up, Mr Faraday."

Unaccustomed as she was of being dismissed, no matter how civilly, Kitty nodded to him, and, taking her book, left the room without delay. She found the sunshine in the conservatory dazzling and sat for a moment, gathering herself.

IN THE DAYS THAT FOLLOWED, KITTY RENEWED HER ASSAULT upon Mr Faraday. Uninvited, she attended him in his corner of her father's library, offered him refreshments, wrote letters at the small desk in the corner, and read her book with an air of ostentation on the nearby chaise. All to no avail. Whilst he was polite, he ventured no stories or unnecessary words. When, over the dressing table, Violet privately enquired as to the purpose of these attentions, her mistress was unable to furnish an answer.

At the end of this unsatisfactory week, the family's visit to the theatre with Lord Trefusis loomed. It had been planned that Aunt Margaret, together with George and Philomena, would gather at Veronica Gardens in the late afternoon, and His Lordship would join them there before they departed for the gaiety and colour of Drury Lane.

So it was that the ladies and George were laughing over tea in the drawing room late on Friday afternoon as the sun outside the window slowly disappeared and clock hands in the hallway wound round. Kitty, who had deliberately avoided the company of the resilient Mr Faraday, sat in the centre of the chaise, a cousin to each side and facing her aunt, whose vivid fan fluttered as she spoke.

"What a fine gown that is, Kitty. That shade of blue was so becoming on your mama as well. How it suits you! Blue and gold, like the country in summer."

"Thank you, Aunt." Kitty glanced at Philomena's downturned face beside her and reached out for her cousin's hand.

"Philomena and I have been thinking of a trip to the British Museum now that the King's Library is open. We have a fancy to see some old stones and imagine ourselves ancient ladies. We are selling tickets if either of you wish to join us!"

George indicated, chuckling, that he should love to come. But Aunt Margaret tightened her grip on her fan and frowned.

"Well, yes. Maybe that would be interesting, Kitty. I have

heard excellent reports of the exhibition from Mrs Furnival. Have you considered inviting Lord Trefusis? It would be kind, would it not? And a fitting act of gratitude for his having been so excellent as to take us all to the theatre tonight?"

"I have already thanked His Lordship, Aunt, rather profusely. And I may consider loaning him my copy of *My Lady Ludlow*, which I enjoyed very much indeed. But I believe that taking him to the British Museum may be a bridge too far. I hardly know the man. It might be considered improper apart from anything else."

"Not if George and I were there, or even George on his own to chaperone you. And Philomena, of course."

Aunt Margaret looked to her son, whose grey eyes had been fixed on his teacup for some time.

"George?" she said, plainly expecting to be supported.

He raised his eyebrows and leaned towards his mother as he spoke.

"Shall we reserve judgment, Mother? It is not in my mind to be against His Lordship. I know that our uncle is *in favour of him*, shall we say. But let us not be hasty. It is, as Kitty says, currently a short acquaintance. I know nothing of the chap and neither do you. Let us see how we get along with him this evening. When the evening is over, if we are inclined to extend our acquaintance to friendship, then we may do so, no?"

The clock in the hall outside ticked, and Kitty felt warm. What a brick George could be when one needed him. Still, something in her aunt's resigned but steady expression frightened her. Aunt Margaret tilted her head to one side and nodded as she selected a biscuit from the plate. She said nothing, but Kitty resisted the silent pressure of her approval of Lord Trefusis leaning against her. It was of no consequence. She had contrived her way out of unattractive prospects before, and she would do so again. She squeezed Philomena's hand and made a bid to change the subject.

"George, did you know that your young friend has been working away in a corner of Papa's library this last week? Your young clerk friend. I'm afraid I've forgotten his name—"

"Faraday. Has he indeed?"

"Faraday? Who is Faraday?"

"Alexander Faraday, Mother. Knew him at Cambridge. Serious sort of fellow but a good man. We were friends, quite good friends actually. But I haven't seen him these three years, at least."

"What has he been doing with himself since you came down from Cambridge, do you think?" ventured Kitty, seeking to sound as disinterested as possible.

"I've no idea. All I know is that he is working for Haworth, of all men."

Aunt Margaret's eyes widened.

"Working?"

"Yes. He is his clerk."

"Isn't that rather odd, George?"

"I wasn't expecting it, Mother. But I don't know that I'd call it 'rather odd'. He is a clever man and an industrious man. I fancy he's the sort of chap who would throw himself into some manner of work, even if he didn't need it. As it is, I understand that his family fell on hard times. I don't know any of the details." He shot a look at Kitty and then turned back to his mother. "But I suspect that he has established himself at Mr Haworth's as he has no other means."

An odd discomfort stole over Kitty. She had devoted her week to establishing Mr Faraday's story, and she was determined to do it. But something about her aunt's frown irritated her beyond reason. She had no wish to see his tale paraded before others. Kitty liked to be party to things to which others were not; the whispered confidence was the thing for her. She did not like to think of Mr Faraday being boxed away, working by the hour for money, while his equals sat in the drawing room, sipping tea and admiring one another's clothes. She found herself unexpectedly confused by matters.

Shortly thereafter, the door opened into the room and Havers appeared, bowing.

"Miss Catherine, Sir Roland wishes to see you in the conservatory."

Kitty excused herself and made her way to the great vaulted glass prism at the back of the house. The edifice, which was rare in town, even in houses as grand as these, had been intended by her father as an unambiguous sign of his wealth. No visitor to the house was allowed to get away without being bathed in sunlight within it, chilled in the winter and baked in the summer, nor given chapter and verse on its design and construction. It was expansive and high and, being full of foliage, did give one something of the impression of being outside without the English climate. For Kitty, any attractions it may otherwise have had were diminished by its purpose and use. It was generally the place her father summoned her if he wished to give her a dressing down.

"You wanted to speak with me, Papa?"

He looked at her, pinching his eye glass tight. The fading light of the day filled the room and a maid watered a large plant in the corner. It was not Sir Roland's way to save Kitty's pride, and she was not surprised to see a servant present.

"Yes Kitty, come in." He placed his papers down on a small table and began pacing the room. Had it been reported to him that she had been keeping company with Mr Faraday? Kitty prayed not, as for all of her defiant talk, her father would not be pleased. Most of the household staff were sooner friends to her than to Sir Roland. But there were those who were especially loyal to him, including Havers. And, of course, in the final analysis, it was Sir Roland who paid their wages.

"Fetch me my tea."

A certain expectation settled in Kitty's mind. They had been through this dance before. She moved with deliberate slowness towards a corner table on which there stood a tea service and began to pour. His eyes were on her, but she would not show any sign of fear.

"Where would you like it, Papa?"

"Here."

He nodded towards the table beside him but otherwise moved not. When Kitty placed his cup and saucer in the middle, he did not miss a moment before barking, "Closer!" The maid in the corner jumped in shock, picked up her watering can, and fled the room as the sound of Sir Roland's roar reverberated around the glass roof. Kitty, who had been expecting the outburst, did not so much as flinch.

As she moved towards her father, he reached out one hand and gripped her about the waist, his fingers tightening ferociously. She could have moved away, could have wrenched free. But, she did not. The pain of his fingers boring into her middle shot through her body. After an unnecessary length of time, he removed his hand and began to talk.

"Now. Lord Trefusis shall be here in half an hour. I see that you are already dressed for the theatre and that pleases me."

He looked her up and down but not at her face.

"I wanted to speak with you before he arrives and to impress upon you, Kitty, the great importance of His Lordship. To you, I mean."

Kitty's body stiffened and her thoughts flew to the room beyond the wall of green, to Mr. Faraday, tucked away like a handkerchief. Was he in there? Was he listening or so fixed on his pen that he could not hear? Did he even think of her when she was not there?

"You can stare at me all you wish, young lady. But it shall avail you naught. Whatever you may say, however bright you may glitter, however many tin pot admirers you may collect, I am the master here, Kitty. I am the master of this house, and I am the master of you. Have you ever thought of that? I cannot imagine that you have."

"Papa—"

"Silence. Your mother left you none of her money, and do you know why? It was because she didn't have any. When she married me, everything she had became mine. That was so because I made it so. I am not a man who is willing to be played for a fiddle, and you would do well to remember that. I had not expected your mother to die without providing me with a son. If I had known that would happen, I would never have married her, aristocracy or not. There are not many men like me in the world, Kitty. I have built a great undertaking from nothing. I have created. Most men create nothing. Now, in my twilight years, I will have my only child married to the most eminent man I can find, and my grandchildren will be of the highest circles. Do I make myself clear?"

Kitty did not look down, as others may have done. She stared right at him, matching him glare for glare.

"There will be no repeats of last year. If I feel that you are too much in the company of George and Philomena, or that you are not acting your part, then I shall not stand idly by. You shall not bury yourself away with books and pens and nonsense. I shall take action. Now. Lord Trefusis is interested, Kitty. He has shown a preference for you. And that is very fortunate, is it not? There are a number of advantages. You will be a titled lady with your own estate. You will be rich, for I intend to settle considerable wealth on you. I will not have men say that a child of mine married like a pauper. You will have to submit yourself to the will of your husband, and that will be good for you. You have run free for too long. There is a further, obvious argument in favour of marriage. And it is this. The longer you remain unmarried, the longer you must remain at home with me. That cannot be any more agreeable to you than it is to me, Catherine, and do not pretend that it is."

"I make no pretence, sir. But I do not agree to marry a stranger simply because you have selected and approved him."

"Then you make a very grave error. Do not test me. You shall not win." He gripped her waist again, this time with two hands and squeezed her, fiercely. Kitty sensed that if she had been a cat, he would have thrown her against the wall.

Neither spoke as he left the room.

Kitty exhaled sharply as she watched him retreat, leaving her in his leafy, glassy cage. Her side stung where he had gripped her, she suspected enough to bruise. In all their years of practising hatred and resentment of one another, he had never injured her person. It was a sign, she was certain, of new seriousness. Heat and panic rose in her for a moment, and she felt trapped. The tinkling sound of her aunt's laugh drifted towards her, muffled by walls and doors, and she took heart. For were the Christies not her greatest supporters? Had she not evaded her father's wishes before? And did she not, in any event, have a plan? Kitty straightened her shoulders and flattened her hands against the blue silk of her skirts, as if readying for battle. She took a deep breath and made to quit the room.

As she did so, the door of the study squeaked open, and there appeared the towering figure of Mr Faraday. She noted, again, the deep blue of his eyes; it was a deep blue, verging into purple. Upon his face sat an inscrutable expression. For a moment, they simply stood there, regarding one another in silence. The air, now slightly chilled, was thick with questions. Just when she had almost given up hope, he spoke, his voice softer than she had yet heard it.

"Are you all right, Miss Cathcart?"

"Yes, thank you, Mr Faraday. I am quite well. I have grown up in my father's house, and I have found that familiarity breeds expectation. And that, in turn, gives birth to defences."

"I'm sure it does, miss. But I still enquire. It is only humane to do so, is it not?"

She had the impression that he asked not simply as a rhetorical flourish but to discover what she really thought.

"It is. And I thank you." Kitty paused, studying the furrowed brow of the man before her and the tightness with which his large hands were balled into fists. Suddenly, she felt uncertain, thrown asunder, as though matters were not quite as she thought they were.

"Please excuse me, I must return to my family."

In barely a breath, she was gone.

✿ 4 ✿

JOSIE

FEBRUARY 2018

JOSIE WAS AT THE PLAYGROUND WITH THE PETERSON GIRLS when her phone rang like an alarm. She reached inside her over-filled handbag to find it.

"Hello?"

"Hello. Is that Josie Minton? Diana Cavendish. We spoke yesterday. You sent me your CV. I'd like to meet you if you don't mind."

"Oh. Thank you." This surprised Josie as she had only emailed the CV that morning and had also forced herself to call some of the other jobs. In a fit of panic, she had even phoned a woman about a position on the Isle of Wight.

"Hello, is anybody there?"

"Yes. Sorry. Sorry. Yes, I'd love to meet you. Thank you."

"Good. Well, how about this afternoon? At three o'clock? 50 Veronica Gardens, SW7. It's a short walk from South Ken Tube. I assume you have an *A-to-Z* or one of those iPhone things."

Josie did in fact have both.

"Thank you. I'm sure I'll find it. See you then."

The line went dead before she had quite finished speaking.

SOME HOURS LATER, SHE FOUND HERSELF GAZING UP AT THE enormous double-fronted house on the edge of Hyde Park and wondering why Mrs Cavendish had wanted to interview her so urgently. It came with the territory that Josie's employers were always reasonably well off. If they were not, they would not be hiring a nanny. Tom was a banker, although his career had been far from perfect, and he was being forced to move to the Dubai office or lose his job altogether. Annie was a lawyer for a big city firm. Her previous families had been similar. But she had never worked for the super-rich. She glanced down the street and took in the gleaming sports cars and pristine gardens and great stucco-fronted houses with their bright polished doors. They looked like so many lacquered nails standing in a row. Remarkably, there was a small church opposite the house, ancient gravestones with daffodils in between, a stone spire reaching up into the blue sky. It was odd, out of place amid the luxury. A thickset guy in a leather jacket was strolling up and down the street watchfully, and Josie wondered why. She looked down at her best shoes, pulled her faux leather handbag tighter on her shoulder, and climbed the steps to the front door. It was opened with alarming speed by a well-presented elderly lady in a beige roll-neck jumper.

"Hello," said Josie. "I'm here to meet Mrs Cavendish. My name is Josie Minton. She is expecting me."

The lady looked slightly affronted and said, "You must call me Diana." She tilted her head, and a hint of humour swept over her expression. "Why don't you come in and meet my grandchildren?"

Josie gulped the gulp of a person who had misunderstood the situation and, racing to compute this new arrangement, she stepped over the threshold and into the capacious hall. She followed Diana along the wide passageway, walls hung with carefully chosen modern paintings in all colours, side tables decked with vases of lilies, blond wood on heavy, expensive wallpaper.

"The twins are in their playroom. I suggest that we go and see them, and then you and I can have a chat in the kitchen. I have a girl from the agency here to look after them, but she isn't permanent material."

Josie nodded as they entered the playroom to find the pink-clad twins sat in a multicoloured wigwam playing with Duplo and making the only-just-distinct sounds of two year olds on the brink of language. The sight of them cuddled up in their matching cardigans warmed Josie. They were a pair of little pickles, and she knew that they could get on. A smile, uninvited, came to her face and she crouched down at the wigwam entrance.

"Good afternoon, ladies. My name is Josie." She held out her hand. "How do you do?"

After a moment of still, one of the twins, the slightly smaller one, for they were not identical, held out her hand, glanced at her grandmother, and said, "'llo."

For a while, Josie forgot that Diana Cavendish and her beige roll-neck jumper were there. She let her handbag slip to the floor and helped the twins, who it turned out were called Maggie and Santa, with their Duplo hospital. She noticed that Maggie was much better with the bricks than Santa, but it was Santa who, with little preamble, climbed on her lap for a cuddle after ten minutes of play and who thrust a small book into her hand and demanded, "'tory!"

"Well, this looks like a very good book. But I had better ask your granny if I have time to read it to you." Josie glanced up at Diana to see a more tender expression than she was expecting, and, after some hesitation, she croaked out a response.

"Yes, I'm sure we've time for one story."

And so it was that Josie cuddled a girl on each thigh and read the story of *The Owl Who Was Afraid of the Dark*. When it was over, there was a moment of silence before an unknown young woman appeared in the doorway and Diana spoke.

"Thank you, Josie. Well girls, I think that Josie and I might leave you with Lucy now." She nodded at the girl in jeans who advanced towards them, and Josie took her cue to follow Diana out of the room. The kitchen into which they then stepped was a vast vision of marble tops and blinding sunlight pounding through glass. Josie blinked and said nothing. Diana began clattering about with a cafetière.

"Would you like a coffee?"

"Yes, please. Lovely."

"Right, well. Sit down." Josie did as she was told and tried not to gasp as she looked around the huge kitchen and outside into the walled garden beyond the French doors. Diana poured the coffee and thudded it down on the table before speaking.

"Now. I understand that you have been working as a nanny for ten years but don't have formal qualifications. Is that right?"

Josie's stomach tightened. She clasped her coffee for warmth.

"Erm. Yes. I have quite a few references. They are on my C—"

"Yes, I know that. I've been in touch with them, of course. I have spoken to Mrs Peterson and your previous families. Although I find it very odd that a girl like you should be a nanny without having been trained, you may as well know that they were glowing in their recommendations. You have been with the Petersons for four years and have looked after their twins from birth, is that right?"

"Yes. I will miss them very much when they go to Dubai."

Diana let out a sound a bit like 'hmm' and looked away.

"What about your personal life?" She looked pointedly at the nakedness of Josie's left hand before continuing. "No fiancé? Do you have a boyfriend? Can we expect you to dash off to god knows where five minutes after starting?"

"Erm, no. I've no plans to dash anywhere. I don't have a boyfriend. Or a girlfriend." Diana's eyes, sage green, flashed towards her in an expression of suppressed something. "Or a cat or a dog or anything really. I'm just plain, old Nanny."

For the first time, Diana smiled a half-smile and poured more coffee.

"I know that you are not trained *exactly,* but do you subscribe to any particular school of child rearing? Are you a would-be Montessori or Norland? Do you deny them naps or make them sit on a cold stone floor of an evening or anything like that?"

"No. I just look after them. I use my instincts. I think we all do."

Diana looked at her, steadily, and a muscle in her cheek twitched.

"I agree. And you can start almost immediately, is that right?"

"Yes."

"Well, I must say that would be useful. The young thing we have at the moment is no good."

The girl had looked inoffensive enough to Josie.

"I should say that I don't actually live here. My flat is a few streets away, but I shall look in when I need to. You will see me probably more than you see my son. He is something of a workaholic, but I expect your paths will cross in the mornings. The twins are up at six most mornings, and James has always been one to start the day with the sunrise. He works late too. You've little prospect of seeing him, really, unless you are completely nocturnal."

No mention of a mother. An alarm rang in Josie's mind. She had always worked closely with the mother, even one who was at work all day. The idea of a motherless household, where her boss was a man, seemed all wrong. It was like a ship without a rudder. A sense of unease mushroomed up in her.

"The girls are quite reasonable little dears, really. They nap in the afternoon. They eat most foods. Santa, as you know, likes stories and watching cartoons. Maggie is fond of building things. I doubt that a woman of your experience will find them challenging."

A cog in Josie's mind paused. A woman of her experience. It seemed like yesterday she was completely wet behind the ears, a failed professional, a loser in love, propelled into an occupation of last resort by her circumstances. Now she was a woman of experience.

"James, you might find...well. Their father lives for his work, and he has had a difficult time recently. He can be rather frank speaking, if you know what I mean."

I know where he gets it from.

She considered saying no. The idea of putting down her coffee, picking up her handbag and saying 'thanks, but no thanks,' sang through her head. So easy, so freeing. Then she remembered that the departure of the Petersons was only days away. She recalled how she had dealt with odd personalities and bizarre, unreasonable, unfathomable fancies before. The recent memory of

49

Santa and Maggie and *The Owl Who Was Afraid of the Dark* soothed her.

"I'm sure I'll be fine."

IT TOOK A DEPRESSINGLY SHORT PERIOD OF TIME TO PACK UP her old life. Annie helped her clear out her bedroom in Notting Hill. She took a few bags to the local charity shop, and after holding the twins, their sister, and their parents in vice-like hugs, and forcing herself not to cry, Tom drove her and her two suitcases to Veronica Gardens. In the car on the way over, he talked almost incessantly. Everything was a riotous joke, no quiet allowed. That, Josie had learned, was how Tom behaved when he was nervous. When they pulled up outside the house, he looked at her with new seriousness.

"Wow, Josie. This is—well this is a bit of a step up. I hope it's more homey than it looks."

"It'll be fine. And it's not that bad. There's the park, and the shops. And look at that church. Isn't it sweet?"

He smiled, unconvincingly.

"James Cavendish is a pretty well-known guy in the City."

"Well known for what?"

"In finance, people are only famous for two things. Fraud or being a superstar. Some people tick both boxes. Most tick neither. Cavendish, as far as I've known, is superstar only. Clever, ruthlessly successful, lucky. I can't picture him sitting on the sofa watching *Love Actually,* if you get my drift."

Josie suddenly felt flattened, like he had completely emptied her bucket. She forced herself to look cheerful. She nudged him with her coated elbow and un-clicked her seatbelt.

"Good job I saw it with you guys then, isn't it?"

As arranged, Diana was there to meet them, and for fifteen minutes, they stood around in the uncomfortable luxury of the house, making small talk before Tom said goodbye. After she had shut the huge front door on his retreating figure, Diana turned to Josie.

"The twins are having their nap. I expect that they will wake up in about an hour. My son had to go into the office today."

"Does he often work on a Saturday?"

"Yes, quite often. I wonder, Josie, would you mind if I left you?"

"No, of course not."

"It's just I've a friend I'm meeting for lunch and I really ought to run a few errands first. I'll give you a call later, and you have my number. You know where everything is, don't you, and you haven't lost the key I gave you?"

"No, no. I've still got the key, and I shall be fine. Thank you."

Josie had been given a tour of the house, or parts of it, the previous day. Her memory of it was entirely of the sight of Diana's wiry, beige-clad frame bolting up and down stairs in front of her, charging along corridors, pausing in doorways, and giving out instructions. She couldn't even remember where they kept the tea, surely the most important thing to know in any house. She sighed and stretched. She would work it out. After checking on the twins, who were sleeping with their bottoms in the air, she retreated to her own bedroom, next door to theirs (and tastefully, almost worryingly, beautifully decorated in neutral shades). Tom had deposited her suitcases next to the bed, and she began unpacking them, opening the wooden wardrobe, smelling the smells of another person's home. She noticed with a start, and then a smile, that Annie had slipped the lacy Jigsaw dress into her things, and she felt tears pressing against her eyes as she hung it up. The suitcases unpacked, she pushed them under the bed and padded downstairs to the kitchen.

Gleaming marble tops and chrome devices stretched out on all sides, and the stools were placed so neatly beside the breakfast bar that Josie wondered if they were ever used. The sterility and the silence threatened to upset her, so she moved to the French doors and regarded the garden. Something inside her settled like a bird plopping down on a branch for a rest. She had never seen such a lovely garden in Central London. It was square and sufficiently large that the tall wall around it did not exclude the sunshine, which presently beamed down on the riot of early spring flowers and shrubs emerging from winter. To the left stood a deep herbaceous border, and to the right a rockery, giving onto a good lawn. She began to think of fun outside activities for the summer, of water play and butterfly painting. At that moment, the quiet of the house was broken by a child's cry, creeping up in volume from above.

By the time Josie reached the nursery, both twins were awake and standing in their cots.

"Hello, Maggie. Hello, Santa. Remember me? I expect you'd like your lunch!"

She smiled at their confused faces. After a moment of hesitation, they smiled back. She got them out of their cots, changed their nappies, and, a girl on each arm, she headed downstairs to find some food.

Altogether, the day passed very easily. Josie made cheese sandwiches, and after a few stories, she loaded the girls into their double buggy and went for a walk to the park. When they returned, Josie half expected somebody to be in. But as she opened the front door, the stillness inside told her that no soul had come in since she went out. It was five o'clock, so she began to prepare a pasta supper for the twins, which they enjoyed messily in their highchairs, before spending a last hour in the playroom, then bath time and stories, and finally dropping off to sleep in Josie's arms. Laying down sleeping twins without waking them was an art she had not forgotten and having turned on the night light and leaving the door slightly ajar, she crept down the stairs to her own evening.

Josie was standing in the kitchen wondering what to do with herself when the phone rang.

"Hello?"

"Hello, Josie. It's Diana."

"Oh, hi."

"I'm sorry not to call earlier. Is everything all right?"

"Yes, fine. The girls have just gone down to sleep, so nothing to worry about, all under control."

Josie laughed nervously and twiddled her hair.

"Super, thanks. Bye then."

The line went dead, and Josie looked at the telephone disbelievingly.

Outside dusk was falling and since her tummy was rumbling, she set about getting some dinner. The fridge was stuffed to bursting with all sorts of foods: platters of smoked salmon, ripe avocados, and a packet of uncooked, organic chicken breasts. It all seemed a bit extravagant for a Saturday night on her own, so she scrambled some eggs and toasted some bread before settling down on one of the shiny, polished stools to read her Kindle between mouthfuls. She tried not to rush but had never quite got the hang of eating alone. The time seemed to gallop and through some combination of hunger and shame, she bolted it down, washed up her plate, and scampered to bed with indigestion.

In bed, the night crowded in on her. She thought of her faceless employer, and he began to take on all sorts of monstrous shapes in her head. Was he as abrupt as his mum? Did he have appalling habits or smell of rotting fish and B.O.? She didn't even know where his bedroom was, but it couldn't be on this floor of the house as there was only her room, the twins' bedroom, a bathroom, and a curious room full of toys, still in their boxes. She curled her body up beneath the duvet and listened to the strange, subtle noises of the house. The bright light of her charging Kindle, the only familiar sight in the room. She closed her eyes against the odd objects, the looming shadows cast by grand furniture.

At some unknown, half-slept point in the night, there was a sharp click and a door opened somewhere near. The sound of a man's tread on wood, of something being put down in the hall, of the door closing, and the latch going down woke her. She reached for her iPhone. It was a quarter past midnight. She glanced out of the window and saw the red taillights of a black cab, orange oval clicking on in the sodium glow of the street outside. At least he wouldn't think she was mad for going to bed at practically the same time as the kids. She lay in bed, still as a statue, scarcely breathing, listening for clues. Who is this man? Where is his wife? She missed the Petersons and wanted to cry. Before long, the quiet was broken by a muffled male voice from below. Only one voice.

He must be on the phone. Silently, she sat up and strained to hear as the voice came closer.

"All I'm saying is, I can't believe you hired someone without even telling me..."

Josie held her breath and closed her hands into fists. His voice was crisp, educated.

"Yes, all right, all right...Mum, I've got to go. It's late...What's her name again?"

The words smacked Josie about the face. She pulled her knees up and clasped her arms around them. She was wearing the customised pyjamas that the Petersons had given her for her last birthday, and, in the dim light of the street, she could just make out the embroidered message on the bottoms: *We love Josie.*

"Mum, I've got to get to bed...yes, okay, okay. Bye."

He hadn't taken his shoes off and the brash sound of leather soles on wooden stairs clicked above her head and into nothingness.

5

ALEX

APRIL 1859

THE NIGHT WAS COAL BLACK AND THE RAIN HAD BEGUN IN earnest by the time Alex approached Battersea Bridge. His overcoat was not warm enough for the hour nor the season nor was the umbrella Mrs Haworth had given him sufficient. Still, he marched on. For, as in many aspects of his life, he had no choice. A fine horse drawn carriage clattered by on the road beside him, and the rackety sound of a well-attended inn crackled some way ahead. Not looking up, the amorphous roar of drunken humour and commonplace aggression keened in the air as he progressed past the rowdy establishment.

Alex had waited until he was certain that the family had departed for the theatre before taking his leave of Veronica Gardens. He had endured a great many humiliations in these last years and grown to consider himself hardened to embarrassment. But when he imagined the Cathcarts and the Christies readying themselves for the theatre, gathering cloaks and hats, and tittering frivolities, he could not bear to witness it. For that reason, he had preferred the loneliness of Sir Roland's study for a full half hour after he had heard the heavy, certain clunk of the front door closing. Having reviewed another few pages of the paper mountain before him, he closed the file, put away his pen, thanked the ashen-faced maid in the hallway, and departed. Stepping out into the grandeur of Veronica Gardens, now cloaked in early darkness, he was possessed of an inexplicable desire to walk back to his lodgings. The feeling of the cold air battering his face and the prospect of observing the city as night fell combined in his mind, and he began to stride. And, though he was hungry, increasingly so, and although a number of omnibuses passed him in his direction, he could not stop.

It was no mean journey. His lodging, which had been arranged by Mr Haworth upon his arrival in London, was a room in the home of a Mrs Patting on Battersea Bridge Road. That was a part of the city that Alex would wager Miss Cathcart had never seen and never would. Terrace upon terrace, thinly built and cramped with crowds of people, smelling of the Thames. He thought of Mrs Patting in her yellowing, thread-bare parlour with one log on the fire for the evening. He thought of his own room, neat and barely adequate, with a thin sheet of cotton not quite covering the narrow window onto the dank passage behind. It had become a form of game to Alex, that no person whom he met in the course of his professional life should know the dire straits in which he had found himself—apart from Mr and Mrs Haworth, of course, who knew every particular. Excluding them, it was his daily challenge to present himself as the educated, respectable man of the world that he was. For that reason, he kept his clothing, the last vestiges of his former life, in immaculate condition. He would not ordinarily have walked in the rain in this way, but every soul must have its frolics.

As he walked away from the city, his body tensed. He had been warned many times of robbers and thugs, of footpads who would lay in wait to attack a well-dressed person for anything they could get. He could fight if he needed to, but the wish was not there.

How different was this place to the airy, white beauty of Veronica Gardens, with its polished front doors and its wrought iron railings? The little church standing opposite the house, the motion of orderly carriages in the road outside. It was another world.

He had, already, had occasion to recall the singular advice given to him by Mr Haworth before entering the Cathcart household.

They had been alone in Mr Haworth's cluttered Fleet Street office, some weeks ago, pouring over the collected papers of *Brindle versus Cathcart*. Being the assiduous student that he was, Alex had read every inch of script available to him. He had devoured the papers, speedily, but no less effectively, taking in all the salient points, ordering them and his thoughts as he went. Mr Haworth, who had lived with the case for some years, had paced the room as he announced that Alex was to work for a time on the papers of Cathcart himself, searching for evidence, scouring for counter arguments. It was to be an inventory of hitherto unexamined details. Alex had felt the compliment of being allowed to undertake this task, for he knew Sir Roland to be one of Mr Haworth's most eminent clients.

"Thank you, sir. I am obliged to you for trusting me with this work."

"No, no, my boy. I'll have none of that. I've no doubt you're up to it, no doubt at all. And you need to establish yourself, Alex. Need to build your reputation, case by case, victory by victory. Cut your teeth. You can start with Cathcart. But I shall not deceive you. Between the two of us, the man is a difficult fish. He can be rude. Curses as a matter of routine, which may shock you. He has, what shall we say? A remarkably strong notion of himself. If he takes against you, you shall soon know of it."

He paused and looked at Alex for a moment too long and took a loud, considered breath before continuing.

"However, I see no reason that he shall not approve of you. He has been my client these twenty years, but I shouldn't say as I know him in any meaningful way. Clever, he undoubtedly is. He can be capricious and downright destructive. All I say is this: be guarded with the man. He is not a gentleman to charm others, but he has a way of knowing what is going on about him."

"Does he know my history, sir?"

"No. He does not."

And with that, the conversation had been closed. The two

men had returned to their papers, and the matter of Sir Roland Cathcart's character swept under the carpet like a pile of dust.

Now, after a week spent in the gentleman's household, Alex well understood why his employer had thought fit to warn him. The household, which gleamed from the outside, was beneath a warren of oddities. The staff appeared to rattle about in terrified obedience. Nobody gossiped; nobody laughed behind closed doors. He had, on his very first day, observed Miss Cathcart's maid leaving by the back door and carrying a suspiciously large parcel in her arms like a baby. Other servants worked in silence, even when their masters were absent. Sir Roland was the worst aspect. Belligerent, aggressive, cold. The sound of his raised voice was commonplace, and Alex had observed more than one maid to tremble in his presence. He had seen the man together with his family, his sister in law, Mrs Christie, and his nephew and niece. They, none of them, bore Sir Roland any warmth visible to the outsider, and Alex was inclined to think love a thing one cannot entirely conceal.

His MIND FLEW TO MISS CATHCART AND THE MEMORY OF that afternoon. How steady her voice had remained when others would have shrieked, how solidly she stood when others would have run. The wide skirts of her fine gown might have been cast in clay and her slender body rendered in bronze. Prior to seeing her, Alex had winced to hear her father speaking to her through the partially open door between the conservatory and the study. Facing her, he had felt a rare sympathy. He recalled the faint blush that came to her cheeks when she said, "I thank you," and he could not shake it.

The rain teemed down upon him even more ferociously than before, and he was relieved to see the weathered front door of Mrs Patting's boarding house hove into view. A dim light glowed from the front parlour window, and Alex began to imagine the warmth within. His tired feet climbed the steps and as his hand reached up for the knocker, the door swung open to reveal the portly lady of the house, smiling broadly and exclaiming:

"Mr Faraday! Mercy be upon us! I fancied you dead in a ditch, you poor boy!"

THE FOLLOWING MONDAY MORNING AN ODD SIGHT HAD greeted Alex upon approaching his desk in Veronica Gardens. The great pile of papers was exactly as he had left it, and the chair tucked neatly under suggested that no soul had touched it during the weekend. But squarely upon the top of the desk, atop his own notes, sat a small book. The brown of the cover was pristine, unmarked, and Alex fancied it new. He picked it up, feeling its weight, wondering at its providence. He opened it to find a title page: *Thomasina* by Ethel Turner Everett. *Never heard of her.* Turning it over, he found nothing more. It cannot have been intended for him. No person within this house took the least interest in him, save for Miss Cathcart. And he was quite certain that if she intended to suggest reading material, she would do so in person. It was possible, of course, that somebody had left it on the desk by mistake. Looking about him and concluding that this was a mystery he may never unravel, Alex placed the book upon the bookshelf beside his desk and got to work.

Later, when the library door opened, he was too engrossed in his work to notice. It was the sweep of wide skirts on the floor and a deliberate cough that took his attention away from his papers. Miss Cathcart swept into the room, her blonde hair fastened in a neat arrangement at the back of her head, strangely dulled by the dingy light of the room. She did not break step as she moved towards him with a small silver tray, a tea pot balanced atop it. When she arrived beside him, she plumped it down on the desk and smiled triumphantly. He noted the porcelain clarity of her skin and the scent of lavender that arrived with her.

"I didn't ask if you wanted it, for I believed that you would decline. And I am not accustomed, Mr Faraday, to taking 'no' for an answer. So, here is your morning tea."

"Thank you."

"You are welcome." She raised her eyebrows as if she had asked a question. Alex exhaled and placed down his pen. How tenacious this rich young woman was. Surely, she had suitors and bored relations and wispy aristocratic friends with whom to convene?

"When I saw you on Friday, we were about to attend the theatre."

Alex nodded but said nothing. After a pause, Miss Cathcart continued.

"It was an admirable performance, and one I had not previously seen. However, I cannot say that it was wonderful. I have never been a great one for the theatre. All that pitch black and watching actors strutting about. Not enough space to move—"

"Not enough talking?" He smiled as he said it, without thinking.

"Do you call me a chatterbox, Mr Faraday?"

"Certainly not." He was not displeased to see her laughing smile beaming back at him. Her eyes...like two great gleams of aquamarine. He almost blinked at the sight of them.

"May I ask how you spent yesterday? I always go to church with my aunt and cousins when we are in town. And then I read a book called *Thomasina*. Have you heard of it?"

Alex reached for the volume left on the desk and held it up.

"I had not heard of it, until this morning, miss. Here, I believe you may have misplaced it?"

"Thank you. But I have finished it. You may borrow it if you like. It is rather good. No end of fluff, of course. But that is to be expected in novels, especially those written by lady writers."

He wanted to laugh but refrained. There was precious little time in his life for reading novels. But when she handed it back to him, he took it.

"Thank you, miss. I went to church with Mr Haworth and his wife and children. They are kind people."

Immediately, he reprimanded himself, for he had said more than he intended. Left to his own devises, he would not attend church at all, for these past years had made him cynical. He did not tell Miss Cathcart this, of course. Nor did he tell her of the hours he had spent attempting to restore the appearance of his clothing after his long walk in the pouring rain.

"I am sure they are. I have not met Mrs Haworth, but I should like to do so. In fact, this reminds me. Mr Haworth called while you were on your visit to the post office this morning."

Alex looked up in surprise.

"He did not stay long but asked to see you. I told him that you were out posting some letters, and he said that he would ordinarily wait but could not do so as he was expected elsewhere. So, he asked that you attend him at his office at a convenient moment this afternoon. He shall be there from three o'clock, he said."

"I see."

Alex looked down at the mound of papers. It was odd that Mr Haworth had not sent a note instead of calling, but perhaps he had been called to that part of town on some other matter. Alex had, in fact, come to something of a natural break in his reading. An expedition to Fleet Street was unexpected and would likely take some hours out of his schedule. He began to plan the additional hours he would work in the morning, anxious as he was not to lose a moment, not to miss a line.

"It must be vexing to have to leave your work for a trip into town, but he was rather insistent. I like Mr Haworth very much. Some people invite trust, do they not?"

"Yes, they do. I am lucky to have him."

"Shall you depart here after luncheon? There is no point in going before, for Mr Haworth shall not be back in time, shall he? In any case, as fortune would have it, we may be able to ease your journey."

"Ease my journey?"

"Yes. Well, George and Philomena and I are going to the British Museum this afternoon. We shall set out after lunch and, if you are agreeable, we would happily take you as far as Fleet Street." Her blue eyes locked with his and softened. "Say you shall, Mr Faraday. It shall be much more comfortable than walking the streets in poor weather."

Her words struck an odd sound in his head, and he recalled his weary trudge home in the rain not a week before. Did Miss Cathcart know of this? Surely not. Thinking steadily, he was forced to concede the attractiveness of her offer. It would do no great harm to travel with them, and it would reduce the time he would take.

"Thank you, Miss Cathcart. If Sir Roland is content for me to travel in the carriage with you and Mr and Miss Christie, then I am pleased to accept the offer. I shall be happy to sit with the driver."

"Nonsense. I shall not hear of that. You are a university friend of George's, and you shall sit with us."

She made to depart the room, but he could not let her go without commenting.

"Please, Miss Cathcart. I appreciate your efforts to include me. I really do. It speaks well of you. But I am not here in my capacity as an acquaintance of Mr Christie. I am here as a clerk. You must see that it is not appropriate for me to—"

"I *must* see nothing of the sort. What is this capacity of which you speak? A lot of nonsense. You are George's friend, whatever may have happened to you in these last years, and whatever you may say. I shall hear nothing more about it. Tempt me and I shall have you sitting on the back like a boy..."

She smiled, and looking at him through heavy lashes, he wondered whether she had winked. Again, surely not.

By reason of this unexpected development, Alex declined the invitation to join the family for luncheon, concluding that his duties required him to work through the meal. This he did and, shortly before two o'clock, was readying himself to depart when the carriage was brought around, and Miss Cathcart appeared with Mr Christie and his sister.

"Here is Mr Faraday!" Miss Cathcart beamed, bobbing a curtsey and accepting her cloak from Havers who glanced towards Alex in an appraising manner. "Mr Faraday is to travel some of the way with us," she said by way of explanation to her relatives, who looked not a bit disconcerted. To Alex, the lady continued. "I am glad you are here in any case, for I shall need you to assist me with the Christies. They have been arguing about Charles Darwin throughout luncheon and my skills as a mediator are all but exhausted."

With this, she trotted towards the front door, her fine cloak clinging to narrow, purposeful shoulders, and forming a rich bell, swooping down to the floor. Alex did not doubt that Kitty Cathcart had her talents, but he should never have supposed diplomacy to be one of them. George Christie was agreeable and solicitous as they entered the carriage after the ladies, and Alex could not deny that he was grateful for this small taste of his prior life. The coachman clicked the heavy door shut, and as the carriage was turned about in the street, the four young people discussed the weather and the increasing number of carriages clogging the byways of the city.

"Mr Faraday, I hope you do not mind. You are coming to the museum with us."

"To the museum? But what about Mr Haworth?" he replied, sharper than he intended, but he was reeling. "Forgive me, Miss Cathcart. It is a generous thought, but Mr Haworth has asked me to attend him in Fleet Street."

"No, he has not."

"I'm sorry, miss?"

"I made it up."

"You made it up?" Alex glanced from her perfect face to the sight of the streets sweeping by outside, incredulous. He sank back in the seat. Miss Cathcart avoided his eye and the Christies peered at them both, their expressions inscrutable.

"I did. It was the only way to get you to come. And it shall be so interesting, Mr Faraday. I am sure that you shall enjoy it. We shall all enjoy it more if you are in our company. Is that not so?"

She looked to her cousin, whose neat hands were folded in the lap of her great skirt. Philomena Christie's eyes moved like small birds as she spoke, giving her an agitated appearance.

"It is indeed. It shall be excellent to have Mr Faraday among our number. But I cannot approve of your methods, Cousin. You could, for example, have simply invited him. Rather than procuring the gentleman's presence by deception."

George nodded and leaned back in the carriage, crossing his legs.

"Indeed. You, Kitty, are altogether too fond of tricks. Still, it is a pleasure to have you here, Faraday. All those years up at

Cambridge, poring over Latin and Greek, should not be for nothing, what?"

And so, the tone for the trip was set. Seeming to understand that his cousin had gone too far, George stepped forward and kept company with Alex for most of the afternoon. He spoke with such ease, as a man in his position might, of this and that. The two gentlemen reminisced but not too deeply; they talked of mutual acquaintances. They strolled between armless statues and great rocks carved deep with strange languages. At length, Alex found himself to be enjoying the expedition. It was as though a gap had opened in his ordinary world, and he had slipped out of it into a fantasy, a dream of sorts. A small bespectacled man approached him clutching a pocketbook. He asked the way to the Assyrian collection in English, but his accent was plain enough. Alex smiled an easy smile and replied:

"Bien sûr, monsieur. Vous le trouverez dans la pièce voisine, le long du couloir. Je prie pour que vous l'appréciez autant que moi."

It was as the man hobbled away that Alex felt an almost imperceptible tap upon his arm. He turned to find Miss Cathcart, broken free from her cousins. She pointedly studied the exhibit as she spoke.

"You speak French, Mr Faraday? How impressive. You are wasted in my father's study. For you shall find no romance languages in there, I'll wager."

"I would have you wager nothing, Miss Cathcart. It is a skill I am happy to let slip into abeyance. I hope you do not think that I dislike my work."

She turned and nearly smiled. The gold of her hair shone bright in the light of the window and her eyes positively sparkled blue. There was an angelic aspect to her appearance that belied her character.

"I cannot say."

And then she turned and walked away.

THE NEXT DAY ALEX HAD BEEN BENT OVER HIS WORK FOR

some hours when Molly appeared with a request that he speak with Sir Roland in the garden. His brow crinkled.

"Of course. Erm..."

"The easiest way is through the conservatory, sir."

She smiled warily, bobbed, and was gone.

During Alex's time at Veronica Gardens, he had been careful to confine himself to those parts of the house in which he was permitted to be. The property itself invited exploration, being towering and expansive. A great grand warren of rooms and corridors and sweeping staircases. But he kept himself to a tiny corner of it and the narrow path that led him there, like a mole. He had seen the conservatory, of course, a great glass green-tinged orb. But he had never properly seen the garden beyond.

When he stepped out into it, blinking into the spangled light, he could not help but be surprised. He paused, as though caught by an invisible thread. How foreign felt the sun upon his skin, warming the fabric of his clothes, lighting up undiscovered trifles. For a moment, he just looked. It was far larger than he had anticipated and surrounded by a square wall. Muted yellow London brick, creeping plants, branches twisted like old man's fingers. The air was heavy with scent and a bird sang. There was a little pond, an apple tree, a wide border of flowers clipped back for the winter. There was some trick of design, some slight of horticultural hand that made it seem wider than it was, broader. He exhaled and his body lost some of its tautness. Momentarily, he felt freed.

Recalling his purpose, he glanced about for Sir Roland. He was not there. But in one corner, standing by a naked wisteria waiting for spring and filling a birdbath with water from a large can, was Miss Cathcart. The sun caught the blonde of her hair like spun gold, and her pale skin glowed. Her slim figure, which he had long noticed, appeared subtly different. He saw for the first time that she was not so delicate as to be frail, as so many girls were. Kitty Cathcart was strong, able. She did not look around as she addressed him.

"There is a blackbird. And she and I are friends. So, I fill this for her each morning. It gives me such pleasure to see her hopping about merrily."

Then, she looked up at him. Smiling, artlessly. He looked about for traces of Sir Roland.

"There is no point in your looking for my father. He is in Birmingham."

"But—"

"I thought you might like to see the garden." She grinned, brightly, forcefully. He could argue. He could claim to object. But it would be a lie. Memories floated back to him, assailed him. A sun-drenched day in July, the feeling of dry grass under his head, the scent of the harvest. How far away that was now.

Suddenly, he asked: "Do you miss Yorkshire?"

He had read about Sir Roland's estate in the papers he was studying. The odd mention here and there, references to York and the Humber. And although he knew almost nothing of it, he had built an idea of it in his head.

"Longhaven? Yes, greatly. Any person who has been there would wish to go back as soon as possible. It is that manner of place."

She placed the can on the stone floor and straightened. He nodded, sketching the scene in his head. Sketching her in it, too.

"Some locations are like that, are they not? One cannot stay away from them, and when one does stray, one is pulled back. Do you comprehend me?"

"Yes. I comprehend you."

"Do you have a home in the country, Mr Faraday?"

"I do not. But I grew up away from London, if that is what you really ask. In Herefordshire."

Miss Cathcart stepped forward swiftly, closing the gap between them.

"Yes, that is what I really ask. I had a feeling about you, and I was right. It is gratifying when that happens, is it not?"

"I suppose so. Gratifying that you have been correct on a whim, maybe. But dangerous too."

"Why so?"

"Well, if one guesses and strikes lucky, one may come to believe that one is always correct."

A string supporting a well pruned rose had slipped, and Miss

Cathcart pulled it up. She avoided the thorns. There was a faded bloom the gardener had missed, so she pulled it off with her fingers. And then she laughed.

"Perhaps you are right. I shall be on my guard against this peril."

Alex was suddenly too warm, sweat beaded on his back. He had spent too many hours closeted within doors, pen scratching upon paper, eyes straining.

"Do you think you shall ever go back? To Herefordshire, I mean."

"I have no plans to. My life is in London. Or wherever else my work takes me."

"That sounds rather an adventure. I hope you see it so."

He tried to. For pessimism is the death of effort, and without effort, there can be no hope.

"Are your people still in Herefordshire?"

In the distance, he heard a door opening and closing, voices, footsteps. But he could not look away from her.

"I do not really have any people, Miss Cathcart. It is a long story. And too depressing for such a fine day as this."

Their eyes locked and, for a moment, he could not disengage them. Suddenly, he railed against it all. The unplanned candour, the feeling of proximity. He was busy, living the life he had been given, building an existence against the odds. She dropped the faded rose blooms into a wooden tray on the floor. A lock of her hair had come loose from its pin and fell across her cheek. She looked as though she had been painted into the scene, in oils, forever.

"You must excuse me, miss. It is a beautiful garden. I am glad to have seen it. But I think it may be best for both of us if I return to my work."

"You are cross with me, Mr Faraday. About yesterday."

In this, she was not far wrong. He was frustrated by her; he was confused by her. Anger also rose up inside him, but was it for her? He was inclined to think it the vicissitudes of fortune that angered him. The straitjacket of convention that placed him on one side of the wall and her on another.

"I am not cross with you. It is not my place to be cross with you, so I am not."

"Well, that is as good as saying it right out."

She laughed again, but he cut her off.

"I disagree. There is no replacement for saying it right out. I used to be able to speak as I found. And now I find that is not possible. My place in this house is as a professional servant, Miss Cathcart. I am here to work. I do not know what you mean by your —kindness—to me. But I am not your plaything."

She coloured, and her eyes steeled.

"I have sought to treat you as a friend."

"If you wish to be my friend, then I am flattered. But is not the essence of friendship, sympathy?"

"There is more to friendship than sympathy. What of sharing? What of companionship?"

"Those are fine words, Miss Cathcart. But you must look to your own self as well. I would not wish to get you into trouble with your father."

Another door in the distance and a bell. Alex's eyes flicked towards the house, but Miss Cathcart ignored it.

"You shall not."

A voice sounded in the house and came closer.

"You enjoyed our trip yesterday. Admit it."

"I did. Of course, I did. But it cannot happen again."

However much he may wish it.

"Good day, Miss Cathcart."

He bowed and pulled himself away from her. She said nothing as he returned to the house, but they both noticed the stern profile of Havers in an upstairs window. A knot of determination formed in Alex and tightened. He strode back through the conservatory, green, hot, and into the house where shadows fell upon him.

6

JOSIE

FEBRUARY 2018

As Diana had promised, Maggie and Santa woke up at six o'clock and began their chorus of squeaks and half-formed words to summon Josie from her bed. She dressed herself in her best jeans and a plain pullover and tied her runaway hair back in a band. Looking down at her toes, she decided there was something disturbing about letting a strange man see her bare feet and so slipped on some socks before taking the washed and dressed children downstairs for breakfast. Both children were in their high-chairs and Josie was just taking toast out of the toaster when James Cavendish appeared in the doorway.

"Good morning. You must be Josie." He advanced towards her holding his hand out to a chime of simultaneous 'Daddy' from the girls.

"James Cavendish."

"Oh, hello." Josie turned and was momentarily silenced. He was tall, like Diana, and he had something of her about his face, the handsome plain lines, the pale tan. His eyes were different though, hazel shot through with green. Josie looked away from them. "I'm just making toast."

"I can see that."

"Erm...would you like some?"

69

He looked mildly shocked by the question and answered quietly, "Yes, please."

"Your mum showed me where things are."

"Yes, she's fond of doing that."

"I mean, I didn't snoop around or anything..."

He looked up from kissing the twins good morning and a confused expression crossed his face.

"Erm, good. Look, I'm sorry I wasn't here yesterday. Things have been a bit hectic at work."

"Don't worry. I was fine. I mean, we were fine." She smiled fleetingly at Maggie and Santa before turning back to the buttering of toast and the pouring of tea.

"No, I should have been here to welcome you. How about we do something fun today to make up for it? London Zoo?"

Once this was said, Maggie started roaring like a lion. And so, even if she had wanted to, Josie could not possibly have refused. As it happened, she loved zoos, so after the twins had eaten and had been cleaned up, they all got their outside clothes on and headed out to the Tube station. By the time they arrived at Regent's Park, both girls were asleep. Realising that their slumber left her alone with their father, Josie began to miss them greatly. He was not the horror she'd expected, but he was pretty short on words. They did not have to pay at the entrance as James flashed a family card. Josie, who was at war with silence, saw her chance.

"Do you come here a lot then?"

"It's a great day out for the kids. Maggie loves the tigers. I'm at work so much, I try to make sure we do interesting stuff when I am home. Here, have the card." He pulled out his wallet again and handed it to her. "You can come whenever you want in the week." He said it casually and she felt oddly dispirited.

"Thank you. It'll make a change from the Tower of London. My last family was mad on that. All the staff there know me, and I think I could do the guided tours myself. Getting up to speed on the zoo will make a new woman of me."

He completely ignored this attempt at conversation. No smile. No polite quiet laughter. No nothing.

"My mother said you looked after twins before?"

"Yes. They have an older sister as well."

"What did the father do?"

"They both worked actually." It sounded sharper than she intended. "He's a banker. His bank sent him to Dubai. I don't think he had too much say in the matter. And Annie, his wife, is a lawyer. She managed to get a transfer to her firm's Dubai office, so there they've gone. I've promised I'll go out and visit them in the summer. I hope you don't mind?"

He looked at her blankly. "Why would I? You do get holiday, you know." The whisper of a smile crossed his lips.

In relative if not easy harmony, they looked at the reptiles before Maggie woke up, followed by Santa. They made their way to the big animals, the girls walking as far as they could and taking turns on James' shoulders to get a better view. After a lunch in the zoo cafe, the girls played on the swings for a while before they set off back to Veronica Gardens. Maggie, who demanded to walk from the Tube station, slowed their pace down, and by the time James put his key in the lock of the front door, it was getting dusky. They had only just stepped into the entrance hall when James sauntered away, looking at his phone. He walked into the study without a word.

Josie blinked before attending to the girls' coats and shoes. James's voice, obviously on the phone, began to rumble from the other side of the study door. She looked at it and wondered if it would open again that evening. Beside her, the twins were quiet.

"Right, ladies. Who fancies chicken for dinner?"

The question met with hearty answers in the affirmative, and Josie and the children headed into the kitchen. After another round of feeding and cleaning and laughing as they tried to spoon food into one another's mouths, they trundled upstairs to start the bedtime routine. Josie knelt by the bath and tested the water with her elbow before stripping them of their little dresses and multi-coloured tights and lifting them in. Santa dampened a bright red foam letter *A* and stuck it to Josie's forehead before collapsing with laughter. Josie began to giggle back but was surprised to hear his voice behind her.

"Sorry about that call."

"That's okay. We had dinner, didn't we, girls?"

"*You* had dinner as well?"

"No, sorry. I mean, it's just Nanny-speak. The girls had chicken for dinner, and I had a cup of tea. I didn't want to disturb you but if you want to take over bath time, I'll go to my room. Or if you want me to get them ready for bed, I'll bring them down to say goodnight. Whatever you like, really."

His gaze trained on her like a page of foreign script.

"Is that a joke? I would never ask you to go to your room or bring them downstairs to say goodnight to me. This isn't a Victorian novel. How about we go for a combined effort?"

And that was what they did. After an interlude of towel cuddling and toothbrushing, the girls were snuggled on either side of James on the low sofa in their room, and Josie was readying their cots and fetching their stories for him to read. Santa thrust *The Owl Who Was Afraid of the Dark* at Josie and said, "'tory!"

"I think maybe Daddy might like to read it."

She glanced at him, and he nodded before she flicked on the night light, kissed their soft foreheads and disappeared downstairs. Although she knew she should get herself some toast and make herself scarce, Josie couldn't help but observe the garden for a while before it lost the light altogether. The yellow of the daffodils seemed to sing through the dingy light. She checked her phone. She had 'How are you?' messages from Annie and Lauren and even her sister, Hattie. She would respond later. She didn't really know the answer.

The kettle was just about to boil when the doorbell rang. Josie made her way along the wide wood-lined hallway and glanced up the stairs. There was no sign of James, so she concluded that she had better answer the door.

"You must be Nanny," came a shrill voice, cut like a diamond, from the doorstep. "I'm Marcia Andrews. I work with James and live not too far away." She regarded Josie with open intrigue.

"Would you like to come in?"

"Only if he's here, which I shouldn't think he is. Who would be in at this time on a weekend evening? No, he'll be out, no doubt, but I wanted to drop this off." She thrust a lever arch file full of papers towards Josie. "It is some due diligence that he'll want to read before the morning. He knows what it's about."

Josie looked down at it.

"Thanks. Erm, actually..."

She was about to say that he was in if she wanted to wait when Marcia cut her off.

"I'll be off then. I often pop round so I'm sure I'll see you again. Make sure he gets that file. Bye." And she turned on her low block heel and was gone.

Josie closed the door and heard the unmistakable rasp of a snore from upstairs. It was understandable. She crept into the nursery and discovered the twins asleep in their sleeping father's arms on the sofa, storybooks slipped onto the floor. Very gently she placed her hands under Santa and lifted her before placing her in her cot and tucking her up. Getting to Maggie was a bit more tricky. She had to lean in very close to James's face and ease her hands at an odd angle underneath the little girl. Just when she thought she had made it, her hair sprang into his face, and he woke with a jolt.

"Sorry," whispered Josie as she lifted the sleeping Maggie up and into her cot. She tried to remember the last time her hair had brushed against the face of a sleeping man, but it was too long ago to contemplate.

James sat forward on the sofa and blinked at her.

"Thanks for putting them down. I just sparked out."

"I didn't mean to wake you."

"Well, I'm glad you did. Let's go downstairs."

Josie left the door ajar behind them, and they made for the kitchen.

"Someone called round while you were up there. Marcia. She said she worked with you, and she gave me a big folder. She said you'd want to read it before the morning."

"Did she indeed?" James opened the fridge door and took out a bottle of white wine. Josie was alarmed to see him take two glasses off the shelf and set them down on the shining marble surface.

"Well, not right now. Right now, I am going to cook us dinner and find out a bit about you. And then, maybe later, if I can't think of anything else to do, I might read Marcia's file. If she comes around again, you can answer the door as long as it is understood that I am not at home, right?"

Josie let out a quiet laugh.

"Of course." She was used to pretending people were out when they weren't and passing on messages to other people's family, neighbours, colleagues, lovers. He began taking ingredients out of the fridge and assembling them.

"Thank you. I was going to have some toast and go to bed with my Kindle."

"Well, I hope I can improve on that." He began taking out more pans than he needed and sorting through knives and condiments while Josie, feeling rather useless, sat on the seat by the French doors and gazed out into the garden, now shrouded in night. Before her eyes, a set of garden lights flicked on, shining through leaf and bramble, and Josie turned to see James moving away from a switch on the wall. They said nothing as he cooked. Silence sat down in the room like a lazy stranger. James didn't ask her before he refilled her wine glass, and she began to worry that she was not controlling herself as she should. Unwelcome memories flew into her face.

"You seem interested in the garden?"

"It looks lovely. I haven't been out in it yet though. Do you have a gardener?"

James blinked before answering, somewhat hesitantly.

"Erm, yes. He comes—in the week, I think. So, I guess you'll see him then." He seemed to want to say more but turned back to his cooking in silence.

"I wonder...do you think he'd mind if the children had a little plot each for planting flowers? I have done that with my previous families and the kids loved it. Especially at this time of year, it's an easy win. They get results very soon."

"Sounds great. Do it."

"I'll ask him when he comes. Make sure he doesn't mind me carving up his masterpiece!"

He turned back to her, saucepan in hand.

"You should ask him *where* would be good. But you're not asking him for permission. I say you can do it. The garden's for living in, not for looking at."

His expression was so serious, but she found herself wanting to laugh.

"Roger." Josie smiled and took another sip of her wine. She ought to ask what the guy's name was and who paid him and whether she was expected to organise him in anyway. But somehow, between the glistening surfaces and the smell of the lilies on the breakfast bar and the disconcerting feeling of being alone with this man, she could not.

The kitchen in which he was bounding around was ostentatiously modern, but just beyond, the high ceilings and elaborate sculpted cornices of the main house gave away its age. It had fireplaces, too, and Josie bet they hadn't been lit in a million years, but they were there all right. Great, grand frames that one could lean against, surrounded in immaculate tile. It amused her to think of how resilient the old Victorian features were. Someone with lots of money had really gone at this place but they couldn't hide the richness of the age it was built in. The lovely details, the great wide doorways, the lavish bay windows. Josie wanted to curl into it. She sipped her wine, and James looked up from his meal prep.

"I love old houses. Old gardens too."

She gestured outside, and he looked completely bemused.

"Just imagine how many people have lived in them and when. These walls must have seen a fair bit over the centuries. Bet they have some memories."

"Walls are walls. They don't have memories."

He looked pretty steely about this.

"You may think that, but I reckon places can have a memory. They can get imprinted with things that happen to them, just like people. If you ask me, buildings, especially houses where people have lived, have characters of their own. You get me, right?"

"No, I don't. Houses do not have characters. People have characters. Houses are just what people make them."

Time passed in a clatter of dishes and scraping of wooden

spoons on saucepans and before long Josie was sitting down in front of a chicken supper, facing James Cavendish.

"Looks lovely. Thank you."

"No problem. I enjoy cooking, although I don't get time to do it much."

"I'm guessing that you work late quite often?" She smiled to mellow the question.

"Yep. Anyway, enough about me. What about you? Tell me about yourself."

"I'm a nanny, but you know that..."

"Family?"

"Yes. But not many of us. I have a sister and a little niece. My parents are both dead."

He looked her right in the eyes but did not express any sadness as a normal person might have done.

"Do you see much of your sister and niece?"

"I try to see them every few weeks. They live in Surrey—about half an hour out of Victoria. Hattie's a single mum so I try to help her out with things..."

"What kind of things?"

"I helped her decorate her flat, and I give her a hand with Emily. She is a lovely girl, but she can be a handful. She is clever and demanding if you know what I mean."

Josie looked up to see a slight smile cross his face, and he nodded.

"So, I take her for days out every now and then and try to help with homework, things like that. I took them on holiday to France last summer and her French really came on."

"I bet. Did *you* enjoy it?"

"Of course." Josie smiled and ate a mouthful of her chicken. She noticed the outline of his body under his pale shirt and glanced back to her plate.

"What about you? Do you speak French?"

"Only the schoolgirl variety, but I can manage on holiday."

"There are people I know at work who get bilingual nannies so that their children grow up with other languages. What do you think of that?"

Josie blanched. If he had been choosing, would he have chosen her?

"Well, I think it depends on the family and how old the children are. With kids who are Maggie and Santa's age, I like to sit back and see what they are into, rather than force things on them."

"Sometimes you need to have things forced on you, don't you? I mean we force school on children, and we force them to go to the doctor when they're ill. A bit of coercion is a necessary thing, isn't it? It is important to help them be the best version of themselves and sometimes, that means giving them a push, surely?"

"I didn't say that I wouldn't encourage interesting things. But you asked about languages, and Maggie and Santa are not yet two. They don't even speak English yet. I know that it is fashionable, but, personally, I don't hold with it unless they come from a bilingual family, and it is part of their culture anyway. If I thought they were showing signs of interest, I'd encourage it."

Josie felt her face flush, riled.

"Fine," he said, dismissively. "If you think there is anything they might enjoy or be good at, just tell me, and you can have it. That's all I'm saying."

The flecks of green in his eyes seemed brighter for a moment, and Josie felt unsteady. He topped up her wine again and went back to asking her about her family.

"How old is Emily?"

"She's thirteen and raring to learn everything it seems. I have promised her a trip to the science museum in the Easter holidays, and she'll love that. She's a budding scientist."

"Does she go to a good school?"

"Yes, well, it's the best one that I can afford."

He appeared to choke on his food but made a quick recovery.

"The best one *you* can afford?"

"Yes, well, my sister, Hattie, doesn't have much cash, so I help out by paying the fees. Fortunately, Emily has a partially paid scholarship, which makes things easier. I make up the rest."

He raised his eyebrows and looked at her steadily. His stare made her feel as though she were being held under a sharp light.

"Nice of you."

"She's worth it. It's like I said, she's clever and demanding, so she needs to be stimulated. She doesn't come from a high achieving family but that doesn't mean she can't achieve things herself."

"Of course not."

An odd look passed across his face as he said this, and for a moment, their eyes locked over the empty plates in the white light of the perfect kitchen. The silence lasted a beat too long before his phone began to vibrate against the marble surface beside them. He answered it, standing up. Dismissed, thought Josie.

"Marcia?"

His brow furrowed, and he turned to the wall as he spoke.

"I've got it, but I haven't read it yet...No. There's no need for you to come round...I'll call you if I have any questions...Okay. My car comes at six. I'll pick you up at five past?...Great. Thanks, Marcia."

He placed the phone face down on the surface in front of him and took a deep breath before turning to see that Josie had busied herself with loading the dishwasher and wiping the table clean. She realised that he was watching her and focussed on the dish-washer tablet and the dial on the machine.

"That was quick work. Thanks."

"Well, thank you for supper. It was delicious. I think I might turn in now. My two little alarms will be going off at six, so I'd better get some shut eye."

She smiled jauntily and scrunched her shoulders but immediately felt like a child herself. His eyes *on her* were inscrutable.

"Sure. I have to read Marcia's file."

Josie looked at the art deco style clock mounted on the wall and was amazed that it was nearly midnight. How had they talked so long? Had she said too much?

"Okay. Night-night then."

He looked away as he replied, "Night, Josie."

⚜ 7 ⚜

ALEX

MAY 1859

ALEX DID ALL HE COULD TO PUT HIS VISIT TO THE BRITISH
Museum and the discussion in the garden out of his head in the
days that followed. He decided, for he had no choice, to trust in
Miss Cathcart's assertion that she had settled matters with Mr
Haworth. In any event, he should be embarrassed to explain the
matter to his employer. It was, no doubt, a case of the least said, the
better.

One morning, some days later, Alex was sat at the back table in
Sir Roland's library once more. His progress with the papers
provided to him was good but had yielded no new evidence. Alex
refused to be put off. He urged himself to keep going. Miss Cathcart had not paid him her customary visit that morning, which
assisted his concentration. He had observed her maid—Springer—
leaving the house carrying another package and wondered at it
afresh. What could the girl be doing, and was it connected to her
mistress? Where was the young miss herself? The clock in the hall
ticked and the motion of the house was underway. Alex told
himself to mind his business and ignore all save for his work.

He was doing just that when the door swung open with a dull
thud and the portly form of Sir Roland appeared.

"Ha! There you are," came his greeting.

"Sir." Alex stood, and the two men regarded one another.

Alex was the taller by a matter of inches, and he had been told before that his stare could unseat a man, could make a person feel unnerved. Sir Roland's moustaches quivered, and he began to move about the room.

"I have had little time with you, young man. The demands of business, you know. I returned from Birmingham only last eve, but I am here now. Now, tell me"—he turned to face Alex—"what have you found?"

"Thus far, precious little, I am afraid. I wish it were otherwise. However, there is still much to go through."

"Hmm," grunted Sir Roland. "Tell me. When you are about this work, what do you believe yourself engaged in?"

"I am gathering evidence for your case against Mr Brindle, sir. I am searching your private papers, as supplied to me, for matters that may assist in proving your case that the invention of the rotating frame was yours."

"And where does it go? Where is it leading?"

"A formal document, setting out that evidence. And one day, to a trial of the issues in question."

"So, a court case?"

"Yes, in layman's terms, sir."

Sir Roland, who had re-commenced pacing the room, paused. Standing near the glass and foliage of the conservatory, he was bathed in green light.

"It is not a court case." His voice was calm, measured, cold. "It is a war, boy. A war of attrition. No man steals from me that which is mine. And if he does, I shall find him out. I seek him out, and he shall regret it. Brindle is such a one. He cannot afford to continue this fight, even if he were right. Do you understand what I am saying to you?"

"Yes, sir."

Alex understood perfectly well. He was young, and his training not yet complete. But he knew how a rich man might use all manner of methods to continue a legal action, to extend the life of the dispute from months, years, decades, even. How the smallest new matter must be dealt with in excruciating detail until nobody could remember why it was raised in the first place. So often, the case would be concluded by one or both parties exhausting their resources, rather than justice being served. The law was a snake that squeezed the life out of its protagonists. Sir Roland knew, and he abetted it. A sour taste lingered in Alex's mouth.

"Good." A ghost of a smile appeared on Sir Roland's face. "Too many men in this world do not know what they are bloody doing. You will go far."

At that moment, the men were interrupted by a hue of noise from the neighbouring conservatory. A booming cry of surprise was joined by a shriek and the crashing sound of an object falling. Sir Roland strode across the room and opened the door.

"What the devil?"

Leaping to his feet, Alex followed the man of house into the conservatory. He appeared at Sir Roland's shoulder and observed the scene. Before them, stood Havers, red-faced and caught between bellows. Upon the floor, by the chaise, sat a maid and a table on its side. The maid, Alex recognised as Molly. Her face was ashen, and she trembled. Upon seeing her master and Alex at the door, she began an ungainly scramble to stand up.

"Get up, girl, at once! Look at the spectacle you make before Sir Roland!"

As she rose, unsteadily, there were tears in her eyes. If there was any sympathy in Sir Roland, Alex did not observe it. He appeared to be looking upon the bizarre scene as a passing curio.

"What is it? What is this nonsense?"

"Asleep, Sir Roland. Laying on the chaise, asleep, if you please. That is how I found her. Shocking. I apologise to you, Sir Roland, for having raised my voice. But I was shocked to my core."

The butler took a great breath and pushing his chest out, seemed to calm. He looked to the poor girl, unwaveringly.

"Come, Molly, to my office. I shall know how to deal with this."

Her sobs, which had been quiet, grew loud.

"There is only one way in which to deal with this lack of discipline."

Sir Roland gestured to his butler, as if in agreement and something in Alex rose. A sound in his ear that he could not stop. Just as Havers was about to push Molly from the room, he spoke:

"Sir Roland, I..." Alex eased his expression as the man turned. "Forgive me for involving myself in what is a domestic affair. But I wonder if this young woman is quite well?"

Molly's eyes looked up to him, pleading and grateful all at once.

For his part, Sir Roland appeared thoroughly bored by the whole business. Havers' brow crinkled as he regarded Alex.

"If I may say, Sir Roland. She appears perfectly well to me. Aside from being upset. And that is not to be wondered at. She shall be even more upset when she is dismissed!"

Alex was surprised at the emotion the man showed over the affair. He was exhibiting a kind of indiscipline himself. What a most peculiar house this was. At that moment, the opposite door swung open, and all heads turned to face it.

"Who is being dismissed?"

Miss Cathcart's voice was bright and cheerful, but she was short of breath and flushed. She raised her eyebrows playfully at her father and then turned a weighty expression on Havers.

"Miss Cathcart, how fortuitous. This young maid has, just moments ago, been discovered in the act of sleeping on the chaise. I came upon her myself. Now, if you will excuse us, I shall escort Molly to the servants' quarters—"

"Thank you, Havers. That will not be necessary. Molly was on the chaise because I asked her to lay there."

The man's colour rose, and his cheeks began to wobble.

"Asked her?"

"Yes. I asked her to pose for one of my drawings. I was just going to fetch my sketch pad and charcoals when I heard the racket in here."

She smiled broadly and sweetly. Miss Cathcart had the sort of face that changed radically when she smiled. Frowning, she was attractive in a mechanical sort of way. Smiling, she was beauty and it was her. Alex felt a lightness in his head growing. Moving swiftly towards Havers, Miss Cathcart placed her hand upon his arm.

"I am sorry to have taken up time in your day, Havers. You are so busy and run the servants so effectively. But it is all my fault. I must beg that you indulge my hobbies and give me, maybe half an hour with Molly. I am sure that Mrs Cooper shall spare her."

For a moment, he looked as though he might argue. But just as quickly, his expression changed. His arms straightened by his sides and acquiescence stretched across his face.

"Very well, Miss Cathcart. Molly, you must wash your face before sitting for Miss Cathcart. Come."

With that, the two servants bundled out of the room in a haze of black and white.

Sir Roland regarded his daughter sceptically.

"I did not know you had taken to sketching?"

"I have, Father. It is such a fitting hobby for a young woman, do you not think? Calm, contemplative, decorative."

"I should like to see the fruits of your efforts. One day."

The daughter's chin tilted up. The father stared at her, severely. Alex began to feel as if he were an intruder, listening in on a private code.

"And with the added advantage of producing something pretty for others to look at."

"That depends on the subject. And the skill of the artist. Enough of this." He raised his eyebrows enquiringly, even doubtfully, before turning away and ushering Alex back into the darkened cavern of the library. The last thing the young clerk saw was the smile on Kitty Cathcart's face as her father closed the door on her.

CHARLES HAWORTH SQUINTED AS HE POURED TWO MEASURES of whiskey and then leaned back in his leather armchair. Alex thanked him and drank. The amber liquid burned his throat and warmed him all at once. Beyond the baize door, the men could hear Mrs Haworth instructing the servants, the scrape of chair legs on the wooden floor, the clatter of plates being tidied away. The men sat on either side of a small window from which there streamed the hazy sun of the late afternoon.

"How do you find Veronica Gardens?"

Mr Haworth knocked out his pipe as he asked the question, but Alex did not believe that it was such a casual enquiry. He exhaled and half laughed in response.

"Honestly, sir, I can scarcely answer. It is certainly memorable."

"Memorable? How so?"

"I find the household, well..."

"You need not be coy with me, Faraday. Be as candid as you wish. We need to be frank with one another, and I would be more comfortable if we were."

The two men's eyes met, and Alex nodded in understanding. Recent years had taught him gruelling lessons. That everything one had may be lost in an instant. That social connexions one thought were solid may count for little, nothing in fact. But he had learned to trust the word of the man beside him. And if Mr Haworth asked for honesty, then honesty he would get.

"The household is odd, sir. The servants are not a happy party. The butler is a tyrant, and most of the others appear to be afraid of him. I know it is commonplace for there to be politics below stairs, but at Veronica Gardens, it is somehow out of the usual way. An atmosphere of malevolence pervades the whole house—but I cannot say exactly why. I only know that, for all my disadvantages in this life, I am pleased that I do not live there."

Haworth smiled. "That is one way of putting it. I have felt the same at times. Have you seen much of the famous Miss Cathcart?"

He made no expression as he asked, and Alex's eyes flicked to what was left of his drink.

"Is she so famous?"

"Oh, yes. Catherine Cathcart is quite the talk of fashionable society."

Alex shifted in his seat. Fashionable society did not deserve her.

"Miss Cathcart is one of the most unusual features of the house, sir. Although I do not find *her* at all malevolent. If you had asked me three weeks ago, I might have said she was a rich young lady in want of occupation. Now, I am not sure I know what she is.

Different, contrarian even. Thoughtful, possibly to a fault. Certainly verging into nosiness. Confident to the point of arrogance. But admirable, for all that."

He could have said more, much more. He reminded himself that Kitty Cathcart occupied a different world to his. For was she not a great lady, a wealthy beauty? The sort of girl who would be a chatelaine of some stately pile in years to come? Who would pick up good and interesting causes along her way and put them down again just as easily?

"I cannot claim to know the girl at all well. As you know, I only met her at Margaret Christie's soiree. But to some extent, her reputation goes before her. Her physical beauty is widely admired, but her character has been called wild. She is known for being unconventional and independent. Her relationship with her father is said to be troubled. And one cannot wonder at that. He is not the sort of man who easily tolerates disobedience." The older man made a great display of lighting his pipe, and smoke billowed between them.

Alex smiled at his employer's talent for understatement. "No. Indeed, I believe that kinship to be a tempestuous one. Of course, it is none of my business. But..."

"Spit it out."

Alex asked outright one of many questions that had occurred to him:

"Do you know what happened to Miss Cathcart's mother? Mrs Christie's sister."

"Yes. What a tragedy that was. I saw her once, years ago. It was before she was married. She must have been just a girl really. I was courting the future Mrs Haworth at the time—and had suggested to her and her mother a trip to the Royal Academy. We had seen most of the paintings and were just lingering in the long gallery when they swept in. The Honourable Miss Esther Alton, together with her father, Lord Fortescue. I can see them now. There was a certain hush when they came in, for they were the best sort of *ton*, as people used to say then."

Alex leaned forward in his comfortable chair, unaccountably interested in this reminiscence of an afternoon, long ago.

"She had the blondest hair—it was like sunshine. And when we passed father and daughter at the entrance to the next gallery, I heard the old lord call his daughter by her pet name, 'Star.' It sticks in the memory. You know, as things sometimes do, even if one cannot quite say why. Now, it revisits me. Each time I have seen the young Miss Cathcart in the street or alighting her carriage, and when I met her at Mrs Christie's, I have thought of that moment."

Alex let out a mirthless laugh. "I cannot imagine Sir Roland calling his child 'Star' or anything else kindly. In my experience of the house, he rarely addresses her in a civil manner."

"That is a great shame. I cannot say that it is a surprise to me. I believe that Esther Alton was married to Sir Roland in the same year as Mrs Haworth and I. It was only months after our near encounter at the Royal Academy. I cannot know the details of that union, but Lord Fortescue was said to be in financial trouble. His estate, in his family since the Conqueror, was failing. Portions of it had been sold off over the years until there was only a shadow of the original left. But they had their titles and they were undoubtedly one of the best families. Sir Roland, on the other hand, had money and plenty of it. He was only knighted some years later. When he married Miss Cathcart's mother, he was a wealthy commoner. Of course, I know none of the details and much of this is speculation. But it has always seemed to me that a bargain was struck between the lineage of the lady and the resources of the gentleman, and that was that."

A discordant note sounded in Alex's mind, for he had never adjusted to the notion that marriage could be a bargain.

"After that, it was never my good fortune to see Mrs Cathcart, or Lady Cathcart, as she became. One read about her, glittering at this or that ball. And it was announced in the news sheets when Miss Cathcart was born. I believe that I was first retained by Sir Roland a couple of years later, but of course, my role did not involve meeting his family, or even discussing them. He is not a man for pleasantries."

"Do you recall when his wife died, sir?"

"Yes, very well. It was the winter of 1847. She took a fever that carried her off. I believe her daughter was around the age of ten.

The Cathcarts had no more children, unfortunately. It may have assuaged Sir Roland's temper had he a son!"

Mr Haworth laughed gently, but Alex's mind was circling. Circling and diving.

Alex drained his glass and re-crossed his legs. He knew perfectly well that Mr Haworth's client was a titan of industry, a great engineer with a flair for business. His invention, the rotating frame, was used in factories up and down the country. Accurate, uncommonly fast, and enduring. From that one object, the man had built a fortune. He recalled Sir Roland's own words to him on the subject of his work. Vicious, uncompromising words. At the same time, he recalled Miss Cathcart, bathed in the golden light of the walled garden. What darkness lurks beneath the carapace? And if one knew beforehand, would one ever have the strength to lift it?

❧ 8 ❧

JAMES

FEBRUARY 2018

THE NEXT MORNING THE FAMILIAR JANGLE OF JAMES'S ALARM filled the room, and he reached his hand across the crisp cotton covered pillow to turn it off. It was five-thirty, and his car would be pulling up outside in half an hour. He had finally gone to bed at two a.m. after reading Marcia's file. And spending more time than he would care to admit considering his household's new resident. Fatigue wrapped around his limbs, but he fought it, kicked it off. He pushed back the covers, exposing his naked body to the discomfort of the morning air and sat up. After checking his diary, blinking into the grey-white light of his phone screen, he showered and dressed. He had trained himself not to notice the empty emperor-sized bed and the empty walk-in wardrobe and the other tell-tale signs of wealth and loneliness. As per his routine, he made his way down the polished wooden staircase. As he rounded the corner on to the first floor of the house or, as his mother would have it, the 'nursery floor,' he heard a babble of laughter from the twins' room. Through the door, the softness in Josie's voice struck him again.

"Where's that bunny gone to? Is she hiding in Santa's bed? Aha! Are you ready to get out, darling? Oh, there's a warm, lovely girl."

88

The noise continued, and, on the other side of the door, a smile broke involuntarily across James's face.

Since he had found himself in this position, they had had two agency nannies, both oddly disengaged. He even had to have his mother staying in the house for a week, although it was fair to say that as a childcare-giver, she left much to be desired. For all that, he had never wanted to stay at home rather than go to work. But here it was, breaking out over him, like a sweat. He knew his car was waiting outside and, no doubt, Marcia was paused three streets away in her first floor flat, pinch-faced and clutching her Mulberry handbag. He didn't have time to linger.

James tapped lightly on the nursery door and entered to find Josie standing in the middle of the room cuddling Santa and her bunny while Maggie, obviously the earlier riser, was sat on the floor drinking milk from her bottle. Josie smiled nervously but something about her beamed at him like a laser. The hullabaloo of her chocolate brown hair raged around her shoulders and down her back. She wore pale blue pyjamas that, unless he was seeing things, had 'We love Josie' embroidered all over them. Realising he was staring too obviously at her person, he made himself look away.

"Good morning."

"Good morning," she replied brightly. "Look, Daddy is an early bird, isn't he? We are a bit behind schedule, aren't we?" Santa giggled and pushed her bunny into the riot of Josie's curly hair.

"Shall we ask Daddy if he has time for a cup of tea with us?"

She peeked up, smiling. Santa had messed up her hair. James looked away, sharply. Her allure was not consciously done; he could tell that. But it was not his style to leer at women in his employ.

"I'd love to, but I can't. Sorry. Car's outside."

"Oh well. We'll just have to say have a lovely day at work, won't we?"

Maggie stood unsteadily, holding onto Josie's leg, and all three grinned at him in the early morning light.

"Okay. Have a good day, girls." He knelt down to kiss Maggie and then stood up to kiss Santa before looking Josie in the eye as she replied, seemingly on their behalf:

"Have a good day, Daddy."

"Thank you. You don't have to address me through them, you know. I do accept direct communications."

"Sorry. It is just—"

"Nanny-speak?"

"Erm, yes. Sorry. On behalf of myself, have a good day."

"Thanks. You too."

With that, he left them to their bunnies and breakfasts and was soon in the back of his car, laptop open, discussing the latest fund with Marcia, who had, as he suspected she would, burst out of her front door like a bullet from a gun before the car even stopped outside her flat. She crossed her legs, and her pencil skirt rode up slightly as she leaned in towards him.

"I met your new nanny. Prettier than the last one."

"I hadn't noticed."

THE DAY PASSED AT A PACE, AND HE RICOCHETED FROM meeting to meeting, from one set of demands to another. His secretary, Helen, held back clients and other partners and juniors like a human firewall. She knew him and how he worked, and he felt a sense of symbiosis with her that he struggled to attain with others. When she appeared in the doorway with his usual salad, he knew that the day was half gone and cursed all the things that he hadn't even started yet. He thanked her, not looking up. He battled through the various documents, red penning them with a determination that was slightly extreme even for him, hurrying but never doing an inferior job as a result. He was a good investor, he knew that. The white heat of his intelligence combined with a certain creativity of mind, an ability to see things side on. In the beginning, it was what had distinguished him from every other well-educated and presentable professional of his age. Now, it was the reason he was where he was. People said that he was unequalled in the City, but he mistrusted flattery on principle. Helen deposited a black coffee on his desk without being asked.

Later, he formed the idea that he would do something unusual. A vision of his front door came to him, and he decided that for the first time in months, he would try to get home before the dead of night was cutting into the morning. He had a million and one things to do, but he judged that it was possible. His inbox flashed up another ten new messages. He rang Helen.

"Hi, Hel. Can you arrange my car to collect me at nine this evening?"

"Of course. No problem. Where should it take you?"

Embarrassment flushed through him that she assumed he must be going out rather than going home. He tried to recall the last time he had left the office before eleven for any reason other than a social engagement or an after-hours appointment with his lawyers. Christmas maybe? It couldn't be.

"Just home."

He could imagine her look of surprise, but he didn't have time to think about it. Putting the phone down and clicking onto the next batch of emails, he powered through the afternoon and the evening. Time passed, and the time on his screen said it was five minutes past nine. Involuntarily, he recalled Josie's profile as she had gazed dreamily into the garden the previous night. There was salmon in the fridge, and he began to plan the meal he would cook for them as he packed up and made for the door. He cursed out loud when his phone rang, and he saw the number of one of the Fund VI investors flash up. He answered automatically, assuming it would not take long. That assumption, it turned out, was wrong. The clock ticked, and the voice on the other end of the phone talked. He got embroiled; one thing led to another. Everything is important; detail is the mother of success. An old boss had told him that when he was fresh out of university, and he never forgot it. The minutes trickled past and by the time James found his way to ending the call and racing down the stairs and into the street for his waiting car, it was almost ten. Still, he told himself, it was only a fifteen-minute drive home and not too late to eat. A smile whispered over his face.

The Banham lock clicked to the right and the big red front door opened into an empty hallway. He could neither see nor hear evidence of life and so marched into the kitchen, where he found nobody. Only clean shiny surfaces and tucked in chairs. He wondered where she might be, curled up somewhere reading her fabled Kindle, waiting for company? With that in mind, he barged into the spacious luxury of the living room, a rarely frequented place of offensively firm soft-furnishings and state of the art technology. No Josie though, and no evidence that she had been there. He checked the snug, thinking that she might be watching TV, and the conservatory on the side of the house, as well as the study, and even the grand, barely used dining room. The enormous table, which could comfortably seat twenty, was shrouded in dimness, gleaming through the black. James felt something sink inside him.

He went back into the hall and stood at the foot of the stairs like a runner about to burst forward. On the first floor, he heard water and the yellow light of the landing bounced down the stairs towards him. He crept up them so as not to disturb the twins, whom he assumed were long asleep. Under their door, he saw the glow of the night light and beside it, Josie's bedroom door was open. Her bedside lamp was on, illuminating the small double bed, slept in by a number of agency nannies over the last two years, never previously considered by him, even for a second. His eyes fell on her jeans and pullover slung on the turned down duvet. A simple white bra was visible beside them. Conscience pricked him, and tenderness and guilt. Suddenly, he was an intruder. She should be left in peace, but it was too late. He heard a light clicking off and behind him a door opened. He spun around to be greeted with a cloud of lavender scented bath steam and the sight of a damp Josie, pink nosed and shiny skinned, wrapped in a towel. Her hair, so much darker and flatter when wet, hung over her bare shoulder. Simultaneously, they each let out a 'hi' and looked to the floor.

"Here you are. I'm home early. I thought we could have that salmon for dinner?"

"Dinner?"

"Yeah. I'd like to cook. You can tell me how the twins are while we eat, sound okay?"

"Erm—" A look of incredulity spread across her damp face and she blinked. He noted her eyelashes were dark brown and unusually long. Turning, he caught the display on her bedside radio. It was twenty past ten. People don't get undressed and have a bath before dinner at home on a weekday night, do they? What a fool he could be.

"You've already eaten, haven't you?"

She looked relieved by the question and nodded, regarding him with something akin to amazement, but he wasn't sure that it was the flattering kind.

"Sorry. I'll leave you in peace, but if you aren't too tired, I'd like to hear about the day."

She agreed to get dressed and come down, and he flushed with embarrassment at the sight of her bath-warm feet as she padded into her bedroom and closed the door behind her. Downstairs in the kitchen, he replied to a few late emails whilst cooking for one. Recalling the previous night, he broke with his usual custom and flicked on the garden lights. The greens and yellows of the outside world seemed to bounce into the vast shiny space of the kitchen and, all of a sudden, it felt like a different room. Memories of drunken rages and end of evening arguments and the clattering sound of stiletto heels being flung across the marble floor receded in favour of a new feeling. With this thought, he noticed a change in the flower bed outside. Next to the path, near the daffodils, a number of wooden markers and a plastic bucket sat to the side. His brow furrowed and he turned at the sound of the door opening behind him.

"Hi," said Josie, wrapped in a towelling dressing gown, her pyjamas clearly visible at the top and bottom and her feet peeking out in pale blue slippers. Her hair, still wet, hung down one shoulder, and she clutched a Kindle to her chest with her right hand. She looked nervous, and since he wanted her to be happy in his home, he made a deliberate effort to be relaxed.

"Evening, Josie. Red or white?" He reached for another wine glass from the cupboard.

"Erm, whatever you're having. Thank you."

He poured and handed a glass to her.

"No problem. So, do you know what's going on in the garden?" He looked out of the window, puzzled.

"Yes. Capability Cavendish and her twin." Josie moved to the window and stood beside him, wine glass in one hand, Kindle in the other. "So, the gardener comes on Mondays and his name is Bob."

James looked down at her and she smiled, not in a critical or gloating way. She just smiled and he felt it.

"He was very enthusiastic. And after the kids had had their morning nap, he helped to mark out the plots and we got digging. It was fun. They enjoyed it."

"Great. I'm glad to hear it. What else has happened today?"

"Nothing much. Mrs Cavendish came around in the afternoon."

"Mrs Cavendish?" He almost coughed out the name.

"Yes. She says to call her Diana, but it feels wrong."

He relaxed and smiled at the thought.

"I get that. I have the easy option of calling her 'Mother'. Having an actual name doesn't suit her. What did she come round for?"

"I think she was just checking up, you know. Making sure that the twins have been fed and I'm not a serial killer or teaching them to swear in Swahili or play the banjo. Things like that."

"Well, every family worries about that."

"Course they do."

"And did you reassure her? Or did she catch you with your banjo?"

"She caught us covered in mud, digging up the garden. But apart from the mess, I think she was fine with it."

His smile faded.

"Fine. Well, she likes to check up on things, but don't let her breathe down your neck. Since...well, Mother has taken it upon herself to play *lady of the house* here recently, but sometimes she takes it too far. You don't have to answer to her."

"Don't worry. I know she's a bit fierce, but she's friendly with me, kind of. We get on all right. And it's nice for the girls to see their grandmother, so I don't mind if she breathes down my neck a bit."

It confused James that anyone who could avoid it would volunteer for his mother's supervision. The months that he had been subject to it had been far from smooth.

"Well, on your own head be it. Are you sure you don't want any supper?"

"Yes, it's kind, but I had toast and scrambled egg. I'm fine."

"Toast and scrambled egg? Is there something in your contract that says you have to eat like a child as well as look after them?"

She laughed, but he wondered whether there was some truth in it. She didn't speak.

"It's fine if you like it. Each to his own. But if I'm not here, you can help yourself to any food you like. If you insist though, I'll ask Helen to up the egg order."

"Helen?"

"She's my secretary. She orders my food every week, so if you have special requests, you need to make friends with Helen."

"Thanks for the tip-off."

James began serving out his supper and piling pans into the sink before sitting at the quartz island and topping up both of their wine glasses.

"You've always got your Kindle in tow. What kind of thing do you read?"

"Novels mostly. I will read pretty much anything, but I really love the Classics. The great Victorian novelists are my thing. You know, Dickens, Charlotte Bronte, Mrs Gaskell, Ethel Turner Everett."

James looked up from his salmon. "Who?"

"Ethel Turner Everett," replied Josie confidently, chin raised, a smile playing across her face.

He frowned as he scanned the recesses of his brain, opening untouched pages and up-ending grey boxes of half-forgotten facts. James was an educated man, a Renaissance mind. He had the confidence of the expensively educated son of the upper classes, of a man who could hold his own in any conversation. A man who could never be embarrassed by lack of knowledge. He knew his

Classics, even if he hadn't actually read them all. Turning the name over in his mind, he began to question himself. How could it be that the twins' nanny was better read than he? A flash of amusement in her eyes caught his attention.

"You're winding me up."

"Not quite. Ethel Turner Everett was a real writer, and I do like her books, but she isn't very famous now. She was very successful for a while, and in the mid-nineteenth century, she was a famous name. She wrote two novels, both of which are amazing, and then her output just completely stopped in 1859. No one knows why. It's really weird. Her writing was improving, and she was getting a real following, but it just dried up. I'm a bit fascinated by her actually. She is my comfort novelist who I read when I need something I know I love."

"Like now?"

Josie looked abashed, and he regretted asking. Too harsh, too forthright, too true. He changed tack.

"So how did you discover her? She sounds pretty obscure."

"She is obscure. I read her work at university."

"You went to Oxford, right?"

She smiled and nodded, and he got the sense that she didn't want to talk about it. When his mother said that the nanny had been at Christ Church, he assumed that there had been a mistake. But he had checked it out, and it was true. More than that, she seemed like an educated girl. His confused thoughts were stopped by her speaking.

"I was doing a paper on lesser known Victorian novelists and my tutor recommended her. A few years later, long after I left Oxford, I tried to do some research into her life, but she seems to have covered her tracks pretty well. Basically, nobody knows anything about who she was or why she stopped writing. It's like a Victorian literary mystery..."

"Sounds like she needs a champion. Why has no one heard of her if she's such an amazing novelist?"

"Well, I guess she just fell out of the canon and got forgotten. That happens all the time, doesn't it? Tastes can be fickle, and nobody stood up for Ethel. She stopped writing and kind of disappeared from view."

He put down his knife and fork and considered her for a moment.

"Okay, so what makes her writing so great? Why do you like it? Sell it to me?"

Her eyes sparked up as she began to speak.

"Well, on one level, it is just solid nineteenth-century novel writing with shades of gothic and social commentary. There are always a lot of characters, from all walks of life—so a bit like Dickens. But the focus of each story is a woman—a wealthy woman moving about among the well-to-do but not being satisfied. Think George Eliot but for high society."

"If you're so interested, why did you stop researching?"

"I didn't find any information."

"Where did you look?"

"Well mostly the internet, where nobody knows anything. And I went to the British Library on my day off and looked her up in the *Dictionary of National Biography*."

"And?"

As she took a sip of her wine, light bounced through the yellow liquid and onto the soft curve of her face. James refused to be disconcerted by this.

"There was an entry, but it just said that nobody knows anything about her. Ethel Turner Everett is believed to have been a pen name but her real identity is a mystery. So, it was a bit of a waste of time in the end."

"Who wrote it?"

"I can't remember."

"Hmm. It is probably online now, so you could find out. You should have contacted them and asked about their sources. She must have had a publisher, right? They might still exist. There must be records somewhere. She can't have just disappeared into thin air."

"I know, but it's time as well. Researching the lives of unknown Victorian writers isn't a great fit with looking after small children. I was with my last family and the twins were tiny and the eldest child was potty training. There is always something to do. You know what kids are like."

His eyebrows raised slightly, and his eyes locked on her face like a vice.

"Despite having two, I don't actually. I've never looked after them on my own. They have had a nanny since the day they were born. So, when it comes to everyday stuff, I wouldn't know what I was doing at all. I don't know how you do it."

Josie laughed and her eyes twinkled.

"You'd work it out. Everyone does. It isn't difficult."

"I'm not sure you are right about that. I'm pretty good at my job, but I'm not great at anything else. Speaking of which, there is going to be a dinner here on Friday night. It's a work thing. Whenever the firm makes up new partners, I always have a dinner here to celebrate. It's just the core team plus partners. There's a lot of work chat but..."

"No worries. I'll get the kids to bed and go to my room with Ethel Turner Everett. Your colleagues won't know I'm here." She smiled brightly but he thought there was a flicker of something else, like a light bulb playing up.

"They will know you're here. I'm not having you hiding away—"

"You'd like me to cook? How many people? I've never cooked for more than ten but I'm sure I could manage it. How formal does it need to be? I'd—"

"No!" It came out sharper than he intended, and he blinked, incredulity rising in him. Josie took a sip from her wine and looked nervous. "I wasn't suggesting that you cook anything or hide upstairs as if you weren't here. I thought you might want to join us? The kids are in bed at six thirty, and I can't have you sitting upstairs with scrambled egg and Ethel Turner Everett, so why don't you eat with us?"

"Thank you. I'd love to."

"Great. I hope it isn't a disappointment. There is usually a lot of work chat. Helen organises outside caterers, and they will come in the morning. You are banned from helping."

"Command accepted."

He blanched at her joking tone, but he knew that he was rather assertive, too challenging with people, even when he didn't intend to be. One hundred occasions when he had struck the wrong note and managed things awry shot through his memory like racing dogs. Josie moved her head and her drying curls sprang about, catching the light, moving like creatures. Something about her discombobulated him, but he couldn't say what.

His meal completed, he loaded the dishwasher, having declined Josie's offered help, and watched her disappear up the stairs. James leaned back in the half-lit kitchen and sighed. Emails flooded his iPhone. He knew, even as he looked at it, that at least half of those would be Marcia unnecessarily copying him into emails to show that she was working late. The others would be matters that he actually had to deal with. Opening his laptop in the empty kitchen, he strained not to think of the curly-haired conundrum upstairs.

❦ 9 ❦

KITTY

MAY 1859

KITTY CLASPED HER HANDS ON HER LAP AND LISTENED TO THE clattering of the carriage as it swept through the streets. Alone, with the curtains drawn, she felt hot and her bonnet sat uncomfortably on her head. She longed to take it off. Lord Trefusis was expected for dinner at Veronica Gardens that night, and her head ached with it. Resolutely, she pushed the thought away.

Her gloved finger twitched at the curtain, and she saw that they had reached as far as Great George Street. At that, she began to watch the crowds. Top-hatted men walked along and ladies in billowing cloaks glided, floated almost, in crinoline shapes. Street stained skirts battled with ragged children and news sheet sellers called out stories onto the clogged air. A great excitement rose in Kitty, and her body tensed. For was not this the city in action, the real world about its business? Her eyes were keen, and when she saw him, she rapped on the carriage roof for the driver to stop.

Leaning out, she opened the door into his path. It was a great amusement to her to see the look of astonishment upon his face.

"Miss Cathcart!"

"Mr Faraday, what a surprise. I am going this way. You must get in."

"That is not proper, miss. As you know."

"I do. But I do not care. In any case, it is also not proper for you to make a scene in the street. And you are well on your way to doing that. If you do not step in, that is. I can take you home."

"Miss...I..."

"Please?"

The wind blew with renewed strength and the ribbons of her bonnet flapped about like flags. She smiled her most imploring smile and knew exactly the moment he relented.

"Very well. Thank you, Miss Cathcart."

"You are welcome. And you have nothing to worry upon. As you see, the curtains are drawn, and the carriage is unmarked. We are some distance from my home. Nobody shall know, and you shall be beyond reproach."

"If I were beyond reproach, I should have refused you. You know that."

"Where do you wish to go? Where do you live, sir?"

"Battersea. But that is too far for you to go, Miss Cathcart. It will be kind of you to take me as far as you go south, and from there, I can make my own way."

Kitty gave an order to the driver. As she sat back on the bench, she took off her gloves.

"I wanted to thank you for your attempt to defend Molly. She told me about it. Of course, you were right. She was feeling unwell. The poor wretch is sick and exhausted and somehow collapsed on the chaise when she was cleaning the conservatory. I have sent for a physician to see her on her morning off. But, thank you. I want you to know that I am indebted to you for your act of kindness."

"I take it, therefore, that you are no more a sketcher of servants than I am?"

"No, indeed. That was a story concocted under pressure. And probably not my best one, to be frank. I am an appalling artist."

He laughed, and she felt a dizzying, almost overwhelming sense of victory.

"Let us hope that my father forgets about the whole scene and does not make good on his promise to inspect my collection. For he shall be sorely disappointed."

"You could always learn. Take up drawing, I mean. Why not? I feel you are the sort of person who could do anything you turn your mind to. Why not that?"

"What if I told you that I was too busy?"

He turned his deep blue eyes on her, and she moved towards him. It was a subtle change, but it startled her.

"Forgive me, Miss Cathcart, but can that possibly be true? You are a wealthy lady, living in a beautiful house with an army of servants. You have your own maid. Visitors come to you. You go to them. You read. I have no doubt that you write letters."

"Yes. Very amusing ones actually."

"You attend the theatre. You visit galleries. With and without others whom you have tricked into accompanying you. You care for your blackbird. You take a great interest in those you meet, that is clear."

"What is your point, sir?"

"My point, Miss Cathcart, is that I find it difficult to credit that you are too busy to take up a new hobby. Now that I have said it out loud, I realise it is rather a bold statement."

"For 'bold,' do you mean 'rude'?"

She tilted her chin again, but it was nothing like when she sparred with her father. This was raising a laugh in her adversary. She laughed too. For gently meant insults did not concern her. They rolled off her back as though it had been oiled.

Mr Faraday spoke next. "You may be rude about me. It is less than I deserve. Go on. Do your worst."

"Well, I cannot accuse you of laziness. You make a religion out of work and call it duty. You work all hours. There you are: first thing in the morning and last thing in the afternoon with nary a moment to eat or think of other things. But nobody is there to watch you. Nobody is checking up on you. So, you are doing it of your own volition. And that, I find mystifying. 'Why does he work so unceasingly?' I ask myself. He must be driven by some enormous, unseen force."

"Cannot a lowly clerk be conscientious without inviting such censure?"

"Stop there. I know what you will say. You will say that I am a cushioned young gentlewoman who knows nothing of the world of work. You will have me believe that is your way of being ordinary. And yet, I know that it is not. And that brings me to my next criticism."

"Next? How many do you have, madam?"

"My next criticism. Which is that you are too secretive. You, sir, have a story."

"Everyone has a story."

Kitty raised her gloved hand to his arm and brushed it, feather light. He did not move away but held her gaze. Try as she might she could not read his face. Nor could she look away. "But you do not consent to tell it."

Silence fell between them and filled the air. Kitty heard the horses braying and a shout of exclamation from the street, but still she studied his countenance. It was Mr Faraday who looked away first.

"Why do you want to know?"

"Because I am inquisitive. Nosy, if you like. Because I like people. Especially those who are out of the ordinary, as you are."

"How do you know that, Miss Cathcart? I may be perfectly ordinary, achingly so. You may discover that I have no more to recommend me than the average hardworking clerk. How do you know that there is anything to interest you?"

"I know."

The carriage juddered to a halt. On the outside, voices were raised. Kitty leaned closer.

"I will make you a bargain, how about that? A trade. I will tell you a secret of mine, for a secret of yours. Is that fair? I will even go first."

"I cannot allow that, Miss Cathcart. What sort of gentleman would I be? No. If you insist, I will lay myself bare. Then, if you still wish to, I will listen to your secret. And, of course, keep it entirely to my own self. That is the only basis upon which I am willing to proceed."

"Done."

The corners of his mouth turned up abruptly.

"I work because I wish to better myself. I wish to build my life up from nothing, and there is no person alive to undertake that task but me. That is not the state of affairs I was born to—as you have probably surmised. I am the only child of my parents. My mother died when I was young."

"And I, the same." Kitty spoke softly, fearing to break his flow but wishing nevertheless to say it.

"My father was a gentleman with a small estate in Herefordshire. We led an ordinary life for people of our station. Life was perfectly comfortable, even extravagant compared to many. Not to your household, Miss Cathcart. But I grew up with no reason to think myself inferior or less well served than those around me. I went up to Cambridge, which is where I met your cousin and a great many other friends. I had every expectation of inheriting my father's lands and conducting my life as any other gentleman, to the manor born."

"What happened?"

"My father, I learned only later, was a gambler and worse. When I believed him to be visiting his sister in town or friends in other counties, it seems he was doing something quite different. He fell into debt. That debt grew to be great, greater than he could ever pay. His greater weakness was that he sought to improve his position with crime."

And there, he paused. It was as though he had reached a fence, a ditch, a wall. Kitty watched his eyes flicker as he prepared to continue.

"Have you heard of the Marshland Scandal, Miss Cathcart?"

Her hands paused. "The fraud on Lord and Lady Marshland? Yes, of course. I read about it in the news sheets."

Kitty recalled the outline, not the details. How the elderly and unwell aristocrats had been persuaded to invest in a fictional company. Mining diamonds on the other side of the world, or was it gold? Every penny was lost and the Marshlands, who had over-invested, were left with nothing. Their estate had to be sold and their son, then facing penury, took up the banner of justice to discover how this state of affairs had come about. It was then that it unravelled. The young gentleman discovered that his parents had been the victims of a great fraud, a colossal lie designed to relieve the unsuspecting of their own wealth. Kitty strained to remember but could not quite do it. But on the blurred edges of her memory, there was the outcry, the calls for the justice, the rounding up of villains.

"My father, I discovered, had been the ringleader in the fraud. He and two friends of his—men I had known all my life—had conspired together. They had taken the Marshlands' money and kept it for themselves. There were other victims, too. My father had used his good breeding and his relative obscurity to his own ends. You said you read about it in the papers. Do you remember how it ended?"

A shadow lifted in Kitty's mind and a memory of newsprint, black, white, smudge, came to her. Arrests, jeering in the street as men were carried off in chains. Talk of a trial at the Old Bailey, charcoal drawings of menacing faces. Then talk of the death of terrible men who did not deserve to live in any case.

"Yes." Kitty's voice was even fainter than before. Oddly enough, now that he was telling his tale, she was less anxious to hear it concluded. The warmth of his body radiated through her like an August sun. The inside of the carriage was dark, and suddenly, she wished to find the light, let in the air.

"Then you will know that the ringleader of the Marshland Fraudsters, as they became known, took his own life in disgrace. He died, mired in scandal, and the manner of his death was the biggest scandal of all. He was gone. His property, including our home, was forfeit. And there you have it."

Questions opened in Kitty's mind like so many flowers.

"I came down from Cambridge ignorant of my father's situation and within weeks, the matter unfolded. He was arrested before my eyes. No sooner was he taken than I lost him irrevocably. With him went my home, my income, and all expectation I ever had. Our neighbours, our friends, everyone we had known, became strangers to me."

"To you? But it was not your fault. You had no part in it."

A worm of outrage turned in Kitty's belly and her temperature rose. He smiled at her.

"You know the way of the world, Miss Cathcart. How long are

the arms of scandal, and how they cling. Everyone wants to read about it. Nobody wants to be a part of it."

"But what about your people, your family?"

"My mother's remaining sister wrote to me, before I had even approached her, to say that I would not be welcome. As for my father's family, well... They are few in number, and my letters to them either went unanswered or prompted a similar rejection."

"What about friends? Why didn't George do something?"

"He did not know. I believe that Mr Christie travelled to the continent immediately upon coming down. Many young men in his position do. Indeed, in other circumstances, I may have done the same. He was there for some months if you recall. There were others, but I did not wish to impose upon them. How can one ask one's friends to associate themselves, and their families, with the son of a known criminal, a viper of respectable society?"

Kitty spoke not, but her lips tightened to a line on her face. She would not have deserted him. There is always a way if people will only look for it.

"I am very much grieved, sir, to know this history."

He turned to her and the light from the gap in the curtains caught the blue of his eyes.

"I have not told you the more cheering part. Which is the kindness shown to me by Mr Haworth and his wife."

"Do they know of your association in this business?"

"Every particular."

Kitty's opinion of Mr Haworth, already solid, soared.

"He had known my parents from before I was born and had always shown an interest in me. If his business took him to the area, he would break his journey at our home. Some weeks after my father's death, he appeared, offering me a position. He suggested that I change the spelling of my name, which I did. It was the chance of a new life."

"A new life. How well that sounds. You will think me frightfully spoilt. But I like your idea of a new life. Of turning a fresh page and not reading the previous chapters ever again."

He opened his mouth to speak, but nothing came out.

"Has it ever occurred to you that in some sense, you are lucky.

Your new life requires you to apply yourself with great diligence and tenacity. But you have those qualities, do you not? When you reach the end of it—once you are qualified—you will be a freer man than you began. It will have been burdensome, but the fruits of your endeavours are yet to come."

"I certainly hope so."

A surety rose in her, an iron belief that he would achieve his ambition. She knew it in her bones.

"You asked me for one secret, but I believe I have given you several."

Kitty turned in her seat, discombobulated. The carriage still clattered and bobbed around her, but she had lost any sense of time or place. How long they had been travelling, or where they were, she could not say. Boldly, she pulled back the curtains. Outside shimmered the dirty surface of the Thames, little boats paddled about like ducks in the distance. Buildings of all shapes cluttered the banks. They were crossing the river.

"We must be coming to your home, sir. If you give me the name of the road, I shall tell the driver."

"I am happy to walk, Miss Cathcart. I know you can have no business in this part of the city."

"I do. That business, Mr Faraday, is taking you home."

"Higlers Lane."

The carriage juddered and then stopped outside a row of terrace houses. Kitty looked out to see a great line of bay windows peeling into the distance. Dirty red bricks and ill-dressed glass, as far as the eye could see. Smoke billowing from chimneys, children running on the street below. It should not have surprised Kitty to discover Mr Faraday's home to be so humble, but it did. Her eyes lingered on the sight.

"Does this shock you, miss?"

"No," came the defiant reply. "I find that little shocks me, although I believe that I shock others. It is not my intention to do so but a necessary consequence of my being myself. You see"—she touched his arm again, firmer this time—"I rarely think or live in the normal way. Convention... well, she and I are strangers, fixed. Do you know my meaning?"

"I believe so, although I may have underestimated you. But I know the direction of your words. Admire them too."

His eyes rested on her hand.

"We are here, Miss Cathcart. I should take my leave."

Despite his words, he lingered, his hand resting on the window frame as he opened the door. He slipped out onto the dirty street. The moment moved slowly, drawing out longer than it should. The cacophony of the street grew loud in Kitty's ear, and her face was hot, flushed. She could not say what discomforted her so, but she felt suddenly untethered, released. Finding her voice, she spoke.

"Very well. Until tomorrow then, Mr Faraday."

He bowed and bid her a silent farewell before turning and walking away.

THE QUINTET STRUCK UP THE COTILLION, BUT IT WAS BARELY enough to be heard, such was the cacophony of the ballroom at Lady Fairfax's house. Finely dressed bodies crushed together upon the wooden floor, polished to a shine only hours before. Voices seemed to soar above perfectly dressed heads and become louder still. Hands linked in dance, laughter rang out like so many bells, candlelight flickered upon punch as it was poured into crystal goblets, glugging noisily.

"She has invited too many people," grumbled Margaret Christie as she eased herself through the crowd. "All sorts."

"Mother!" exclaimed Philomena, in a stage whisper, audible to all around. "People will hear you."

"I rather hope they do. The sooner standards are restored the better. The Season did not used to be like this. One used to be able to rely on only the best people being here, but now so many men rise above their station. They want good marriages for their daughters, so along they come. Good heavens. If every shopkeeper and every miller in England can send his daughter to Court, where shall we be?"

"Keeping shops and running mills?" George was behind his mother, who turned abruptly to face him.

"Oh, George. You cannot mean to joke about such things? Your father would turn in his grave."

"Now, now, family. I must be the arbiter here. I have a foot in both camps after all." Kitty brushed her cameo with slim fingers as she spoke, and her cousins and aunt looked to her enquiringly. "You are my family. And so is Papa. I am old money and new. And I say, let us leave our qualms at the door and enjoy the evening?"

Her smile was quite irresistible, even to her aunt.

"Of course, dear."

At that moment, new musicians, who had been opening their instruments and arranging chairs alongside the old ones, began to play. George held out his arm to his cousin who took it and they were gone, absorbed into the crowd of dancers. Kitty danced with George, twice, and with various of his friends. Sweet, eligible boys, men really. Sir Anthony Cadogan and young Viscount Sheen. Others whose names she confused, forgot. When Lord Trefusis ambled towards her, bowed, and gestured to the throng, she could not very well refuse. She laid her hands as lightly as may be upon his person as they danced.

He spoke of his family and their travels on the continent, his horses, and a great estate in Cornwall with rivers and streams and cliffs by the sea.

"You must have a desire to travel yourself? A young gel like you, eh?"

"I have already been to Cornwall, my lord. And very beautiful it is too."

"Didn't mean that, although, god knows, it takes long enough to get back to the old place! No, I mean further afield. What about Paris, Rome, you know, all that, eh? Is that not what all the young ladies want?"

The mention of Paris brought *him* to her thoughts. The sound of him speaking French gently, confidently, tripped through her mind. A wild notion came to her. They would go there together. Why should they not? By what authority has she been told such a thing is not possible?

Lord Trefusis groused, awaiting an answer.

"I cannot speak for others, but I am sure travel on the continent would be wonderful. Or even further afield."

"Now, steady on. Not sure about that. There is such a thing as too foreign you know, Miss Cathcart, eh?"

"I defer to your wisdom, my lord. Of course, why does anyone travel, if not to broaden the mind in some way? If it were not so, then travel would just be a succession of roads and rivers and seas. Pretty views and remarkable buildings, and so on. Those who have travelled the most, in my experience, say that there is some greater purpose to it."

Lord Trefusis looked suddenly flustered. His round cheeks flushed pink, and he furrowed his brow. At the conclusion of the dance, Kitty was happy to regain her composure on a chair beside Philomena at the edge of the ballroom. After a short interlude, she was asked to dance by another of George's friends and by the elderly Marquis of Cranby, who had known her mother. In such giddy spirits, did the evening pass. Dances merged in Kitty's mind until they were one giant, swirling beast. Was she a part of it? Or was she not? Lord Trefusis joined the Christies at supper. Kitty's glass of punch was refilled. Acquaintances, old and new, flitted by, greeting and departing. The hour grew late, and Kitty again sank onto a chair beside Philomena.

"You are slightly out of sorts, Cousin." Philomena had a habit of speaking so, of stating the facts without frippery.

"You are the one who has sat out ten dances."

"Twelve, actually. I consider it quite an achievement with Mother present."

The ladies laughed, beholding the twitching fan of her aunt on the other side of the room.

"You must be very proud."

"She may have given up on me, of course. You, on the other hand, are never out of sorts in company." She leaned closer, whispering. "What is it, Kitty?"

Kitty's tired eyes surveyed the room. A maid in the corner struggled to carry away silver platters. One hundred couples drifted in and out of dance. In the distance, a young debutante dropped her glass upon the floor and shrieked. Kitty exhaled and closed her fan. She had felt weariness before, and boredom. But this was different. This evening, she imagined getting up and walking out on her own two legs. She thought of Alex Faraday and his lodgings, his earnest eyes and how they seemed to bore into her. She had lingered too long in a place distasteful to her. A scent of something new was in the air and Kitty had caught it. She leaned to her cousin.

"Oh, I do not know. It is nothing in particular. I am just...I cannot say exactly. I am here, Philomena. But my mind is not. I feel as though I were a spectator to my own life. There is something else waiting for me, somewhere. A life that is different."

Philomena met her cousin's eye and blinked. "Maybe," she said. The ladies spoke no more on the subject.

Later, Kitty grew more fatigued. Seeking fresh air, she stepped out onto a balcony, alone. The balustrade was a low, stone affair and Kitty was relieved to place her hands flat on it and contemplate the sight of Mayfair, shrouded in darkness. A night watchman called out the hour, and a dog barked in the distance. Kitty closed her eyes. She recalled the image of Mr Faraday disappearing through the bleak front door of his boarding house, and she could not rid her head of it. Neither did she wish to.

From behind her, an unnatural cough broke the silence.

"Dashed dark out here, eh?"

"My lord." Kitty turned to face him. "Yes, it is. Maybe we should return to the ball?"

"No, no. A moment out here will be quite satisfactory. You look very fetching by moonlight, if I might be so bold, Miss Cathcart."

Kitty hesitated. "Thank you."

"Miss Cathcart, you must have noticed that I...favour you. I do, my dear. Obvious, eh? Never was good at speeches. But—well. What I mean to say is why not make a match of it? You are not as young as you could be. I imagine most of the gels you came out with are married, eh? I am rich enough to keep you in the style to which you have become accustomed. Marry me and I will take you to Paris, what? Your father agrees to it."

He smiled, toothily. Kitty straightened her face and began to rehearse her polite refusal. Well used phrases rolled about in her thoughts, unfolded like visiting cards. How flattered she was, and how honoured. How her conscience forbade her to accept, but that the secret would always be theirs. That was entirely true, for Kitty was an excellent secret keeper.

"My lord, I—"

"Wait, Miss Cathcart. Catherine, if I may." He shifted about beside her. He was a heavy man with a heavy tread. But he seemed no less large for being still. "Do not just refuse me right out. Think upon it. I know that I am older than you are. Maybe older than you would like. But I offer many advantages. Your father, I know, supports my suit. I will leave it at that. You consider it, eh?"

With that, he retreated, and the cold air quickened against Kitty's face.

In the carriage on the way home, she leaned back as Aunt Margaret held forth on the new fashion for bodices to be trimmed with great heavy fringes. "I cannot imagine what Lady Arbuthnot is thinking, for it favours her very little." Somehow, Kitty could not fetch the words to speak, and so she remained silent. Her own bodice gripped her body like a vice and the comb in her hair hurt her scalp. It felt like a claw and she longed to take it off. She longed for much that was not readily obtainable. In her head, she saw him again, walking away from her carriage. Proud, fierce, defiant. Calling her. Her aunt continued to talk. Kitty closed her eyes until there was only sound upon movement upon sound.

⚜ 10 ⚜

KITTY

MAY 1859

KITTY HAD BEEN IN THE NARROW ROOM FOR AN HOUR AND A half by the time he arrived. Footsteps in the passage, and she stood, attempting to look as nonchalant as possible. In a moment, the rickety handle clicked, the door opened and there appeared Mr Faraday, his greatcoat already removed, his boots spattered with rain.

"Miss Cathcart!"

He did not bow, but his mouth fell open, eyes widened.

Kitty made a mannered curtsey and smiled broadly. She sought to seem as comfortable as possible in the cramped little room, brown, beige, grey. Her fingers played about the brim of her bonnet, long removed. Unfamiliar ribbon trailed on the wooden floor. Silence yawned between them and a door in the distance slammed shut. Their eyes met for a brief brazen moment before he looked away. He closed the door behind him.

"What are you wearing?"

Kitty looked down at the plain gown and flattened her hands against the faded blue of the skirt.

"It is one of Violet's. I rather like it actually. It is not the sort of thing that Miss Cathcart would ever wear. I hoped to disguise myself for your sake. To reduce the embarrassment you may otherwise feel at my visit."

"It is not a question of embarrassment. Nor of my feelings or welfare. *You* risk a great deal in coming here."

He did not say what she risked, for he did not need to. Kitty knew very well that respectable unmarried ladies did not pay calls on gentlemen alone in their rooms. Nor did they sneak and lie in order to do so.

"I told Mrs Patting I was your sister." Kitty stepped closer, Violet's half boots clicking on the bare floor. She could not say whether the older lady had been persuaded. But she had smiled and ushered her in warmly. Did she really believe her? Or was this house full of counterfeit cousins and false aunts sitting upon the beds of bachelors?

"There is nothing improper, is there, in a man being paid a visit by his own sister?"

Kitty thought she saw a spark in his eye but could not be sure. His face remained inscrutable, but by degrees, his appearance altered. The broad shoulders tensed, lowered. The hands, held in fists at his sides, released. Placing his greatcoat over a chair, he looked straight at her, perfectly still, perfectly calm.

"You enjoy pretending to be someone else?"

"I do rather. I know that many people might wish that they were me. I hope you do not think me ungrateful for my lot."

He shook his head and Kitty, taking heart, continued.

"That is not why I am here. I wanted to speak with you. In private and without interruption. Our secret."

Alex blinked, but he did not shrink away from her. He gestured towards the one chair in the room and she sat on it. He perched himself on the edge of the bed. Kitty knew in her heart that he was listening more deeply than ever before, that she had her stage.

"First, thank you for telling me your story. I shall never ever tell another soul. I know what it cost you to say it, and I am more honoured than I can say. I promised you that I would give you a secret in return and I come here with two."

Beneath her bodice, her belly fluttered. How small was the room, how hot.

"The first"—she paused as she reached into a small bag that she had beside her and pulled out a small book—"is this."

His eyes followed hers to the book and he took it. A flicker of recognition swept over his features.

"This is the novel that was left on my desk at Veronica Gardens. You mentioned that you had read it. I am sorry, Miss Cathcart, I have not yet had the time."

He looked kindly, and a lock of hair fell across his forehead.

"I did leave it there, hoping you would find it. But the reason is a strange one. You see, this book, and a couple of others, are my secret."

He examined it and peered at her, enquiringly. She moved towards him so softly she may have been an animal in the wilderness. With her delicate fingers, she touched his and opened the book in his hands. She was nervous, of course, anxious, but having begun, she could not stop. His hands were warm and dry. Confusion chased across his face, but he did nothing to stop her as she brushed her fingers over the title page.

"It is my book. I wrote it. I am Ethel Turner Everett."

He smiled and his eyes stirred.

"Then you should be congratulated."

"I am not seeking congratulation. It is, I suppose, another occasion of pretending to be somebody else. You see, Mr Faraday, I have never wanted to be the girl that I am. I dream that one day I may have my own establishment, built on my own efforts."

"You want to escape your father, I understand that. Any person would."

"That is true. But it is not the whole truth. You see, I could escape him at any time I liked. I could marry. Various gentlemen have asked me. My father would be thrilled. But I refuse to be sold like chattel. When I leave, I shall choose the manner and timing of my departure."

He nodded, and she knew that he understood.

"So, you have become a secret author. That is...impressive. I wish you good fortune."

"I have refused every match my father has sought to make for me, and do you know why?"

"Why?" His voice was suddenly brittle as glass, about to break.

"Because I did not love them, not even a little bit. I have always been determined, that when I marry, I shall do so for love, and love alone. And that brings me to my other secret."

Her hands still held his, holding her book, and for a moment, neither moved. Kitty heard a ringing in her ears, rising, clanging, bashing, and a heat soared in her body. She knew the thing that must be done, but even after everything, it seemed too bold. An extraordinary beat was thronging through her and she knew it must be let loose, given life. Putting the book aside, she leaned towards his face. And the last thing she saw before she kissed his lips was a spark of fire from blue eyes lifting to her face. As it was, he kissed her back, and her fears slipped away, like water through fingers, like ice into fire. Strong, warm arms rose around her and pulled her to him.

❧ II ❧

JAMES

MARCH 2018

THE DAYS APPROACHING THE DINNER PARTY SPED PAST JAMES like a series of gunshots. Up at five each morning, he was working until late every night, looking up only occasionally. He didn't see Josie until Friday morning, when leaving for the office at the slightly delayed time of quarter past six, he bumped into her in the kitchen, warming up milk for the twins.

"Morning, Josie."

She spun around, tippy cups in hand, hair awry.

"Morning!" she replied, slightly too brightly to be really convincing.

"Everything okay? How have the twins been?"

"Great! Fine! You know, just normal. Are you looking forward to your party?"

"Party?"

"Tonight. The dinner."

"Oh that. I don't really think of it as a party." He frowned, unconsciously. The last occasion he had hosted a partners' dinner he had been a single man for less than a week and the time before that he had had a wife sitting at the head of the table, glowering at him and spoiling for a fight that surely happened. He recalled the embarrassed expressions of his colleagues and something inside him died. A fresher memory of Marcia, hanging around in his office earlier in the week, discussing what she planned to wear while he worked, came back to him. Inwardly, he groaned. He had mixed feelings about the event.

"Yes, I suppose I am looking forward to it. After a fashion. I hope you don't find it boring."

"I'm sure I won't. Helen called me and arranged a time for the caterers to come in. She asked if I wanted extra eggs in the food order, but I said that you were encouraging me to eat like an adult."

Good old Helen. She was such a brick. Had he really told her about the egg thing? He must be getting loose tongued.

"Great. I'm glad. She's a very organised woman. I'm lucky to have her."

Josie turned slightly to screw the tops on the tippy cups, and the morning light caught the down on her neck and collar bone. The rise of her bust as she moved echoed about his vision, and he felt suddenly unworthy. He clenched his fists. It was unthinkable, impossible. She was his employee and the twins' nanny. Plus, she was an aimless and vulnerable young woman, living like a captive under his roof. There was some indefinable innocence about her. He couldn't put his finger on it, but it was there. She was not the kind of woman he was used to or who was used to him. Josie turned to him, smiling. The feeling in his gut had not gone away.

"I have to go to work. I'll see you later."

Later, after his third meeting of the day, he returned exhausted to his desk to find that Helen had deposited a salad and a coffee there. She appeared in the doorway as he sipped it.

"If that's cold, I'll get you a fresh one."

"It's fine, Hel. Thanks."

"You have had calls from Goldman and Credit Suisse, and the New York office has been on the phone as well."

"Thanks. I'll call them."

She pottered to the corner of the room and began assembling various files and putting Post-it notes of different colours on them.

"Helen, thanks for calling home about the dinner tonight. It was thoughtful of you."

"No worries. I had to make sure someone would be in when the caterers arrive." Her eyes flickered to him and, in her task of piling the files up, she broke step, only for a moment. "I always did call. Before, I mean."

"Did she answer?"

"No. And she didn't call back, so I made sure the caterers had a key and the code. She sounded like a very nice girl. This Josie, I mean."

James looked at his computer screen, staring at its angry brightness.

"She is. Thanks for keeping her in the loop. She's going to join us tonight actually, once the twins are asleep."

Helen looked up from her files. He could not quite read her expression.

"Helen, have you got half an hour this afternoon?" he asked, knowing full well that she had whatever time he asked her to have.

"Yes, of course."

"Would you mind doing a spot of internet research? I want all the information you can find about a Victorian novelist by the name of Ethel Turner Everett. I'm sending you an email now with the spelling. Just search everything you can find. Look for academic articles, anything. If you need to, pay for them. Use my card. Email it to reprographics and get them to print and bind it. Okay?"

"Sure," she replied, looking more than a little confused.

"Mr Cavendish, we have set up to serve drinks in the conservatory. Would you like the doors left open?"

James thundered down the stairs, fresh from his shower and in a crisp shirt to find the girl from the catering company standing in the hallway looking expectant. He hadn't given it any thought, but the weather was unseasonably warm, and it might make Josie feel more at home.

"Why not? Sounds great. Thanks."

He walked through to the conservatory and cast his eye over the table of sparkling glasses, young girls in black and white uniforms straightening bottles in ice buckets and arranging champagne saucers on silver trays. The evening light bounced through the glass and around the room. When he bought the house, he had assumed that having a fully restored Victorian conservatory, complete with vaulted, iron supported roof, and acres of glass, would be a liability. However, it had not been. It turned out that it had been very carefully modernised to preserve its original character, whilst at the same time being made quite habitable from a modern perspective. The main reason that he rarely used it was that it was so big. It stretched out like a giant on the side of the house, and even James found it a little expansive for his tastes. It afforded a perfect view of the garden though and it was easily warm enough for people to have drinks outside or with the door open.

He looked at the clock and wondered how Josie was getting on with bedtime. He had seen her disappearing into the twins' bathroom in her jeans and t-shirt earlier. The recollection was stopped by the sound of the doorbell chiming through the house, and he headed to the door. It was no surprise to see Marcia, always the first to arrive, standing on the doorstep.

She came flouncing through the door as soon as it was opened, air kissing her greeting, and slipping off her jacket to reveal an oddly designed and obviously, achingly expensive black dress clinging to her form. One of the girls from the catering company leapt forward to take Marcia's jacket and she took James's arm and escorted him to his own conservatory. He was spared solitary conversation with Marcia when further guests arrived, one after the other like buses. Wives, girlfriends, boyfriends, and partners were introduced and, looking around them, blushed at the grandeur of the place. The air filled with activity; the volume of the collective chat and clink of glasses rose like a loaf in an oven.

James's team, like the whole world of high finance, were mostly male. Guys who he worked with, all of them rich and tired and having had just enough time to change their clothes, meandered around the conservatory and garden, talking about their deals. Their various wives and girlfriends were dressed up, and smart heels clicked about on the tiled floor as their perfectly made-up faces beamed up at the glassy roof. The only women on the team were Marcia and another senior, Jessica, who hadn't yet arrived. James reminded himself that Marcia was a good investor, a hard worker, and in a minority group of two. He tried to ignore the fact that she was showing people around his house as though she lived there herself. Charles, who was a junior director and a man in need of a holiday, had begun describing the ins and outs of his latest deal, regaling James with an account of the board meeting that afternoon and slopping champagne on the conservatory floor.

On the other side of the room, Josie appeared, and the babble of Charles talking reduced to indistinct noise in James's mind. She was wearing a blue shift dress with a lacy bit at the top. It occurred to him that he had never, apart from the incident outside the bathroom, seen her legs. He was seeing them now. They were slim and shapely and, on his estimate, bare. Her face, she had made up subtly, and the increased colour lifted her features from pretty to mildly ethereal. She looked about her, smiling and blinking, and thanked the server who offered her a drink.

"Would you excuse me, Charles?"

James didn't wait to hear his response before moving towards her beaming face. He arrived before he had thought of an opening line.

"You look—erm, great."

The words fell flat, plopped down in an embarrassing way. He felt a fool, and she blushed.

"Thank you. It was a five-minute job as Santa wanted an extra story and then resisted going to sleep."

"You should have told her you had a party to get to."

Josie laughed and his mood lifted.

"Ha! Can you imagine? If they knew there was a party here, they would never have let me go! You have a pair of party animals, I'm sure of it."

A number of questioning eyes had fixed on them. Charles and his French wife Marina had somehow drifted across the room and planted themselves beside Josie. They were looking at her with barely concealed intrigue.

"Josie, let me introduce you to people. Charles, Marina, this is

Josie. Charles is one of our directors and Marina is his long-suffering wife."

They all said hello and detecting Marina's accent, Josie got her talking about where she was from in France and how long she had lived in London. While Marina was telling Josie about their ever-growing family, James noticed the final arrival, the other female associate, and her fiancé wandering into the room, arms linked.

"Hi, Jessica. Welcome..."

He held his hand out to the guy accompanying her, trying to recall whether they had met before. There was nothing memorable about him and James decided to assume that they had not.

"Chris Daniels." His handshake was firm, but he had an odd look in his eyes. "I'm Jessica's husband-to-be."

"James Cavendish. Good to meet you. Have you met the rest of the team? Charles, here, is my second in command and this is Marina." They each smiled and shook hands. He was about to introduce Josie when he turned to see that she looked as though she had just been winded. James observed her whitened face and blinked. Her brow was furrowed and everything about her body was suddenly tense. He leaned close to her ear.

"What's the matter? You look like you've seen a ghost..."

Before she could answer, Marina's accented high-pitched voice broke out above them both.

"And this is my new friend, Josie! We've only just met but she seems fabulous."

She looked up from under a blanket of unruly curls and laughed at this accolade before facing the man in front of her.

"Hello, Josie. Long time, no see."

James did not miss the mild aggression in his voice. He wanted to know why, and then he wanted this guy out of his house. Josie held out her hand to him.

"Hi, Chris. Yes, it has been a long time. It's nice to see you. Congratulations on your engagement."

"Thank you." He turned to a somewhat confused looking Jessica and squeezed her hand. She regarded Josie with open suspicion.

"How do you guys know each other?"

Josie looked at him and smiled. Something about the way she stood told James she had found her confidence.

"We were at university together. A long time ago."

He nodded in response, as if to approve this obviously inadequate account of events.

"It certainly was. What brings you here anyway, Josie?"

"I work here."

"You work at Cavendish Partners?"

"No, I mean, I work in this house. I'm nanny to Mr Cavendish's children."

There it was. Said. James felt, rather than saw, a room of eyes on him.

Sometime later, supper arrived. After a bit of shuffling around the table and squinting to read name places, everyone was seated. The dining room, which was far too large for a household of four, two of whom ate in highchairs, was barely used, and James felt the familiar sensation of looking around as though he were in somebody else's house. He had no hand in the seating plan, and, with Marcia to the left of him and Jessica to the right, he wondered who had. Josie had been placed directly opposite him.

The starter had not long been served when Marcia's voice chimed out.

"James, how is Lady Cavendish these days?"

James observed Josie's eyes flick up.

"She's fine. Thank you."

"I am sure I glimpsed her the other day at South Ken Tube, but she is always in such a hurry. Such an impressive woman, and it's wonderful how she keeps herself so busy in retirement as well. She's not the sort to just sit at home, is she? I read that she is on all sorts of committees doing non-stop charity work and so on..."

"Well—"

"She really is an example to us all. Although, I am not sure that I could ever be a domestic sort of a woman. You know, a stay-at-home."

Jessica was nodding away and glancing across him as Marcia chattered on.

"And these days, there isn't really any excuse for it, is there? I mean women have all the same opportunities as men. All the same qualifications, and the same careers are there for the taking, aren't they?"

James paused before answering but he didn't look at Josie.

"Well, I suppose they are, but be careful before you are too blasé about it. You and Jessie are the only women on the team after all. And it's the same all over the City. You've got to question that, surely?"

Marcia laughed and sipped her wine. She placed it back on the table with a loud clang, and her voice, when it came, was louder than before.

"I think a lot of women are just shy of hard work. I mean the hours are long and the standards are high. At the end of the day, it is easier to do something else."

"That may be true, but surely that would apply equally to men as to women. Some people want a quiet life and some people don't."

What did he want? In that moment he was not sure.

"Women tend much more to that attitude though. Because, culturally, there's this idea that a woman can just stay at home, so a lot of women aspire to that. But what could they possibly be doing at home that is worthwhile? I mean, you can't change the world from the living room, can you?"

There was a collective clink as a few of the ladies let their cutlery down against their plates, absently. Poor old Marina looked as though she may be about to cry. Josie showed nothing.

"I'm not so sure. I don't think you can assume anything about how other people use their time. There are many profitable things that can be done away from a City office. And even if people are not 'changing the world,' as you put it, well, maybe to some extent, that is none of your or my business?"

Marcia leaned back and smiled sheepishly. He knew her well enough to know when she was retreating, pulling back her armies. When he glanced at Josie, she was just quietly eating her supper.

Charles spoke as he ate: "What do you mean, old man? If you were at home all day, or some of the day, how would you use your time?"

"I'd read."

It was a spur of the moment answer.

"But you read the *FT* every day. I've always admired how you make time for it—"

"I mean, I'd read things other than the *Financial Times*. I'd read novels, histories, you know. Accounts of the human condition. You can't consider yourself properly educated unless you are well-read, and I've always been a bit insecure about how much I haven't read. So, I'd read."

The two men grinned jovially at one another, and the evening continued.

12

KITTY

JUNE 1859

HER HEART HAD POUNDED AS SHE MADE HER WAY TO HIS lodgings but to be there was worth any quantity of anguish. For the third time in as many weeks, she had dressed in Violet's old blue dress and slipped from the house, unremarked upon. It was Sunday, but Kitty had cried off church, pleading a headache. Aunt Margaret had gently stroked her temples—"You poor, darling girl." Philomena had glanced at her boldly, almost knowingly, even though she had not been told the truth. It was their secret and theirs alone. Kitty and Alex. Alex and Kitty. They were an army of two.

Now, in the early afternoon, they lay entwined in a narrow bed. She felt the warmth of his naked body touching hers and a cry of joy sang through her head, through her whole being.

"Have you ever done this before?" she asked.

He laughed.

"Of course not. This is the kind of happening that visits a person once in a lifetime. Or, at least, I prefer to think that."

Kitty turned and placed her hands on his chest, smiling. She had a sense of being washed over by waves or spun like gossamer thread. It was as though every secret resolve, every transgression, every refused proposal, every word published under another name, had been leading to this moment. She had been in training, learning how to live differently, because one day she would need to. Here, lying in a room south of the Thames, was the reason.

"I suppose that is right. It does feel rather like that."

She said nothing of her past history, for she knew in her bones that he did not think her loose or fast. For all of the callow boys who had proposed to her and the old men who had stroked her shoulder whilst removing her cape, she had never been touched by a man like this, nor wished to be. It was as though Alex knew everything already. There was no need to explain, to give an account of past years, to fill in gaps and counter fallacy. She was the woman she was, and he accepted her. Her heart ached at the thought of her imminent departure.

"I must go home, or I shall be missed."

"You shall be missed here too. All the time you are away."

He ran his fingers through her blonde hair, disarranged. The light from the small window shone on it, through it.

"And I shall think of nothing but returning. But you know that I cannot be discovered to be missing. If my father knew I was from home and had lied, he would have me followed. My freedom to see you here would be lost. We should have to make do with the library. Just imagine."

A smile lit her face as she pressed her hands to his chest and moved herself up to a sit.

"Challenging, to be sure. Not as comfortable as I should like."

"You give me ideas, Mr Faraday."

Kitty stood, and walked about the room, collecting her things. Her blonde hair, out of its pins fell down her back, shining, sparking with light. Keeping his eyes on her, Alex sat and leaned back against the unadorned wall. He fixed his gaze on her as she began to dress herself haphazardly.

"Kitty."

Wearing only her slip and crinoline, she paused.

"Tomorrow, shall I see you?"

She exhaled, regretfully.

"I have to go to the theatre with Aunt Margaret and George in the evening. But I shall see you at Veronica Gardens. I will visit you in the library."

He shifted on the bed, saying nothing.

"You are troubled."

"Of course, I am troubled. I have no choice but to let you sneak about in this way—"

"I have taken great care. Coachman John sits with my carriage three streets from here. Nobody knows that I am here but you. And when I see you at home tomorrow, I shall be exactly as I always am. I know that we must take care not to appear too familiar in my father's house. I have been deceiving him for many years, Alex. I know how to do it."

"You are so confident." He reached out and stroked her arm. "The obstacles of the world are as nothing to you. That is what makes you so fearfully wonderful. But sometimes, we must deal in realities. Maybe we should not talk at all at Veronica Gardens. You should cease your visits to the library—"

"That would arouse more suspicion than it would allay. The way to fox father is to carry on as normal."

"That is just it, Kitty. Foxing your father is not really what I am aiming to do. If matters were different, it might be. If this were merely some entertainment, some frippery between working hours. If I did not care. But I care very much."

"So do I."

Her voice broke slightly as she spoke. Unbidden, a tear blurred her vision. Alex reached out and held her.

"Then let me go to Sir Roland."

"No. It is too soon."

"Kitty, some would say it is far too late."

"Let them say that. I do not care. I would give myself to you one hundred times over, even if I knew I would lose you, even if there was no hope. What we have is worth any storm."

"The storm will be greatest if we are found out to have been dishonest. If you allow me to approach your father and ask for your hand—"

"He will refuse you. He may do worse. You do not know the man he is."

"Then when?"

"Let us wait. I will reject Lord Trefusis and anyone else my father throws in my path. He will come to realise that I cannot be forced. You will finish your articles to Mr Haworth. I will write as hard and as fast as I can. When you are qualified to practice, we will be married. We will start this new life of which you speak. But first, we must wait."

"Wait. You know that I shall do whatever you ask. I would wait all my life if that was your wish. But I cannot be easy about it. When you wait, Kitty, unexpected things occur. This new life is not something that we shall start after a period of preparation. It is underway. You have changed me, Kitty. As long as you realise that...even when I am more advanced in my career, I shall never be as rich as your father."

"I do not care."

"I shall not be able to give you the life you have now, or close to it."

"I do not want it. I know that I have everything, every gown, every jewel. But I can more than happily live without those things. But for you, I am a prisoner of my father's money. I know that life will be different. But... The world is well lost for love."

Later, the bells of St. George's rang out the hour as Kitty descended the steps of Mrs Patting's house and made her way across three streets to where her carriage was waiting. Although she had resolved not to look, she knew that Alex followed a safe distance behind. She knew her way, of course. And the lowliness of the area did not give her to fear. Kitty looked at the world with new eyes. As she walked, she felt a sense of lightness and joy so great that she might fly.

"What has Evelina Lyndhurst done to her hair?"

Margaret Christie squinted through her quizzing glasses before peering over the top of them. From the orchestra pit of the Theatre Royal, Drury Lane came a low, babbling noise, a beast finding its voice. The curtain kissed the stage floor and shook slightly as hidden figures rushed about on the other side. In the audience, the well-appointed took their seats beside the aspirational. Wide skirts swept and canes tapped the floor. Aunt Margaret kept her vigil from her own box.

"Good heavens, Jane Peabody is here. I should have thought that her brother's affairs were more than enough drama. Do you see her, Kitty?"

Kitty, who had been leaning back in her chair, gazing, unseeing before her, blinked and met her aunt's stare.

"Yes, Aunt Margaret. I see her. Why ever should a lady avoid society, just because her brother has been named in a divorce suit?"

"Sshh! Kitty. Pray do not use that word. People will hear you."

"Oh, really." In a moment, she sat forward and reaching up, took her aunt's spectacles and begun to scour the stalls.

"Where is George?"

"He is sorry not to be here, my dear. But he and Philomena are seeing their late father's cousin, who is come to town. I cannot say that I approve of this new fashion for hair dusted with silver powder." Her aunt Margaret took back possession of her spectacles. "Maria Bridges looks quite absurd."

"That is very much unexpected, is it not? For George told me he was to be here tonight. I know that he is anxious to see the play."

"Come now, Kitty. Let us worry no more about it. Your family, you shall always have. Fix your mind on other matters, dear. Think of the f—"

Without warning, the box door clicked open and the heavy curtain was drawn sharply apart. The two women startled. Kitty's heart drummed as Lord Trefusis strutted into the box, lifting his hat and removing his gloves as though it were the most natural thing in the world for him to be there.

Margaret Christie stood.

"Ah, Lord Trefusis. Welcome." Her smile, objectively pretty, suddenly seemed garish, drawn on.

He bowed to them and made his greetings. When he bent over Kitty's hand, he kissed it. A warm, moist, unwelcome kiss. Aunt

Margaret looked away, remarking upon the programme. Kitty withdrew her hand with an effort.

"Well, thank you for inviting me, eh? Miss Cathcart." He turned to Kitty, suddenly seeming larger than he was. "Your dress becomes you. Yes, well. Time to sit down, what?"

Aunt Margaret fluttered her fan as she spoke and avoided her niece's eye.

"Yes, of course. Your Lordship, please sit here." She gestured to the middle seat. Boys ran about dimming the gaslights and gradually a shroud of black fell. A hundred voices said 'hush' and Kitty straightened herself. "Kitty, dear. You sit to His Lordship's left. And I shall sit on his right."

She plumped herself down and stared studiedly ahead.

"A rose between two thorns, eh?" Lord Trefusis roared, slapping his thigh and leaning towards Kitty.

Music swelled the air as the audience settled and the curtain lifted. Figures appeared on the stage, then voices. Aunt Margaret's fan rippled cool air against her face, and, in the next box, a lady laughed. All the while, the rasp of Lord Trefusis's breathing continued, like a metronome. Tick, tock, tick. When Kitty closed her eyes, she saw Alex's face, felt his hands on her. Skin on skin, the moment wrapping her up, transporting her. She missed him and that missing was like a sickness in her belly. She could get no rest of it. A howl had started inside her and she could hear nothing else.

Suddenly, she felt a hand on her leg and hot breath in her ear.

"How have you been keeping, Miss Cathcart?"

Kitty's eyes flashed open, alarmed. The stage, bright as it was, receded in her mind, and all she could see was his fat, white hand resting upon her skirts. Heavy, uninvited. Beside her there was a rustle as her aunt stood and made her way out of the box. Kitty's mouth opened in astonishment, but the last thing she saw was her aunt's trim, well-dressed figure eclipsing the light from the corridor and then, the closing door, shutting it out. Aunt Margaret was her chaperone, but she was gone. Kitty felt the knot in her belly grow and pull tight. Lord Trefusis's hand pressed tighter.

"Well? Are you well?"

Kitty shifted her legs and, as though merely brushing her skirts, moved his hand away with hers.

"Yes, thank you. I am quite well."

"I believe there is a matter upon which you and I must speak."

He glared at her, appraisingly, and the set of his mouth hardened. Gone was the hail-fellow-well-met. Gone was the ostentatious bumptiousness. Had it ever been persuasive? Nausea stirred in Kitty.

"Yes."

"But it is not what you think, Miss Cathcart. Did you know that I have been acquainted with your father these thirty years or more?"

"No, my lord."

"It is true. Met in Birmingham. Summer of '29. I had heard about him before that of course. Everyone had. No knighthood in those days, but his reputation for cleverness went before him, eh? Brilliant chap. Ruthless, of course. No, I was a callow youth, you might say. Found myself in that part of the world. An acquaintance invited us all to a card party. Now, what was his name? Yes. That's right. Brindle. William Brindle."

He paused and moved not an inch. In the dark, Kitty blinked, confused, disarranged.

"You are shocked at the name, miss? Yes, of course. I know that there has been some trouble since. Lawsuits and what not. Of course, that sort of thing is over my head. Dashed complex, I am sure. It is a shame when old friends fall out, is it not?"

"It depends on the friendship. And the reason."

"I am a simple man, Miss Cathcart. All I know is that Brindle and your father were friends. And then they were not. Brindle accused Cathcart of stealing his ideas. Now, I shall tell you now that public accusations of dishonour are always poor form in my book. Don't hold with 'em. Dreadful."

He stroked his moustache, absently.

"It's true, of course. The whole damned shooting match."

"What is true?"

"Brindle's accusation. I know. I was there."

"Why are you telling me this?"

"Well, just passing the time, really."

"We are at the theatre, my lord. There really is no call to talk at all."

"Maybe not. But if two people are to be joined"—he paused, seeming to chew the word, to lacerate it before continuing—"there should be no secrets between them, eh? No, indeed. As coincidence would have it, I actually have a document, written by William Brindle, which puts the matter beyond doubt. The original, you know. If it should happen to fall into the hands of the judge hearing the case...well, it would be bad for Sir Roland. But do not worry your pretty head about that, because you have my word that it shall not. I have kept that blessed piece of parchment safe for many a long year, and I shall continue to do so. I made a copy for your esteemed father, Kitty. Just so he knows what the thing says. But the original, it is completely safe in my care. As, my dear, shall you be."

The hand crept back to her lap and grasped her own. Dots in Kitty's mind began to join, shapes formed. It was unthinkable that her father had been bribed with his own fortune to marry her off to this man, but it was true. Her head throbbed and her hands jittered. The sound of the play roared, bellowed in her ear and something inside her hardened. She could not let it happen. Lord Trefusis let out a bark of laughter at some aspect of the performance and slapped his thigh with his other hand. He leaned closer to her in the darkness and the awful mass of his body threatened to move her. The itchy texture of his frock coat scratched her bare shoulder.

Flinching, she moved forward, feeling for the spectacles with her gloved hands. Focussing for the first time on the stage, on the neighbouring box. Looking for something, anything to distract him. She thought of her carriage, in which she had travelled alone, awaiting her in the street outside. Thought of John, kicking his heels against the dusty ground, and how she could leave whenever she wished. The hand that had been resting on her leg came to her back where the silk of her gown ended and her warm skin began. He began to caress her quivering back, to lean closer. A memory of Alex soared though her and she knew what she must do.

"I am so sorry, Lord Trefusis. I am feeling rather unwell."

With that, Kitty stood and fled, allowing him the steadiest smile she could manage. As she departed the box, she observed several sets of eyes from neighbouring boxes fixed upon her.

She told herself not to run, but her slippered feet pounded the carpeted floor and she walked briskly. The air of the corridor was a relief, but its circular shape made her feel trapped, snared as a hare. Kitty pulled her shawl up as she reached the staircase and fled down it. In only half an hour this space would be flooded with people, heaving. Now it was empty. Bleary-eyed doormen looked up in surprise. The air from the street was cold, biting. The wind rustled her hair and she saw John's confused figure appearing.

"Miss Cathcart?"

"I have to go, John."

"Of course, miss. Are you all right?"

He searched her face, seemingly with concern, jogging alongside her as she made for the blue-bodied carriage. John opened the door a moment before she threw herself inside in a haze of silk and crinoline.

"Get a message to Mrs Christie's coachman that I am unwell and gone home. Then take me to Great Suffolk Street. I've business nearby."

13

JOSIE

"SO, WHAT WAS ALL THAT ABOUT?"

His voice was not what she expected, and she startled slightly. Josie had been sitting on a bench in the garden for a few minutes. Light from the kitchen bounced on the wooden pegs of the twins' gardening efforts in front of her, and she noticed that someone had left a glass of champagne on the ground by the daffodils. The party was over. The guests had receded, clicking heels and unbuttoned coats swanning down the front steps into waiting cabs, couple by couple. The clatter of the girls from the catering company clearing up the kitchen whispered into the garden, and the volume thinned. Josie had a sense that they were nearly finished, and she was looking forward to the perfect empty silence that would follow. His question brought her back to a different reality.

"All what?"

"Whatever *that* was. One minute you're fine. Then some guy arrives, and you're not fine. Don't deny it, Josie. I saw it. Who is he?"

"Oh, he's no one important. Just an old squeeze. It's nothing for anyone else to worry about."

"But you're worrying, right? That's why you're out here, in the dark, shivering?"

He slipped off his jacket and draped it over her shoulders. The heavy, felty weight of a too-big man's jacket on her body was something she had not felt for years, centuries. It was warm from his body and smelled of spice.

"I like the garden."

He sat down beside her without being asked.

"I know. But that's not why you're sitting out here now. You're hiding. Look, I invited you because you work hard, and I thought you'd enjoy it. I didn't know that the ghosts of boyfriends past were going to turn up. Sorry. He's not coming here again. There was something I didn't like about him."

Her head sprung back in soft laughter, and she turned to look at him, trying to read his expression.

"There's no need for that! He's okay. He doesn't deserve to be exiled, especially as he is engaged to one of your employees. It was just—a bit of a shock, that's all."

"If he comes here again, I'll set the kids on him. If they thought he'd hurt you, they'd hate him, and there is nothing like a two-year-old with a grudge. He'd never return..."

"He did hurt me, but it was a long time ago. There's no point crying over spilt milk. We were kids ourselves. Chris was my university boyfriend. We had one of those relationships that you form when you're nineteen, away from home, and there are no anchors in your life. I was easy to impress. I fell into bed with a boy who seemed impressive, and it became a habit. It was never love though. It was just a thing that happened. It's ridiculous to be thinking about it over a decade later."

"But you are?"

"I'm just being vain. It was the way things ended. We had graduated and we were living in a shared house with other friends. Everyone else had a flashy city job, but I was doing a teaching course."

She paused, stepping over the land mines in her mind.

"I was going to be an English teacher. That was the idea. I had a little stipend, but I had much less money than everyone else in the house. Although, now I think about it, he always made me pay half our rent."

"Hmm. Fair warning."

"Well, if it was, I didn't see it. We dawdled along for a few months. I was really enjoying the course, and it was fun living with friends. I thought everything was fine. Then, one morning, I was headed to the Tube and a girl in a suit stepped out from the bus stop and told me she was sleeping with my boyfriend. So, the whole thing unravelled with embarrassingly little trouble to him. He admitted it when I confronted him, said he hadn't been happy for a while, and that was that. I couldn't stay in that house. We had been sharing a bed and there was nowhere separate for me to sleep or store my stuff."

"Why didn't he move out?" James asked, sharply.

"Chris isn't the sort to offer things. He gives what he has to give. Being generous isn't his thing. He sat tight. He knew that I would go. And I did. I packed up my cases, my friend Lauren picked me up in her mini, and I was gone. Problem was that I didn't have anywhere to live, and I couldn't afford to rent. I could only afford to live in the house because the rent was split so many ways. Money-wise, I just couldn't do it. So, I camped with Lauren for a couple of weeks. I ate a lot of chocolate and read Ethel Turner Everett over and over. Then one morning, I was thinking about Jane Eyre while eating my breakfast and I knew what I had to do. I walked out to the newsagents, bought a copy of *The Lady* and applied for every live-in nanny position that was advertised in there. It didn't take long to get a job. My first family was great, and, although it was weird at first, it got easy very quickly. Luckily, they seemed to like me."

He looked at her appraisingly, and it was as though he could see right through her. And although she usually avoided examination, she did not recoil. She leaned into it.

"I bet they did. You have a way of making yourself indispensable."

"I don't have any choice but to make myself indispensable."

It sounded far more sour than she intended. She was not in the habit of speaking harshly, especially with her employers. But something about him brought the candour out of her.

"That's not true. Everyone has choices. Don't hide behind it.

You're young, clever, and capable. You can do what you want. You happen to be very good at what you do, but you are not tied to it."

"It has never seemed possible. I had to take a live-in position because I didn't have anywhere to live. Problem is that they are not that well paid—"

"Hang on. Am I not paying you enough?"

She smiled and looked at him doubtfully.

"No, you are paying me a good market rate. I'm not complaining. Although, I bet you don't even know how much, do you?"

His eyebrows rose apologetically, and he nodded to indicate that she guessed right.

"Point is that you get paid less for live-in positions so I could never save because I just didn't have very much money. Then my dad became ill and, before he died, there were a lot of expenses. Then, my sister ran into problems and needed help financially with my niece. I've thought of trying to do teacher training again. But somehow, it never happens. There's always something immediate to do."

She paused and stretched out her arms, as if letting lose an invisible weight before glancing back at his watching eyes.

"So, seeing Chris upset me not because I care about him, but because he reminds me of these things. He had a huge impact on my life. I bet he doesn't even realise. He's one of these people who walks about knocking things over and doesn't even register it."

"And you're that girl who cleans up when it isn't your mess. He didn't deserve you, Josie. By the sounds of things, he doesn't even deserve Jessica, and that's saying something. You know. It happened, but it was a long time ago. Don't be defined by it. You're a person, not a set of circumstances."

"That is very reassuring. Thank you."

She uncrossed her legs.

"You should try living for yourself more. Less of the self-sacrifice, more doing what you want to do."

She laughed.

"I don't even know what that is."

"You must have some idea. Come on. What have you always wanted?"

She picked something at random.

"I used to go swimming in the sea with my sister when I was a child. I always wanted one of those colourful beach huts, you know what I mean?"

He raised his eyebrows. "Yes, I know what you mean." A flicker of humour danced across his face, and she had the impression that he was keeping something back.

"You didn't tell me Diana was *a lady*."

"It isn't important."

"Maybe not, but it *is* interesting. Does that make you a something? What about the twins? Am I the only commoner in the house?"

"Would you care if you were?"

"I don't think so, but I'd like to know. When I was a little girl, I had an imaginary double life in which I was the daughter of the Prince and Princess of Wales, but I'm over that now."

"The twins do not have titles. I'm an 'hon', but I don't use it, and I don't usually tell people. My dad, who you are bound to meet one day, is a lord. I'm not his eldest son, so I'll never be one myself, and I like it that way."

"I bet that's unusual. I bet most people who are an 'hon' can't wait to tell people. I bet it slips out the whole time."

"Not with me. I don't consider it interesting or important. All that sort of stuff is just noise. It never tells you anything that matters. It's a distraction. I'm a person. End of story."

The air that had been unseasonably warm had chilled and she shivered, even under the weight of his jacket. She reflected on those words. *End of story,* he said, but what story? She hadn't even heard the beginning. Questions screamed about in her head. What were the answers? Where is this going? Her eyes fixed on the deep, textured colour and movement of the great herbaceous border in front of her. Even at night, the vivacity of it seemed to break through. Briefly, she felt strong and free and snatched a glimpse of some manner of life she hadn't contemplated. She could not have described it to a person who asked, but she had a sense of it in her bones. Josie turned to face James to find that he had done the same. A thrumming in her ear was soaring through her head. Her body, underneath his jacket, underneath Annie's dress, moved of its own volition, inched towards him and he moved too. His hand shifted in her direction, and one hundred questions crossed his face as he leaned towards her—

"Mr Cavendish, we've finished up in here. Everything's cleaned and put away. Can I ask you to sign my sheet, please?"

Josie looked up after a moment of pause to see one of the girls from the catering company bounding towards them, holding a sheaf of papers. James held her gaze for a beat longer than was comfortable before turning and answering.

"Sure, of course. Thank you all. You've done a great job."

"You're welcome, sir. We aim to please—I, oh! I'm sorry this is the wrong sheet. I must have left the thing I need you to sign in the kitchen..."

James stood, somewhat jerkily, and Josie watched as the two of them made their way back into the house. She observed him through the glass as he exchanged pleasantries with them and helped them out of sight with a box of supplies.

Josie felt chilly and foolish and embarrassed beyond description. How could she have been so unguarded, so loose? To have nearly kissed her employer, a man with whom she had to live alone, who held her in his power like fish in a net. What would he have thought if she had done it? She had even imagined that he leaned towards her too, but she knew in the cold, solitary garden that it wasn't so. She had created it. It was her fantasy. She had a fertile imagination and sometimes it bit her on the behind. Feeling the cold surface of the wooden bench, she pushed herself up and stood gazing at the flowers, before retrieving the champagne glass the caterers had missed and making her way into the kitchen. Hurrying in and locking the patio doors, she popped the glass in the dishwasher and slipped James's jacket onto one of the breakfast stools before grabbing a glass of water and rushing towards the stairs.

James turned from the front door as she appeared in the hallway, clutching her water glass, ready to bolt up the stairs to bed.

"Josie?"

She glanced towards him, wishing she were invisible. "Night-night. I think I might turn in. I've locked up."

At the foot of the deep carpeted stairs, she neatly slipped off her heels before starting up towards the nursery floor in her bare feet, eyes down, mortified. Behind her, she heard a casual 'night' and then nothing.

❧ 14 ❧

ALEX

JUNE 1859

ALEX COULD SMELL HER SCENT ON THE AIR AS HE BOLTED down the narrow staircase.

In all of his months at Mrs Patting's, he had held to the same routines. He left at the same time, in the same clothes. He ate at the same place at the supper table, spoke to the same clutch of respectable lodgers: clerks with squinty eyes, older men to whom life had not been kind. The walk from his room to the street he had undertaken many times without thought, like a machine in a factory, rolling, whirring. But now, it felt different. Everything felt different. Only hours before, he had let her out of the front door, easing the latch soundlessly, and watched her click down the road in the half-dawn. Unbeknown to her, at a distance, he had followed. Having seen her board the carriage with his own eyes, watched it trundle into movement and clatter away, he had slipped back. The drab normality of Mrs Patting's boarding house had taken him back, sucked him up and on the surface, everything was as it had been. And still, he worried. As he rounded the last of the stairs and bounded into the hall, he slowed before knocking at the parlour door, and gingerly opening it.

"Come in, Mr Faraday, come in, dear boy!"

Mrs Patting looked up from her ledger, pen in hand, fingertips inked. She was thickly built, simply dressed. Her eyes were quick, her brain too, he fancied.

"You are well, dear boy?"

"I am, thank you, Mrs Patting."

"Good. Hmm."

She gestured to a spare chair, and he promptly sat.

"You have had a caller." She tilted her head and lowered her voice. "I hesitate to say a gentleman, although he may have been. But he looked somewhat...rough. Declined to give a name, which I call rather rude. He said he would be back, but he has not made good on his promise yet." The lady squinted at her untidy figures and then looked up, smiling.

Alex's mind raced, galloped, full of questions.

"When did he call?"

"Yesterday. At two o'clock," she said. "Precisely."

"How did he appear?"

"I couldn't say as he was handsome, indeed not. Nasty great scar on his face. Right across his cheek it was! Slim. Young. But everyone seems young to me, dear boy. He spoke well enough, not refined though. Not like you."

He leaned back in his chair, stroking his chin, but he could not make it out.

"I have no idea who that may be, Mrs Patting. I apologise if I have been the cause of you feeling uneasy."

She laughed, guffawed even.

"Oh, dear boy. It takes more than a vulgar with a gash on his face to make me feel uneasy. Do not worry yourself on that score. But keep a watch, dear boy. Keep a watch."

He nodded and she turned back to her work. It was clear to Alex that she would say no more. Mrs Patting had that quality, not uncommon amongst city dwellers who have seen life, that she rarely ventured unnecessary remarks upon the events to which she was witness. She opened a book of notes and compared it to her ledger, squinting.

"My eyes, dear boy, they do not improve. How vexing age is."

She looked up, laughing, and placed the pen down.

"I am sure you are no age at all, Mrs Patting. But if you ever need extra eyes, I would be happy to oblige."

It was no more than the truth. If only he could repay all his debts so easily.

"What a dear boy you are. Thank you, Mr Faraday. That Mr Archer helped me last week. He is a kind man too, but, my word, what a talker! I have a good number of dear boys here at the moment."

The clock in the corner struck the hour, and Alex went to leave, bowing to her and withdrawing. It was when his hand was on the door handle that she spoke again.

"And it is because you are a dear boy...because I've rather a taking for you that I feel I must speak about something else. Some might call it out of place, but I've only your best interests at heart."

He hesitated. "Of course."

"Your sister, Mr Faraday."

Alex moved away from the door.

"I...she...well. Miss Faraday appears to be a very agreeable young lady. Educated, I can tell. Just like you are yourself. She is a person of quality, is she not?"

"Yes, she is."

"I thought so. There are some things people cannot disguise. No matter how they try. Shows through like bone."

She paused, gazing at him unrelentingly, as though she expected to see some explanation in his face.

"She is the sort of girl who sticks in the mind. Pretty too, of course, but that is of less importance. I must say though that I worry for her. The world is a judging place. I should know. I've lived in it long enough. I have been judged myself, and it is no pretty affair."

Their eyes met and they each understood.

"Being abroad at night. Coming and going." She leaned forward, removing her eye glass. "She should take more care."

ALEX HURRIED INTO THE HECTIC STREET, ON THE HEELS OF his discussion with Mrs Patting. He had an appointment with Mr

Haworth that would take him away from Veronica Gardens for the morning, and he was anxious not to be late. The streets were clogged, heaving. Carriages, dogs, knife grinders, beggars calling out for charity. The stench of cruel chance hung about them like an apron. The buildings were no less cluttered, and dirty fronted houses, sheets flapping from windows, jutted overhead. Alex moved quickly on. And as he progressed, so his surroundings changed. A few cleaner windows, some polished knockers and the streets had become quieter, more refined. He forced himself to think in a rational manner. Who was calling for him and what did they want? He had ruthlessly severed all his ties with his father's associates. He had not spared a soul, even if he liked a man, or thought him more innocent than he was guilty. Alex had stripped himself of every man Jack of them. The faces of men one could not trust appeared in his memory; villainous names spoken in whispers. He had resolved that he should never go back. But these were men who could find things out. A dry bitterness lodged in him for he did not wish to belong to such a world, never had.

Turning into Great Surrey Street, he found a market in progress. Red-faced men called out prices and crushed fruits rotted by the side of the road. Unsurprisingly, the crowd was greater here, louder. Alex quickened his pace to pass it. He was just about to turn down the alley that would lead him to his workplace, when a young woman crashed into him, cursing and jabbing his back with her arm as she fell.

"Are you all right, miss?"

He offered his hand to help her up, but she sprang up without assistance. Her eyes, which briefly met his own, were watery grey. Within a moment, she was gone, absorbed into the crowd. Alex moved on, but the incident had caught him, shocked him out of his previous thoughts.

He became aware of the carriage a moment later than he would have liked. But when he realised, all of his senses sharpened and turned. The noise of its progress was deafening loud, the clatter of hooves, the smack of wood upon stone. It rushed up on him and he ventured the swiftest of looks. What a fearful, heart quickening sight it was. Bearing down upon him was a large conveyance, black, plain, moving briskly. There was a driver, but the brim of his hat obscured his face. Alex moved quickly aside, expecting the carriage to keep its course. But it did not. In a moment, it shifted, barrelling towards him as sure as a dart. On instinct, he began to run, but the carriage was gaining on him and the wall of buildings close. His feet thudded the uneven ground, his breath sawed out of his chest. He ran until his heart strained and his body thronged with the pain of effort. Still the carriage kept on. A scream came from somewhere, and a clatter of objects falling, men crying out in protest. Alex saw the opening when he was almost upon it. Fortune, somehow, through everything, smiled upon him. It was a right turn, a narrow passage, the sort that may go anywhere, contain anything. It did not matter. His whole body tensed, and, at just the right moment, he flung himself into it. He got a bloody cheek against the stone wall for his trouble, but the carriage could not get him. Heart exploding, he ran and ran, turning this way and that. Eventually, he flung out his arms and allowed his body to stop. He had lost his pursuer, but how long would it be before he was found again?

JOSIE

MARCH 2018

EARLY THE NEXT MORNING, THE SUN CRASHED AGAINST Josie's window, seeping around the edges of the white polished shutters and bouncing around the pastel cottons of the room. She shifted in bed and realised that she was naked. A puddle of blue lacy dress sat on the floor alongside her knickers and Annie's old shoes, flung down without care. Josie sat up and gently pulled the shutter open. Sunlight dappled across the roofs of grand town-houses, lit up pocket gardens and gleamed on the tops of cars in the street. Beyond, the green of Hyde Park was just visible over the church spire. Josie stretched and reached for her unworn pyjamas as a solitary little voice in the next room started up singingly: "Oh-sie, where are oo?"

The morning passed in a series of tasks and was, on the whole, much less embarrassing than it could have been. The twins, having conveniently slept through the party, woke up with all the energy of two-year-old fireballs on twelve hours of rest and between them, kept Josie very busy. After breakfast, they played in the garden, digging at their patches of earth and soaking the plants with tiny, wildly coloured watering cans. Josie began to think that James had gone out before she had got up when he finally appeared. The sight of him, standing in the kitchen doorway, occupying it completely, got her at the knees. He was wearing jeans and a polo top, and his eyes trained on her as she paced around the kitchen, filling the dishwasher and fetching the children's toys to their floor play area. After the hail of excited shrieks of 'Daddy' and a bit of frenzied toddler kissing and cuddling, he turned to her: "Good morning, Josie." She could not quite place the tone of his voice, but she sang the cheeriest 'morning' she could muster back.

James, it transpired, had work to do, and soon disappeared into his office, leaving Josie to read a few stories with the girls before taking them to the park. Back at home, lunch was much the same as ever, Maggie stealing half of Santa's pasta but both eating well and happily. In the afternoon, Josie put the twins in their double buggy and made for the front door. There was a knack to getting them down the front steps in the buggy, but she was strong enough, and they were not good enough walkers to go down themselves. Josie felt her stomach muscles tighten as she lined the back wheels up on the top step and gently, steadily lowered it down to the next. The door behind her sprang open.

"Josie, stop! Let me—"

James came to the side of the buggy and picked the whole thing up, much to the amusement of the girls. He lifted it down the steps and set it down on the pavement below.

"Thank you."

"You're welcome. Next time, ask for help. It's heavy with both of them in it. I'm sorry that there's no slope, but there isn't room for one."

"London houses always have steps. It's okay. I'm good for the job."

"Fine. But you're not built for weights." He looked her up and down, and she felt rather affronted. How did he think they got in and out of the house when he was at work? Did he think about it at all? Josie had looked after up to four children on her own. She had lugged toddlers in buggies and babies in slings and bikes and tricycles and toy tractors all over London.

"I'm stronger than I look."

He blinked and looked her square in the face. A moment of silence gaped between them before it was broken by Maggie crying that she had dropped her toy bunny. James picked it up from the ground and gave it back to her, before looking to Josie.

"Where are you off to?"

"There's a fair for little ones in the park this afternoon. I read about it in the free paper. Do you want to join?"

He shrugged.

"Sorry. I've got a call."

"Okay, well, we'll be back about four. Bye, Daddy!" She raised her hand in a wave as she turned the buggy with the other and the twins did likewise. James maintained his smile, but his eyes dimmed.

The fair was predictably popular and after returning home, Josie and the twins played with Duplo before she made them a fish pie for dinner and took them upstairs for their bath. Once they were in their sleep suits, Josie picked them up, one in each arm and padded downstairs to James' study. Tensing her arm, which was also holding Maggie, she knocked gently on the door before crouching slightly to turn the handle.

"We just came down to say night-night."

James looked up from his computer and smiled, stood, and strode towards them.

"Also, I thought you might like to do bedtime stories?"

Santa reached out to him and he took her easily in his arms before turning to Josie.

"How about we do it together?"

She could not say no to this suggestion, and so, that is what they did. When the girls were settled in their cots, James and Josie sat side by side on the nursery floor, reading old favourites and new acquisitions, taking it in turns to be the narrator and 'do the voices.' She was taken aback by how good he was with the voices. She had somehow expected that he was a narrator-only man. Outside in the street, the sun went down. Light creeping through the gaps in the Beatrix Potter curtains winked dimmer every moment and finally fizzled out into an opaque haze. The room, Josie realised, was lit only with the peachy glow of the night light, as she and James were huddled together, almost noses to the page in order to read. When both girls were asleep, the adults stood carefully before slipping out of the room.

"Josie, about last night—"

"It was great! Thanks for inviting me. The fair today was fun. It is still on tomorrow if you want to go."

He opened his mouth to speak, but for a second, nothing came out.

"Great. Okay. Thanks. I haven't forgotten that tomorrow is your day off. Diana and my dad are coming round, so maybe we'll go to the fair. Thanks for the tip." He looked away from her face.

"What are you doing with your freedom?"

"I'm visiting Hattie and Emily."

"Great. Erm, how are you getting there?"

"Train. It's forty minutes out of Victoria, so it's easy from here."

"Okay. Have you eaten?"

"I have actually. I ate with the kids. I made them a fish pie. There's enough for tomorrow as well if you need it. My train is quite early in the morning, so I'd like to get an early night."

"Well, I can understand that." He yawned and tried to stifle it. "I wish I could have one too. I'll see you in the morning."

"Night."

"Night."

Later, Josie lay in bed, wide awake. Her phone buzzed a text, and she reached for it on autopilot.

Annie: *How are things? How is the Dad?*

Josie quickly tapped out a response: *Confusing & Confusing*

Within seconds, the phone rang.

"How's Dubai?"

"Hot. Never mind Dubai. What's going on?"

"Nothing really"—Josie spoke in a whisper—"everything's fine. I'm just being silly."

"Why are you whispering? Where are you?"

"I'm in bed."

"Okay. Listen. What's this guy like? This James Cavendish?"

Josie was certain that Annie would already have a Google folder on him. She smiled at the phone.

"Tom said he wasn't even there when he dropped you off. He said the place was like a palace. He felt pretty bad leaving you, Josie. Said it was glamorous but not at all homey, and we've been kind of worrying about you. Now you text that you're confused..."

"It's okay. He's okay. Bit strange. In some ways, he's really nice to me."

"How nice?"

"Very nice. So nice that last night, I nearly kissed him."

At the other end of the line, Annie exhaled loudly and slowly.

"Is he single?"

"Annie!"

"Well, is he?"

"I think so. He has a female colleague who obviously fancies him but, I'm pretty sure he's not interested. I have no idea where the twins' mum is—nobody has said anything. But she's certainly not here. There is no trace of any woman in this house. It's just me and him when the kids are asleep."

"Hmm?"

"It's not a big deal. It was only once and, fortunately, it didn't happen. I'd had a bit to drink and it had been an emotional evening with one thing and another."

"Is he good looking?"

"Very."

"You need to find out what happened to the mother."

"Why?"

"Well, if she's in a refuge for battered wives, then I suggest you stay away from her husband. But if she isn't, then you shouldn't be frightened. You deserve some fun and some happiness. If it feels right, then do it."

Despite her poor night's sleep, Josie was up at six and in the twins' room when Santa started her morning chorus. To her amazement, James appeared in the doorway only a moment later. His hair was wet from the shower and he had a look of a man who had dressed in a hurry. Taking a confused-looking Santa from Josie's arms, he told her to leave it to him and catch her train. As she left the room, she glanced back to see him looking about doubtfully and was glad that she had pre-made their meals and set out their clothes for the day.

Her own day was good. She caught the rickety train from Victoria and gazed at the sight of South London rumbling by until it ended, and the gentle hills of the Surrey countryside opened out around her. When she stepped down on the concrete of her childhood platform, Hattie and Emily jumped out from behind the sign and cried, "Surprise!" before flinging themselves at her for cuddles. They walked home to Hattie's flat in the blazing spring sunshine, Emily skipping ahead at times and talking about her school projects and latest hobbies and whether Josie could stay until tea. The visit carried on in that vein, and Josie felt herself relaxing. She had decided on the train that she would not say a word to her sister about James. It had been a mistake telling Annie and, if Hattie knew, she'd never hear the end of it, so she said nothing. When Hattie asked how the new family was, Josie just said 'great'—and that was that.

After a late lunch in a local pub, which Josie paid for, they all walked back to the station, and she hopped on the 17:35 to Victoria, settling down in the window seat and making the requisite faces at Emily through the window. The journey was fast and easy, and before long, Josie was wandering back along Veronica Gardens, pulling her cardigan together at the front in the slight chill of the evening. She climbed the grand steps to the front door, but as she was taking the keys out from her handbag, it opened. An elderly man, holding a stick and a copy of the *Sunday Telegraph* looked at Josie doubtfully before Diana sprang from behind him and made the introductions.

"Ah, there you are, Josie. This is my husband, Henry. Darling, this is young Josie."

A look of incomprehension crossed his face.

"Josie," Diana bellowed. "The new nanny, dear!"

"Ahh. Hello, Josie." He smiled and she could not resist liking him. She held out her hand that he shook before Diana bustled him out of the door and down the steps, and Josie came into the house and slipped off her shoes.

After the journey, she was parched, and so she grabbed a glass from the cupboard and turned on the bizarrely shaped avant-garde tap for some water. Cold water, tinged with brown, burst out unevenly. She let it run for a few moments, but it didn't clear.

"Yuck," she said to herself and went to the fridge for some orange juice. After looking into the garden for a while, she sat down at the kitchen table with her Kindle. She could not have said how long she had been there when James walked into the room.

"Nice day?"

Josie looked up.

"Yes, thank you. It was lovely. How were you and the girls?"

"Fine. They missed you. But they are okay. They've had three meals and sustained no injuries."

Josie smiled at him as he put a glass of white wine down in front of her. She did not think he was at all incompetent, just inexperienced. And she was what her mum had always called a 'worry pot.'

"I saw your parents on my way in."

"Yes. They were babysitting me, I think. They usually head home to Ashburton at the weekends."

"Ashburton?"

He hesitated.

"My parent's home in the countryside. Devon. It is their natural habitat."

"How old is your dad?"

"Ninety-three. He's not that well, actually. He has the first stages of dementia, so Mother likes to be with him most of the time. That's why she said she couldn't look after the twins. Although, I guess that's a blessing, for them and for me. You have probably noticed that I find my mother a little oppressive at times."

He raised his eyebrows and looked straight at her.

"She's very forthright."

"That's one way of putting it. She likes you though. She may not show it but if she didn't like you, you'd know about it. I've tried to get her to mind her own business, but she is a stickler when it comes to interfering. And ever since my ex-wife left me, she has felt extra justification."

Josie sipped her wine as that piece of the jigsaw came down in its place. "Ah. I'm s—"

He looked away from her and started getting food out of the fridge.

"Don't be sorry. It was for the best. She wasn't happy and neither was I. It's a long story and not one that you deserve to have ruin your Sunday night. So, suffice to say that you're unlikely to see her very often. We are divorced, which suits us both. She lives a very international life. She is not really interested in the girls, and they are lucky to see her twice a year."

Josie digested this rapid fire of information and tried to make sense of it.

"What's her name?"

"Rosaria."

"Italian?"

"Yes."

"Do the girls know her? Do they call her 'mummy'?"

"They know her as 'mummy,' but they haven't seen her since Boxing Day. They show more affection to you and even Mother." He fixed her with a stare. "Does that answer your questions, Josie?"

She thought about it and concluded that whatever else there was, it wasn't her business.

"Yes. I had been wondering..."

"Do you know what's wrong with the water?" asked James, running the dirty-brown liquid over his hand and looking to Josie enquiringly. She was glad of the distraction from the embarrassing discussion of his ex-wife.

"No, but it was like that when I came in. If it's still like it in the morning, I'll call Thames Water. If you need bottled water, I'll get some from the store..."

"No, you won't. Sit down. It's your day off, and I'm cooking you dinner."

"Thank you." Josie smiled and opened her Kindle, feeling uncomfortably free of household tasks. When he came back into the kitchen with a bottle of water, James wrestled a binder of printed pages out of his laptop bag and put them down on the table in front of her.

"This might interest you. I got Helen to print them off. They are all that is known of your Ethel Turner Everett..."

Josie opened the booklet in amazement. After a short Wikipedia entry, there were a handful of academic articles, printed from online subscription journals, a copy of the *Dictionary of National Biography* entry she had already read, a couple snippets from newspapers. She couldn't believe that he had thought of doing this just because she was interested.

"Wow. Thank you."

"You're welcome. If you want it on your Kindle, tell me. Helen can scan it and send it just like that. It's no problem."

"No, it's great like this. Thank you. It can be my reading when the twins are napping."

"Enjoy it. Maybe you will write the next article?"

His eyes were a challenge, but she stared back, laughing.

"You are so demanding! Am I allowed to just be interested? I can see why you work such crazy hours. You have more energy than normal people."

"Are you calling me a workaholic, Josie?"

"Yes, of course."

He looked disbelieving and continued to throw chopped vegetables into a wok that hissed.

"I know it may look like that. But the truth is, that in my line of work, you have to work those hours if you want to succeed. It's a fact of the job. I could never sit back and just be a rich man who hadn't worked for it. So, I work pretty hard, same as you do, except you work in the home, and I work outside of it."

"Fine. But sometimes it's okay to relax, isn't it? I mean, I'm relaxing now. On orders, of course."

"So am I, actually."

He finished the cooking, and they ate in companionable chat, and, at times, silence. That silence was alarmingly comfortable. Despite the almost kiss, Josie felt herself falling back into step with him. Talking about reading and the twins and the house and gradually pulling back the layers that covered over this strange, handsome, brittle friend of a man. She wondered if she would ever complete the task. Probably not. But when he smiled at her and said 'goodnight,' she felt a sense of contentment rising inside her. Upstairs, in bed, her iPhone buzzed a text.

Annie: *what's going on?*

She texted back: *all fine, no drama*

❧ 16 ❧

KITTY

JUNE 1859

PHILOMENA HAD SENT A NOTE TO SAY THAT SHE WAS CALLED away. She and George were asked to visit the sister of their late father, a lavender scented old lady who lived in Hertfordshire. Their aunt, Philomena wrote, was grievous poorly, and it was feared that she may not survive the week. She would write to her cousin upon her return to town. 'Fondest love' she wrote above the curved scrawl of her name. Kitty folded the letter and placed it down on the counterpane to the side of her breakfast tray. It had a rose scent, and for a moment, Kitty was discomforted. Violet had been there, but now she was gone, gliding through the halls with a pile of linens in her arms. Kitty's chamber was silent, dappled in morning sunshine. She stretched herself out like a cat, bed warm. She was sorry to read of the elderly Miss Christie's ill health, although her memories of the lady were hazy. She would send a note wishing her a speedy recovery. She finished her tea, pushed away the tray.

A timid knock came at the door.

"Come."

Molly appeared, closing the door behind her like a secret and speaking in a low murmur.

"Message from the master, miss. He'd like to see you in his study please, miss."

Kitty folded back the cover and slipped her legs out.

"His study? But— Very well, thank you, Molly. I shall be down directly."

The girl coughed, looking about like a shy puppy. She bobbed a curtsey but did not leave.

"That will be all, Molly."

Her face coloured.

"Please, miss. But I'm to take you down, straight, like."

"Now? But I'm not dressed."

"I can help you dress, miss. Springer is out on an errand for Mrs Cooper."

A worm of worry started turning in Kitty's stomach. What could this be about? A speck bled into a stain in her mind. She rose and hurriedly dressed. Minutes later, concealing her breathlessness, she appeared in her father's study. Molly closed the door, melted away, and Kitty forced a smile as she greeted him.

"You wished to see me, Father?"

Sir Roland, who was sat at his desk, placed a book face down and peered up. His movements were slow, almost languid. Kitty's eyes made a rapid survey of the room. Worn leather and old hatreds. But no Alex. Nobody but Sir Roland and herself. The sickness in her belly grew, bubbled. Her nails dug crescents into the palms of her hands.

"Where is Mr Faraday?"

Sir Roland blinked.

"Who?"

She knew he was feigning ignorance, but it was essential not to overreact.

"Mr Faraday, Father. Haworth's clerk. The young man who has been working here these past weeks."

He rapped his stubby fingers on the edge of the desk.

"Oh him. He is not your affair. Ask only that which concerns you."

Her thoughts began racing, leaping, sweating, but she kept her face blank. She had learned from many years in her father's house that if one wished to survive, one never showed one's hand.

"Is everything all right? I heard from Philomena this morning that her aunt Christie is unwell. I hope that there has not been bad news."

Sir Roland's fleshy face shook in denial.

"No idea." He picked up his book and moved it atop another pile. "Aunt Christie? I cannot recall the woman's name, even. Come now. You know that I am the last man to concern myself with the trivialities of others."

There had been some movement in her skirts as her feet shuffled about, but it stopped now.

"Is something wrong, Father?"

"Certainly not!" He smiled a mirthless, scowling smile. "Nothing is amiss. Indeed, things are *exactly* as I would have them." He stood and moved towards a small table in shadow to the side of his desk.

"Sit down, Kitty."

He picked up a news sheet and began turning the pages, shaking it out.

"Ah-ha. Here it is. Have a look at this, girl."

He passed her the folded news sheet, and she held it with one hand. It took a moment for her eyes to see. Words danced on the page, black, white, grey, smudge. When she read it, a gasp escaped her, unbidden.

"Father, you can't—"

"But I can, Kitty. And I have. It is there, in print. And that which is in print is halfway to being true, is it not? Pass it to me."

She did so, hand shaking, heart thumping.

"I do like the form of words. Engagements. Lord Trefusis of Rosshampton to Miss Catherine Cathcart, daughter of Sir Roland and the late Lady Cathcart, of Longhaven, Yorkshire. It is elegant, is it not?"

Kitty shook her head, incredulous, despairing.

"It cannot be."

"Oh, I assure you, it can. And it is."

"But I have not agreed. I have not consented."

"Yes, you have. For if you had not, your parent would not have placed the announcement in the news sheet."

Kitty looked away, defiant.

"No. Nothing so bare-faced could ever work. For I know my own mind."

"You do. But I am nothing if I am not audacious, Kitty. And I have tired with the effort of persuading you."

"And thought to force me instead?"

He shrugged and moved the book on his desk before sitting down and leaning back into the embrace of his great chair.

"Force. That is an ugly word. I will tell you another ugly word: scandal. And another: exile. You are not a fool, Kitty. You like the riches into which you were born. I do not believe you know how to be without them. You cannot break an engagement to a Peer of the Realm and keep your reputation intact. You would be cut off and that would destroy you."

"And you, likewise."

She could have said more but did not do so. Did he know what Trefusis had told her at the theatre? Or was that a double duplicity on behalf of that man? For her intended had it within his power to ruin Sir Roland utterly, to beggar and embarrass him. Kitty reeled in the cords of her knowledge. If Sir Roland knew that she knew, it may push him too far. Her heart ached to think of Alex, not at his desk as he should be. Somewhere, elsewhere, in peril, or no?

Her father clasped his hands together.

"Wrong. My dream of marrying you to quality would be in tatters, yes. But I myself would be perfectly fine. I am a man, Kitty, and a self-sufficient one at that. I have one fortune and the wherewithal to make another. You, on the other hand, would be ruined. All that you are, would be lost. Do you imagine that the charms of your face would carry you through? Do you think that these callow boys would chase your skirts if you had no fortune to sell? If they thought you were dishonest, fickle, mad, worse? If they suspected you had been soiled and used like a common light skirt?"

A wave of cold realisation enveloped her.

"I do not care what people think."

His face reddened and his coal black eyes were suddenly angry.

"Then you are a fool."

His chin jutted forth as he spoke and his face quivered. Kitty exhaled slowly, silently. She feared. She longed. She boiled with rage. But opening her mouth to speak, she stopped. Her cobalt blue eyes closed, and no words came. Her father filled the silence.

"The thing is done. Accept it."

"I shall resist. I cannot be dragged to the altar."

He stood and without appearing to hurry made for the door.

"Resist, will you? I think not."

He closed it behind him with a click.

If she had been another girl, she would have cried. She would have lowered her head into her hands and sobbed. Her heart was heavy with worry, and her head tangled by unknowns. The initiative had been stolen from her in an instant. For a time after her father had departed the room, she simply sat, rock still, thinking. It was in that state, alone in the shadowy room, unwelcoming at the best of times, that she decided. And she knew that however formidable the task, and whatever it cost her in money and status and connexions, it must be done. Her name, her wealth, even her secret writing, were worldly trinkets all. They were nothing compared to him.

She rang the bell and Havers appeared.

"Good morning, Havers. Please have the carriage brought round. I should like to go out."

He stood straight as an arrow, hands clasped behind his back as he frowned.

"I am sorry, Miss Cathcart. I am afraid that the carriage is not available."

A flicker of laughter crossed his face and Kitty blanched.

"If my father is using it, then I will make do with the phaeton."

"It is not that, miss. Sir Roland himself is to his office in the phaeton. The carriage is here. But I have instructions that you are not to be given leave to use it."

"Instructions! Well, indeed..." The exclamation burst from her, unplanned, and she felt hot, flustered. The reins were loose, flailing in the wind, and she needed to get them back. "From my father, I suppose?"

The question was needless, and he nodded in answer. Kitty flushed with anger and turned away as she spoke.

"That will be all, Havers."

IN HER CHAMBER, KITTY RANG THE BELL FOR VIOLET AND paced. Back and forth, back and forth, slippers stomping on thick carpet. A quiet word with Molly had confirmed Kitty's fear: Alex was not in the house and none of the servants knew the reason.

Footsteps in the hallway, and suddenly the door opened.

"Miss Cathcart?"

Kitty spun about, skirts flying.

"Violet. What a relief. I need—"

"If I may be so bold, miss. Mrs Christie is in the drawing room, wishing to see you." She spoke hurriedly, and her grey eyes flashed about. "I know what is happening, miss. All the servants are talking of it. Mr Havers reads the announcements every morning before he gives the news sheet to Sir Roland."

"My god. All of London must know. What am I to do, Violet?"

"I cannot say as I know, miss. But you could do worse than start by talking to Mrs Christie. It can't do any harm, miss."

"No. You are right. But I need you to do something, Violet. I need you to find out where Mr Faraday is. He is not here, and I am frantic. You know why, I believe. Please find out where he is. If I am engaged with Mrs Christie, nobody will know that you are gone. Have some money for a hackney, here." She fumbled with her leather purse and the coins jangled.

As Violet made her way out of the servants' door and into the sun-filled street, Kitty found her aunt in the drawing room. She closed the door behind her and leaned on it, as her aunt looked up from her teacup.

"Ah, Kitty, darling."

Cup clattered down upon saucer. The older lady's face was so familiar. It sent a pang through the younger just to look upon it. Her eyes twinkled, as Kitty knew her own could, and her fine features echoed those of her poor dear Mama. Kitty held a picture in her head of her mother's countenance. But it was a poor second to actually recalling it, patched together as it was from sketches and portraits. It shamed her that she could not really remember it, as though she had let go of a great prize with which she had been trusted. The likeness of Mrs Christie to Kitty's mama drew the girl to her aunt; it always had. The power of it broke through her reserve. Unwillingly, she sobbed.

"Oh, Aunt!"

Kitty fled across the room and flung herself upon the settee beside her visitor.

"My dear girl."

Her gloved finger wiped away a tear from Kitty's face.

"I came to offer my congratulations."

She spoke slowly, carefully, as though she had measured out her words. Kitty felt suddenly cold.

"I am thrilled. Thrilled, little dove. This is such a fine thing for you, darling."

"But—"

"You know I have always loved you as though you were my own child, Kitty. Ever since your mama died, before even. We have had a special something, have we not? A link."

"Yes, I suppose we have."

They did. But that link could be great or mean. At its best, it might have been honour, loyalty, love. Or it may simply be the understanding that two beautiful women have of one another, like swan winking to swan across the river. Kitty swallowed.

"Even more than I have with Philomena. Most excellent Philomena, but you know what I mean. You and I, Kitty, are birds of a feather."

Aunt Margaret plucked her glove off one hand and laid it on Kitty's arm, holding her niece's gaze. She smiled, but it was not quite warm. Kitty's skin prickled.

"Are we? If we are, then you must know that I cannot possibly do this."

Her aunt Margaret's eyes drifted up and down her niece's

hunched form. "Sit up straight, dear. You have such fine shoulders, but you must show them off."

"You see, I did not agree at all. He asked me, but I did not say yes. I did not."

Her aunt pulled her other glove off and frowned.

"But you did not refuse outright?"

"No, but I was about to. It was only because—"

Aunt Margaret silenced her with a finger to the lips and a 'hush.'

"Aunt?"

"You know that your father only wants the very best for you. He wants to see you settled in the most advantageous circumstances. It is his manner of being affectionate."

"He wants me gone. And he wants me titled. I acknowledge that he is willing to pay for those things. But it is not affection. Do not call it that."

Aunt Margaret shifted in her seat. Her eyes were sceptical, glassy.

"You are overwrought, dear child. I wonder that you are not sickening for something." Her soft fingers traced a line around Kitty's cheek. "For you are not yourself. You should go to bed, dear, get some rest. I'll ask Springer to make you up a tonic."

"I cannot go to bed. I have to extract myself from this engagement."

"That is not desirable. And even if it were, it is not possible."

"There must be a way. A way to do it without embarrassment to anybody. We could say it was all in error—that it was all a frightful mistake. Yes!"

"No, Kitty."

"But it could be put down to a mix-up at the news sheet office. A poor tired clerk who put in the wrong names. That would be quite credible."

"But even so, it would not do. You must see that. Life is not a story that you write for yourself as you go along, dear. You were born to things, great things. You, Kitty, were born to marry well, to breed well. To better your own blood, think of that."

"I do not love him. I do not even like him."

"Love? What do you know of love, child? I shall tell you something about it. Love may grow from practically no regard at all. It is nurtured by comfort and position and security. Most of all, by the advent of children. If a man gives you a child, you shall love him forever."

A thumping nausea rushed through Kitty's frame.

"I do not know of all your attachments, Kitty, and I do not ask. But I was a young deb once. And I know that one may expect to be infatuated from time to time, to fancy oneself in love with some young pup or another. But whoever these young men are, they cannot offer you what you are being offered now. And you must think of your whole life, dear, not just one moment."

Her aunt reached for Kitty's hand and squeezed it. In the distance, a clock sounded, and there was a rumble of voices. She spoke into the young girl's ear:

"Think what you shall be establishing. Your children will be better, even than you. And your grandchildren. Just think how high they shall be, how fine. This is what you were born for, darling. If you turn your back on it, you shall be betraying yourself."

Kitty took a deep breath.

A curtain in her head had drawn closed. It swept up the dust as it went. People, places she had known all her life, would be forever shrouded. She wiped her own eyes. On the other side of the curtain was light. The knot in her belly pulled tight and a wave of determination rose, took her. She would find Alex. They would get out. So much love could not exist just to be dashed upon the shore. Within her, something was readying itself, fighting. She began to plan, to scheme. Pieces moved together, drew pictures in her mind. When she nodded and thanked her aunt, she kissed her too.

Kitty endeavoured to spend the following hours as normally as possible. She repaired her face, reached for her favourite shawl, and sat in the drawing room, ostentatiously reading. When she passed Havers in the hall, she bid him a good morning. The thought of luncheon with her father made her head throb, but it must be faced. If she did not appear, he would suspect her. All her worry was for naught. For when the bell rang, and she made her way to the dining room, she found herself eating alone, cutlery scraping on china, silk skirts swishing as she left the room. The front door teased her, and she imagined walking out of it, brazenly. But that was not the way, for Havers was watching her again, and other servants too. The hours ached past, creaked like old leather, but eventually, the wait was over. Kitty was turning a page of an unread novel in the conservatory when Violet appeared. She was flushed from hurrying and slightly wet from the rain.

"Thank goodness. Did you find the address?"

"Yes, miss."

Violet frowned.

"And? Where is Mr Faraday?"

"Gone, miss. Landlady says he's vanished clean out the house."

KITTY'S HEAD HAD BEGUN TO ACHE THE PREVIOUS DAY. A PAIN had seeded and expanded and now came to be overwhelming. It was an ache of the soul too. Alex was gone, and she knew no way of getting him back. In her bed, at night, she lay awake. Her circumstances, she pondered like an unfavourable news story. The fact of the matter was that her father had placed fetters upon her with great effectiveness. The front door was locked and bolted, and the servants were watching. Aunt Margaret would accompany her out of doors, but there was no other way out. She thrashed in her sheets and turned on her side. The servants were long abed, and silence hung in the house. Kitty felt tears well up in her eyes, but she would not let them break forth. She would continue to think until she alighted upon a solution.

Suddenly, a sound, a sense of movement. She held her breath and the ache in her head pounded. It was the slightest whisper. A hint, nothing more, but it caused her to sit up. Somewhere, the softest steps fell on carpet, a door opened and closed. Kitty stared into the black room, panic rising with intrigue in her heart. A flash of pale light as the door to her chamber opened and closed. It was so deftly done, so quick, that it might have been Violet. But it was not Violet. It was him. She knew the shape of him as he moved towards the bed in his great coat and the rhythm of his breath as he advanced.

The audacity of the thing stunned her. How had he done it? It was almost as though it were affected by magic. Her legs caught in the sheets as she crawled forward. They greeted one another with great ardour. With gasps of incredulity on both sides, they embraced.

"You came! Oh, Alex, I have been so frightened. I know you left your lodgings. I have been frantic with worry. But you are here." She touched his face. "How can it be so?"

"Because I was determined to do it. Because I would not give up. And I must admit that I had some help."

A shadow of a smile crossed his face.

"From Violet?"

"No. I haven't seen her. I asked a man who knew my father. He is...well, he is somewhat practised at gaining access to great houses. We watched the house for two days to establish the best way in. But that is a story that we do not have time for. If I stay long, I shall be discovered."

Kitty's heart hammered. For how could she bear to let him go?

"I read of your engagement."

"But you did not believe it?"

"No, of course not. I knew at once that you could not possibly have consented to it. It would be so unlike you."

"I cannot stay here, Alex. But I cannot leave. My father's servants watch for me to leave. I am trapped."

"No, you are not, not really. Sir Roland believes you are snared, but he is wrong. I have a plan. I will come back here the night after tomorrow. Between now and then, you shall carry on just as before. You need to take Springer into your confidence."

Kitty nodded. In her imaginings, she was gathering her skirts and leaving the house without a backward glance.

"I assume that you should like to take her. And she should not be sorry to break with this household."

"I believe that is right."

"Good. I have purchased three passages to France. I have some money. Not much, but we will make more. We will prosper some-how. Come with me, Kitty."

"I will, oh, I will. What must I do?"

"I shall tell you."

And they sat on the edge of the bed and plotted. In very little time, the plan was fixed. Patches of light appeared in Kitty's mind until all was clear. It was astonishing what could be achieved behind the carapace of respectable society. A new name, a story of life, a crossing to another land. But the price of that was disconnexion. She would not be sorry to leave the house and her father. Aunt Margaret too, for she had proved to be no friend to her. The betrayal of it still sliced her, and confused her too, for why would Margaret side so uncompromisingly with Sir Roland? As for George and Philomena, she would write to them, let them into the secret. All would be well. First thing in the morning, Kitty would appraise Violet. She was suddenly filled with excitement and certainty. For how could they fail to be successful? When he stood to leave, she reached out to touch the buttons of his waistcoat, not willing to let him go.

"Did your father's friend help you to plan this escape?"

"Yes, a little."

Kitty paused.

"Then I am sorry for it. I know you dreamed of breaking free of such people."

"Do not be sorry, darling. For it does not matter compared to you. Compared to us being together."

She stood too and reached up to his face as she kissed him.

KITTY DONNED THE OUTDOOR CLOAK AND BONNET. SHE WORE a cap, too, for it could do no harm. She did not tie the ribbon as well as Violet, but no matter. Tears of panic pricked her eyes, just below the surface. A wave of white-hot determination, laced with fear, followed. The room was just as it always was: lavish, comfort-able, well made. It was all so dependable. The polished wood, the heavy fabric kissing the floor, the gleaming glass reflecting the afternoon sun. Kitty surveyed it for a moment, caught like a fly in a web, balanced over a gaping abyss. She blinked, knowing she may never see it again. In the middle distance, a clock chimed. *Cut the rope, Kitty Cathcart, shut the door.* In speedy inelegance, she grasped at the trinkets box beside her bed and with a shaking hand, pinned her mother's cameo to her bodice. The cloak covered it, and the day was losing the light, so no one would see. It probably would not be necessary. She would look back later and think herself silly, melodramatic even. But she would not be without it. The ache in her belly lifted and the web was suddenly gone. For Kitty, it was as though the path of her life rose to meet her. The plan was laid, the preparations made. Nothing was writ, but everyone knew their part, Kitty most particularly. Burning with indignation, she made for the door.

❧ 17 ❧

JAMES

MARCH 15, 2018

THE RED LIGHT LABELLED 'SECRETARY' LIT UP ON JAMES'S
desk phone as it rang loud as soon as he sat down after his meeting.

"Helen?"

"I've got Josie on the line."

He had left her this morning, much later than usual at eight
thirty. He had had to take a call from Abu Dhabi at five a.m. and it
had gone on for hours. Then it turned out that one of the twins
had made off with his passport, which he needed for a business
trip that evening, and it took Josie half an hour of searching to
recover it from the washing machine. The men from Thames
Water were just arriving as he was leaving, lugging canvas bags of
tools in through the front door. Josie never bothered him during
the day. The unexpectedness of it made his stomach turn.

"Put her through ... Josie?"

"Hi. Don't worry the twins are fine."

"Are you okay?"

"Yes, I'm fine. But, I thought I ought to call you about this
Thames Water thing."

Thames Water thing? The water in the kitchen had been
running brown for two days and engineers had been making a
mess of the utility room plumbing, digging holes in the garden, and

scratching their heads for at least the whole of the previous day. Helen had ordered in loads of bottled water and James was not remotely worried about it.

"What Thames Water thing?"

"Well, the thing is the police are here now as well."

"The *police*? Why?"

"Thames Water called them. They were digging in the garden border to get to the pipe. You know the one they think is leaking. They asked me if they could dig further over, near where the girls' plots are. I didn't think you'd mind and said yes. So, they did. And, well"—her voice wobbled slightly—"James, they've found the remains of a body down there."

18

The Times, July 10, 1859

Fears are growing for heiress Miss Catherine Cathcart who disappeared from her family home in Kensington last week. Renowned beauty, Miss Cathcart is the only child of wealthy industrialist Sir Roland Cathcart and his late wife, who was the younger daughter of the late Lord Fortescue. The lady, who is a well-known figure on the London social scene, was last observed by servants at the London home of her family on Wednesday evening. Miss Cathcart is reported to have supped as usual and retired at ten o'clock. She is presently engaged to be married to Lord Trefusis and their nuptials were planned to take place next month. A search for Miss Cathcart has been made without success. She is an attractive, fair-haired young woman of fashion and readers are asked to notify the police immediately in the event of a sighting.

The Times, August 12, 1859

No progress has been made in the hunt for missing

society beauty, Miss Catherine Cathcart. Miss Cathcart, who is known as 'Kitty,' has now been missing for four weeks. It has emerged that a want of honour in her own conduct may be responsible for her circumstances. The missing girl is understood to have turned down a number of proposals of marriage from eligible and respectable men and to have regularly fraternised with the lower classes. Her engagement to wealthy peer, Lord Trefusis, was announced the week before her disappearance. The pair were observed at the theatre together, before they became engaged, and theatre goers noted Miss Cathcart's forwardness towards His Lordship. Where she is now, is not known, although the police have conducted exhaustive enquiries. One theory has suggested that Miss Cathcart absconded with a male servant from her father's house, and another that she was observed boarding a ship bound for the Americas at Liverpool, dressed in red. Whatever the truth, it is understood that Lord Trefusis has now renounced his engagement to the young woman.

The Times, August 25 1859

CATHERINE 'KITTY' CATHCART, THE DISGRACED HEIRESS AT the centre of what has become known as 'the Cathcart Affair,' remains at large. The young woman's disappearance remains a mystery, however, it is increasingly believed that she has absconded from her home in order to live a disreputable life. Reports have been received that Miss Cathcart has conducted associations with any number of men including the son of the late well-known criminal and reprobate, Mr George Farradaegh. Readers will recall that name from the infamous Marshland Scandal. Members of high society, including some of the lady's own relations, have sought to distance themselves from her. Wherever she is, her name shall always be associated with immorality and criminality. Close friends of Lord Trefusis have suggested that the peer made a lucky escape from one of the worst females of her generation.

❧ 19 ❧

JAMES

MARCH 15, 2018

THE SUITED MUSCLED MASS OF JAMES CAVENDISH THUMPED into the back seat of a black cab, and he slammed the door after him. It had been faster to hail than to wait for Helen to call his car and, frankly, he was glad of those brief moments, belting down Fleet Street, the wind in his face. He stated his home address to the driver and turned his attention back to Helen, who was on the other end of the phone.

"I'm not going to make Paris. Get Charles to go instead. He knows the deal as well as me. Jessie can cover the Project Helium call this afternoon. But tell her I need to know what is said."

He silenced and his brow furrowed, listening to her various questions before answering.

"I'll do that call from home. Email me the dial in details. And I'll look at the Project Trillium document tonight...Get Edward to do that one...Okay, thanks, Helen. I'll call you later."

He tapped the disconnect button and sat back, watching the many limbed chaos of the capital whip past the window. Heading out of the square mile, bound for home in the middle of the morning on a Tuesday, was not something he was familiar with. There was far more traffic than he would have imagined. What were these people doing? Wasn't everyone at work at this time, parked behind Formica desks and blinking at screens? The cab stopped at a pedestrian crossing, and a torrent of people crossed the road to the piercing bleep of the green man flashing. James glanced at his phone, as if expecting to find some answer there. He texted Josie: *I'm on my way home. Are you okay?* He bristled when no instant reply appeared. His eyes closed with much the same sense of frustrated expectancy. He was reminded of the time in his teens when the village flooded, and his mother volunteered to have the misplaced, welly-booted residents in the spare rooms at Ashburton. He smiled, all of twenty years later, to recall her justification to his astounded father: *"We've got a big house on the top of a bloody hill. It's the least we can do."* A familiar ache started in his head. But this time, it was tempered with something else, a weird feeling, a sense of being trapped in a carnivalesque parody of his own life. Many strange thoughts fanned out in his mind like cards...none stranger than the sight that greeted him upon his arrival home: a police car parked outside his house and a uniformed officer standing on the doorstep. James paid the driver and sprang from the car and into the house, slamming the door loudly and marching into the kitchen.

"Hello?" he called out expectantly.

"In here." Josie's voice rang out from the conservatory and James followed it. He found her, perched on the edge of the sofa, facing a suited man sipping tea and a policewoman with a notepad on her knee. As he entered, she sprang out of her chair.

"Ah, you're back. I've left the girls in the playroom with Lena."

"Lena?"

"Yes. Lena. Your cleaner."

She blinked, and James felt ever more as though he had a walk-on part in a situation comedy of the 1990s. He had no notion that he had a cleaner named Lena. Everything in his life appeared at present to be an elaborate, and not especially funny, joke. He didn't smile at her as she left the room, pleading a need to check on the twins.

James turned to the two strangers.

"Mr James Cavendish?"

"Yes."

"Inspector Grange." He held up his identity card, which glinted in the sunlight, before turning to the woman beside him. "And this is Detective Sergeant Stack."

James smiled at her, but she did not return it.

"Mr Cavendish, there is no point in beating about the bush here. We were called here today by Thames Water who have been conducting some excavations in your garden. I'm afraid that when they were digging in your flowerbed this morning, human remains were discovered. Does this come as a surprise to you?"

He tilted his head and raised his brows. James immediately thought of Josie. Had Inspector Grange been this rude and obvious with her?

"It does. A total surprise."

Inspector Grange looked somewhat doubtful. "I see. Well, it's a bit of a turn up for the books all around at the moment, sir. I'd say that looking at it, it's definitely human remains. They've been there for some time. Don't know how long but a while. Other than that, we're in the hands of pathology. They'll be here shortly."

James nodded and D.S. Stack began scribbling furiously in the silence that followed.

"I wonder if I might ask you a few questions, Mr Cavendish? All routine, of course."

"No problem. Fire away."

"Who lives here beside yourself?"

"My twin daughters, who are nearly two, and their nanny, Miss Minton, whom you've met."

The inspector's eyebrows rose on his furrowed brow like a pair of caterpillars.

"Nobody else?"

"No."

"No Mrs Cavendish on the scene?"

"No," James barked, impatiently. A moment of silence followed in which both police officers exhaled audibly. James was in no mood to be played and gave the game short shrift. "The former Mrs Cavendish is alive and well and living in St Moritz, most of the time, if you'd like to have a word with her?"

Inspector Grange didn't look even slightly abashed and James wondered whether he believed a word he had said.

"Thank you. Maybe you can provide her contact details to D.S. Stack here. How long have you lived here, sir?"

"About five years."

"Nice place. Did you inherit it?"

"No. I bought it myself. Look, Inspector, I'm happy to answer any questions, but I suspect that you need to work out more about these remains first for your questions to be useful. So, what is the process? What can we expect from now?"

"You can expect the boys from pathology to turn up, and I'm afraid make a mess of your beautifully landscaped garden for a bit. They will take the remains away for examination. It should take about twenty-four hours to date them, a bit longer to work out other things. Let's go and have a quick look at the scene now, eh?"

James agreed and the three of them trooped out into the mud strewn garden to find two guys from Thames Water sitting on garden chairs and sipping tea. The multicoloured markers that had staked out the twins' garden plots had been tossed aside and the path was littered with crumbling earth. In the sunken crater before him, framed by budding geraniums, broken off at the beginning of life, were a series of hideous pearly bones. Even James, a man with all the scientific abilities of next door's poodle, could see that they were the remains of a human body, sure as you like.

"Good grief."

A flicker of human sympathy came over Inspector Grange's face for the first time. James was glad of it. He was a tough man, a man of the world and nobody's fool. But maybe he didn't have a heart of stone. Had Josie been presented with this grisly sight? She would have kept the girls inside at the first sign of unpleasantness, but had she been asked to stand here and peer at these ghoulish sticks of calcium herself?

"Inspector, my children are very young. I'd like to get them away from here, I think, if there are going to be police crawling around the house and garden."

"Understandable, sir. I'm bound to tell you that you're free to go wherever you choose. However, I'd be grateful if you would stay in London for the next twenty-four hours. By then, we should be able to date the remains. After that, all being well—"

"What does 'all being well' mean?"

"Assuming this is an historical case. Then, there is no reason why you and your little girls can't get away, although I'd prefer if you stayed in the country for the time being."

Having answered further apparently pointless questions, given D.S. Stack his work address and contact details for Rosaria, James left them to their note taking and officious prowling around the garden. While they had been speaking, a large van had emptied a parade of men and women in all-in-one white suits, clutching bags and cameras and the like, on the pavement outside the house. As James reached the foot of the stairs, he greeted this flock of arrivals with the briefest of acknowledgements before bounding up to the nursery.

"Josie?"

He opened the nursery door to find her leaning over Santa's cot, laying down her sleeping form, Maggie snoring lightly from the other side of the room. The task achieved, she looked up. Her hair fell over one shoulder and she smiled with half her mouth. The curtains were drawn, and a sort of half-light sat in the room.

"What a morning!" she exhaled.

"You could say that. Is it okay to talk in here?" He glanced worriedly at the girls. "They won't wake up?"

"Not if you speak quietly. I often talk to myself in here while they are napping, so I'm sure they're used to it."

"Are you okay? Have the police questioned you?"

"Yes, but it didn't take long. They just wanted to know how long I'd been here and a few things about you." Her cheeks reddened slightly. "Where I've worked before, that sort of thing."

"I'm sorry about it. I can't believe this is happening."

"I know." She smiled in that knowing way she had and took a deep breath. "Don't worry about me. I'm fine. The girls have been in the playroom all day. I brought them up to get them away from the sound of the automatic digger and I thought they might be upset to see their plots being messed up. Are you home for lunch? They will be so excited."

"I'm home for the day, Josie, and I'm not going to Paris tonight. I've got a couple of calls that I'll take in my study. But I'm here if the police need to speak to anyone. You and the girls can just stay upstairs, or go out, assuming that the police haven't barred the front door."

"That's kind. Thanks."

"It's not kind. What kind of guy would I be if I left you here with half of the Met Police and the bones of god knows who in the garden? Last time I checked, your job description doesn't include overseeing the exhumation of dead bodies."

"I thought you hadn't read my contract."

"Touché. Guessed that bit."

She moved closer and his throat tightened. A forceful desire to embrace her came over him. Was this a symptom of shock? Or the strange result of breaking from routine? Or the inevitable consequence of prolonged exposure to the way her t-shirt fitted her body? He didn't know, but he fought it. She was polite and sometimes she was sweet with him, giving him a smile or sharing a joke. But she never gave him the impression that *she* lay awake thinking of *him*. She was unquestionably a wonderful nanny, and the thought of her packing her bags and abandoning him under the twin clouds of dead bodies in the garden and him touching her when he should not, horrified him.

"Let's go downstairs. It's crawling with police but I'm not hiding up here all day. I'll make you a coffee for a change."

Josie pulled the nursery door closed as they left and agreed to this plan. From below came the clunk of the front door opening, footsteps in the hall and a loud, "Yoo-hoo! Josie?"

James's heart sank. How did she have such timing? His mother never missed a crisis. She had an instinct for them. He announced his presence from the top of the stairs.

"Good morning, Mother."

"James, what are you doing at home? And why is there a policeman outside? Good morning, Josie dear. Girls napping?" She removed her jacket and hung it on the stand in the hall.

"Morning, Diana. Yes, they've just gone down."

"Mother, I'm making a coffee. I assume you'll join us?"

The three of them sat down at the island in the kitchen while James briefly described the events of the morning to his mother. Josie seemed distracted by the team of white suits in the garden, erecting plastic barriers and marching about with buckets and tape and so forth. She didn't touch her coffee.

"I've never heard of anything so ridiculous in my life!" pronounced his mother loudly. "All these people and forensics and god knows what, and they don't even know if it's a human body at all yet. I mean, it could be a dog."

"Mum, believe me, it's not a dog. I haven't seen it all, but it looked human. I think we can take it as read that a human was buried in that garden. Question is who and when, not what. They were asking about Rosaria..."

"Now that is ridiculous. She was here at Christmas for heaven's sake! Mind you, she is a nasty woman. Ending up under the begonias is no more than she deserves if you ask me."

James, who did have an appreciation of his mother's humour, smiled and thought about how to change the subject. Josie placed her undrunk coffee on the marble surface and broke the silence.

"Diana, are you staying for lunch? We can eat in the dining room, so the girls don't see the garden. I was thinking of making spaghetti Bolognese. Maggie and Santa will be amazed to have Daddy *and* Granny home for lunch. It'll be like a party." She smiled, but it didn't reach her eyes.

"Josie, are you sure? I can order in? Or we can all go out?" he asked.

"No. You ought to be here in case the police need you, and I don't mind the cooking. It'll take my mind off things."

With that, she stood and began shuffling around the kitchen in her bare feet, taking out pots and ingredients and piling plates up.

His mother exhaled noisily.

"I cannot see why there needs to be so many policemen in any case. What is wrong with the security guard?"

"The street security guard?" James looked at her doubtfully. "Come on, Mother. You know as well as I do that the residents pay him to stand about making them look important. He would be the first to call the police if something actually happened here."

Josie clattered about with the lunch things while James and his mother continued to speak.

"So, run all this past me again, James. How long is it before we know how old these bones are?"

"Twenty-four hours apparently. After that I'm taking Josie and the girls away from here for a few days break."

Josie's curly head sprang up from her task on the other side of the kitchen, and their eyes met. James had only thought of this idea a moment before he said it. But, in his experience, sometimes in life you may as well just say the thing and see what happens. It wasn't as though he didn't have a perfectly good justification.

"I can't have them living like prisoners in a house crawling with the police and with people carting human bones through the hall. Helen is rearranging my diary for the rest of the week. Now I just need to find somewhere at late notice."

"Well that's easy, surely. Josie dear, how do you like Devon?"

"Love it."

"Well, then it's settled. I'll call our housekeeper at Ashburton, and she'll have your rooms ready. Daddy and I have no plans to go to the country this weekend, so you'll have the place to yourselves."

The rest of the day passed in a kaleidoscope of unfamiliar activities. At Josie's suggestion, he had gone up to get the twins when they woke from their naps. They were beside themselves with excitement to find him home, and the five of them ate Josie's delicious pasta in the dining room, away from the grisly tableau in the garden. Josie had relaxed a bit and his mother was giving her chapter and verse on Ashburton. Maggie held on to James's little finger throughout her meal, and unexpected contentment washed over him. Later, he took calls and replied to emails in his office while Josie and the girls played in the room above; his mother had long since left to relay the dramas of the household to his father, and no doubt, a great many people besides. Marcia turned up with a file of papers for him to review, although he could not really understand why she hadn't just emailed them. She stood in the doorway, leaning against the frame and twiddling her hair with her fingers, her eyes dashing about nervously as she asked him how he was and whether he needed a quick drink. He declined. He received a hysterical call from Rosaria who had heard from the police. James dealt with her questions quickly and blankly. It was only when the call was over that he realised she hadn't asked after the twins once.

The forensics team had packed up and gone for the day, leaving a network of blue and white plastic sheeting and netting over various parts of the garden. A tent tunnel had been erected along the side of the house, and James had observed various articles being bagged up and carried to and fro. Inspector Grange had returned mid-afternoon and informed him that all was going well and to expect a call in the morning to confirm that there was no reason he could not leave for Devon. Constable Simons, the rod-backed young man on the doorstep was, James had been informed, for the moment, a permanent feature. When he asked why, Inspector Grange had sniffed the air and remarked, nonchalantly, "Routine, sir. And we don't want the press sniffing around now, do we?"

♋ 20 ♋

LETTERS BETWEEN GEORGE CHRISTIE, ESQ.
AND HIS SISTER, MISS PHILOMENA CHRISTIE

George Christie, Esq.
c/o The Royal Oak, Broadway, Liverpool
September 15, 1859

My dear Philomena,
I trust that this letter finds you well, Sister. I write this in my chamber at the inn at which I have been staying in Liverpool. It is a lowly sort of a place, and every step I take within it makes me glad that I persuaded you to stay at home. There can be no sense in heaping discomfort upon heartache.

Here, I have made all enquiries I know to make. I fear that I have made little progress. On Tuesday, I ventured to the dock to the office of the Great Western Shipping Company in order to make enquires as to the passenger list of the *Athena*. It will not surprise you when I confirm what we have already been told: neither Kitty nor Faraday were named on the list. I endeavoured to discover from the young man in the office whether or not a list of ages or indeed other details are kept. He was, alas, unable to assist. He recalled the visit of the constable some weeks ago and claimed to have nothing further to add.

183

I asked him about the report in the *Times*, but he knew nothing of it and was adamant that he was not the source of the information. He then surprised me by suggesting that I visit the tavern across the way and ask to speak to a girl by the name of Mildred. At length, I found her. A very young thing to be working in such a position but seemingly polite and honest, if rather nervous. I explained who I was and that I have a sister named Philomena and that we are both anxious to discover the whereabouts of our cousin, for whom we fear greatly. I took out the newspaper clip-ping, now somewhat distressed by excessive handling. Querying to myself, whether she could read, I read it aloud for her like a school-master. At the part that described the grand young woman boarding the ship, she became rather agitated and began saying she would never speak to another young hack who came to the bar and whatever was the world coming to and the like. I asked her what she meant by this, and at length she told me that a young man who said he worked for the *Times* appeared in the bar and she had told him of the finely dressed young woman whom she observed. To look upon this young girl and think that she may have seen our Kitty, shook me to my core, Philomena. I fought to remain calm and not frighten her, for I knew her to be one of the last hopes available to us. Having discussed matters for a time and content that she was reasonably easy, I showed her a miniature of our cousin. Her reaction was immediate, my dear. Kitty was not the girl she saw.

And, so you find me here, in this lonely place, far from home, and quite despondent. It may be that Kitty and Faraday *were* on that ship. It cannot be discounted if it was somehow within his gift to establish false identities. The idea that Kitty would have under-taken such a thing dressed in expensive clothing and presenting herself as the fine lady she is has always rung wrong to me. Kitty is a peacock of a girl, but she is not a fool. If she intended to flee, she would have done so as inconspicuously as possible. Now, I believe, we have evidence that that particular person was not her. The world is a wide and perilous place. I am torn between joy at discovering that woman was another, and horror at the renewed knowledge she could be anywhere, and we are no nearer to finding her. I have chewed the matter over like one of Nanny's beefsteaks, and I cannot credit that Kitty would have vanished without a word to us. While I have that thought in my mind, I cannot cease to search for her.

I trust that you are well at home, my dear, and that you and Mother have had no further words, nor any visits from our uncle. My plan for the morrow is to visit the attorney at Longhaven village. If you wish to write to me, send care of the inn there, and I shall receive it when I arrive. My intention is then to continue my journey to Gretna.

Your loving brother,
George

22 Queen Anne Gate, London
September 17, 1859

Dear George,
Thank you for your letter, which warmed my soul greatly. I cried when I read your passage about Mildred in the inn and wished that I had been with you. Surely you accept that on occasions such as that, you would do well to have a sister in your keeping. I should placate nervous maids better than a smart young gentleman with the voice of a lord, would I not? Think upon it, maybe. As for the young lady's intelligence, I was relieved but not surprised. It has never been, in my view, a plausible explanation that our dear Kitty would have run away to the Americas, in first class, or steerage, or otherwise. It cannot be right that she would have left us so irrevocably and without one word of communication. I do not believe it of her.

I know you will wonder at me when I write 'relieved.' Part of your dear mind will be thinking it would be better to be out of reach and well than have met another fate. I cannot bear to write it here, and so I shall not. But we both know, dear George, that of which I speak. My eyes sting to write it, but here is what I say. Until I have evidence to the contrary, I believe that our beloved Kitty is alive and, in the world, and while that is the case, I cannot believe that she would abandon our society forever. We must search every dark corner, for somewhere she is waiting for us. Please take heart from that.

You will be pleased to read that our uncle has not repeated his visit here. The door was closed upon his retreating back, and I shall not be the one to open it again. Shall we know him in the future? Have we ever known him at all? I have thought on these questions but to no end. All the sinews of my body recoil from the man, that is the fact of the matter. Between Mama and me, there have passed no words for these two days together. She has written some letters; I know not to whom. I am ashamed to say that I begin to suspect she may have taken some of my letters. For yesterday morning, Smithers thought a letter had come for me, but it was not on the tray. I fear that I am too long with my demons and see enemies in all corners. In the afternoon, she walked in Hyde Park with O'Connor without inviting me to join them. There have been no callers, nor do I expect any. We have taken our meals together, in the shortest possible time and in a sepulchral silence.

I suppose this letter shall find you on your way north. I would prefer, as you well know, to be with you. However, I wish you blessings and God's speed, dear brother, until you are home.

Philomena

21

JOSIE

JAMES SLOWED THE CAR AS THE WHEELS CRUNCHED ON THE gravel, and the pale-yellow façade of Ashburton appeared before them. Josie sat forward from the leather of the passenger seat and exclaimed.

"Wow. How beautiful is that?"

The grass-lined drive led to a small turning circle before a broad, E-shaped house, leaded windows, clusters of red brick chimney pots. A wisteria on the verge of budding stretched across the walls, and a squirrel hopped about before the wide oak, seemingly ancient, door.

They had packed up the car the night before and left early. The twins, still in their pyjamas, had happily snuggled back to sleep in the car seats and the mist of the spring morning had slowly lifted during the long drive, shifting up to make way for the clear bright light of the day, the increasing warmth of the season. Josie had expected a big house and a long driveway. In her mind's eye, she saw horses and awful oil paintings of unknown men. She hadn't expected it to look like this. This was a mansion that a fairy might build. There was something in the wonder of it, the blurred edges and history-worn corners that unravelled her. She knew in her bones that she could stay here.

"It's a nice house." James kept his gaze fixed ahead.

"Nice? It's amazing. This is like, *Howard's End*. This is Mandalay."

"Didn't that burn down?"

"You are so lucky, growing up in a place like this."

He smiled but didn't reply.

The car doors opened with an expensive, heavy click, and they each removed a drowsy twin from the back. Josie, who held the slowly waking Santa in her arms made for the front door.

"Not that way. Round here," announced James as he set off around the side of the house. They paced around to the right, through a stone archway and into a small walled garden, where James nudged the outer door handle with his elbow, and it sprang open.

"Carol?" he called out as Josie followed him in. "We're here."

Josie looked about her. They had come into an enormous kitchen with a pale blue Aga and a vast, rather worn table with mismatched chairs. It was so different to the kitchen at Veronica Gardens that she wanted to laugh. On one of the chairs was a woman's jacket, and beside it, a handbag. Above their heads, there was shuffling, followed by the sound of footsteps upon stairs nearby.

"Where are they then? A-ha!" proclaimed a small, pink-faced woman as she bounded into the room, clutching a can of polish and a cloth. These, she deposited on the table and made a beeline for Maggie who was just gurgling into wakefulness. She took her from her father's arms as one might pop a pea out its shell.

"Come to your auntie Carol, darling. Have you been having a sleep? Yes, you have!"

"Nice to see you too, Carol," replied James, dry as ever.

"Oh, get away with you!" she responded, not looking at his face. Much to Josie's amusement, she swatted him on the bottom before turning her attention on Santa.

"Hello, poppet, looking very well too." Carol kissed Santa on the forehead before looking up. "And you must be the famous Josie."

"That sounds ominous! Yes, hello, I'm Josie. It's nice to meet you."

"Carol Reader. I'm the housekeeper and general dog's body around here. I'm on strict instructions from Lady Cavendish to make you as comfy as what we know how. She says you're a godsend in need of a holiday. And I tell you what, you must be something. A girl goes on a long day's march to get a compliment out of Her Ladyship."

"I expect she was just being polite."

Carol looked at her doubtfully.

"I shouldn't have thought so. Now, let's get you up to your rooms. Girls are in their usual room. Cots all made up. Josie, you are in the connecting room. The bath's fine but avoid the basin. The pressure's awry, and you'll get drenched. Jimmy, dear, I've put you in the spare on the other side of the twins. Thought you might like a change."

As they made their way up the back staircase behind the kitchen, Josie moved Santa to her hip and turned to her employer, smiling. "Jimmy?"

Carol had set toys out in the twins' room, and the girls set about playing with them immediately. Carol gave them each a peck on the cheek and excused herself, saying she had to get her husband to a doctor's appointment, but she'd come in to do the beds and see them 'round and about,' as she put it. James went down to the car to get their bags and Josie took in the space around her like an unexpected fragrance. Under her feet was a thick carpet and over the mantlepiece hung a painting of three young children, two boys and a girl, in pastel coloured smocks and cardigans. She could not have identified the other two, but one of the boys was so obviously James. He had a stare, even as a child. Josie noted that he was as tall as his brother, who she knew was older than him, and that over the years, his hair had darkened. The eyes that gazed out of the canvas had not changed one bit from that day to this. Within moments, the man himself appeared in the doorway, carrying their bags.

"Josie, shall I leave yours on your bed?"

"Yes please." She waited until he had disappeared through the adjoining door... "Jimmy."

"Watch it." He reappeared, dumping a suitcase with the twins' things down beside one of the cots, his lips hinting at a smile.

"I've just been meeting your younger self." Josie glanced at the painting and picked up Santa who had been holding her arms up for a cuddle.

"How did you know it was me?"

Josie laughed, and he looked confused.

"Seriously? You look at me like that every day."

James regarded the canvas, which he must have seen many thousands of times before, as if it was something new.

"Worrying."

After unpacking and a spot of Duplo construction, Josie found her way down to the kitchen to make lunch. Carol had, no doubt on Diana's instruction, stocked the place with all sorts of delicious foods, and Josie selected a couple of quiches to bake and began assembling a salad while the new potatoes bubbled away on the top of the Aga. Out of the back of the kitchen window, she spotted what looked like a small swimming pool, covered over with a blue sheet, and a tennis court with no nets. Amongst the cookery books on the shelf beside the fridge was a copy of the *Canterbury Tales* and an illustrated *Karma Sutra*. Smiling inwardly and wondering slightly about James's parents, Josie set the table for lunch.

Having slept so long in the car, the twins were irrepressible, and to use their energy, James took them all on a tour of the garden. Maggie sat on James's shoulders and Santa walked, Josie supporting her along the freshly mowed lawn towards the tennis court and the stables beyond. There was only one horse, but Josie guessed from the number of stalls that there must have been more at one time. His name was Alfie, and James and Josie held the girls up at the stable door for them to give their greetings to him.

"Does Daddy ride?" asked Josie in a sing-song voice she regretted the moment she had used it.

He turned on her.

"I can ride, but I don't. I'm not a member of the green welly brigade."

"Neither am I. I was just asking."

"Well, there's your answer. Now who wants to see the well?"

There was a great infantile cry of 'me,' and they followed him around the perimeter of the stables, waving goodbye to Alfie until they reached a squat brick well, with a little circular roof, just like in pictures. But it was real. Josie's knuckles whitened as she gripped onto Santa and they leaned over to look down. For a moment, the dinginess disconcerted her and then, her eyes adjusted. She stared into the cavern. None of them could see where it ended or what was in there. Josie recalled the bones in the garden, locked into the muddy earth, unmarked and unknown. She thought of how those bones had been there all the time: when she first arrived and sipped her wine nervously by the French doors; when she guided the girls planting out their plots; when she nearly kissed their dad. All the time.

Suddenly, his hand touched the small of her back. Heat shot through her.

"Hey, I'm sorry I was sharp with you back there. Mea culpa."

"S'okay. Why though?"

"Because I'm a sharp man, who doesn't know how to talk to lovely people. And because there is something about this house that brings the worst out in me..."

"Why did we come here if you don't like it?"

"Because the kids love it, and it's all set up for them, and it's nice to see Carol, even if she does still call me Jimmy and smacks my arse. Because Mum suggested it right in front of you and you looked so happy, I couldn't deny you."

"Maybe you need to look for the fun in it? I think it's amazing. How many people have an overgrown tennis court with no nets and a bottomless well in the garden?"

"And an open-air swimming pool in March?"

"It'll be bracing." Carefully, she leaned over the edge of the well. "Listen girls. Echo!" she shouted down, and, to their great delight, the sound bounced jauntily back up. Not quite able to say 'echo', Santa began making miscellaneous sounds into the black, empty space. James lifted Maggie up, and she did likewise.

"So," Josie continued, not looking at him, recalling the feel of his hand upon her back, "does this tour extend to the house?"

Ashburton had started life as a medieval manor house, but the centuries had added so much as to extinguish the original building in favour of a mostly Georgian series of comfortable day rooms and spacious bedrooms. The main drawing room was lined with books and in each room, the walls were hung with portraits and land-scapes and framed sketches. On top of a covered grand piano stood numerous family photographs—wedding scenes, graduation pictures, newborn babies of all generations—beaming out.

The twins ate early and went to bed at their usual time, Josie tucking them up in their enormous, unfamiliar cots, observing the rise and fall of their tiny chests beneath the blankets as they slept. Before going downstairs, she went to her room. A squat painted lamp by the side of the bed threw a gentle light around the room, and she stood in front of the mirror, taking her long hair out of a hairband and shaking it loose. The light bounced on her and around her, and the air tickled her scalp. There was something about this room, this house, that made her look at herself differ-ently. Observing a blob of Maggie's supper on her sleeve, she took off the t-shirt she had been wearing all day and put on a fresh one: bright white, slightly tight across the bust. Reaching into her tatty make-up bag, she put on some lipstick and then blotted it with tissue. Unwilling to examine why, she scampered down the back stairs to the kitchen.

There she found James going about one of his favourite activities.

"What are we having?"

"Lasagna." He spun around to face her and blinked. "Just gone in."

He poured her a glass of red wine without asking, and she took it readily.

"How long?"

"Forty minutes. Come on. I want to show you something."

She fell into step behind him as he walked out of the room and along a narrow, apparently unheated, passageway. They emerged into a small room, lined with books, and dominated by a massive fireplace at one end and an enormous oil painting of a young woman in jeans at the other. James flicked on the lights and set about lighting the fire, with an obvious air of experience and proficiency.

"Welcome to the snug. Best room in the house." He paused and struck a match against the scrunched-up newspaper and kindling. It curled orange and, at its heart, purple and black. The small sticks of wood, perfectly assembled, shifted about and took, throwing up flickering light, trembling heat. Josie wondered whether a fire was really necessary. It was a warm March, and the heating was on. She could see he wanted it though, and that was reason enough. Perching on the edge of the battered sofa, she regarded his lean back, his strong arms prodding the fire.

"It's a nice room. Good video collection," she said, eyeing the shelves, and noticing on close inspection, many Classics. "It must be the work of many generations...?"

He turned to her and laughed. "They all belong to me and my brother and sister, but we've kept them here to amuse visitors."

Beneath the television, Josie noted an ancient video player.

"I don't get why you don't like it here."

"It's not that I don't like it here. Actually, it's fine, especially now."

He gave her a searching look, just like the little boy in the painting, and she felt the heat of the fire smacking her face.

"It's just that this is my family's house, not my house. I didn't build it. It's not how I do things. I like rowing my own boat, and I'm not that great at being in a team. Anyway, you must have realised that my parents are, well, bloody bonkers?"

"I had. But maybe we're all a bit mad, *even* you?"

"Never." He placed a log on the fire and watched it for a moment before sitting back on the sofa, beside her.

"What do you want to do tomorrow? We can hang out here, go to the beach, go to Exeter if you're missing the big city. We can go for a walk in the wild wood." Josie raised her eyebrows at him. "There's a pig farm we can walk to, over the way. There are bikes in the old barn with a chariot thing for kids. Devon's your oyster."

"Any of those sound great. Are you properly on holiday then? I thought you'd be working from here."

"I've got a call tomorrow. But apart from that, I'm delegating. Today's tally of emails from Marcia, so far: one hundred and twenty."

"Oh my god. I have never received that many emails in one day, never mind from the same person. I don't think I have one hundred twenty things to say."

"Bet you have."

"Maybe about Ethel Turner Everett. I've been busy reading the articles that Helen printed out."

"Good. Anything new? Got any ideas for your PhD thesis yet?"

She fixed him with a silent stare before continuing. He was so pushy, *so rude.*

"Quite a bit of it was literary criticism. I enjoyed reading it, but you don't learn anything about the author. You just think more deeply about her work. But when it comes to the woman herself, absolutely nothing is known of her. She's a complete mystery. Ethel Turner Everett is definitely a pen name. There are no records of a person of that name being born in the relevant period. For a short time between 1857 and 1860, she was very popular, and then she totally disappeared. K-pow. Gone. No more novels, no poems, no nothing. Even when she was actively writing, she never appeared anywhere, never gave talks, never corresponded with other writers or earnest readers. She was a recluse, and then she was gone altogether."

Just thinking about Ethel, made Josie itch. How can somebody be so completely there and then so utterly absent?

"Publisher?"

"Hepworth & Company."

He prodded the fire for a final time and sat back beside her on the sofa.

"Well, that's a lead then, isn't it?"

"Yes and no. Hepworth was acquired by the big publishing house, Bollingbroke in 1964."

"Well, go to them then. If you don't ask, you don't get."

A few moments of eddying silence crept around them. The glow of the fire twisted, shifted, and steadied. Josie's tummy rumbled. But it was James who broke the silence.

"I'll go and check on the lasagna." And he shot off the sofa like a rabbit from a trap.

From: josephineminton@gmail.com
    To: editors@bollingbroke.co.uk
    Date: GMT 22:15, March 18 2018
    Subject: Ethel Turner Everett
    Dear sirs:
    Hello, my name is Josephine Minton, and I am looking for information about the Victorian novelist, Ethel Turner Everett. Everett published two novels ("Thomasina" Pub. 1857 and "Mariah" Pub. 1859) and a small collection of poems (Pub. 1858). Her publisher was Hepworth & Company that, I believe, was incorporated into Bollingbroke in 1964. I am fascinated by Everett and am trying to find out more about her. If there is anyone there who knows anything and would mind corresponding with me, I'd be very grateful. Thank you.
    Yours faithfully,
    Josephine Minton

From: tim@bollingbroke.co.uk
    To: josephineminton@gmail.com
    Date: GMT 09:35, March 20 2018
    Subject: Ethel Turner Everett
    Dear Josephine,
    Thanks for contacting Bollingbroke. You are right that Turner Everett's publisher became part of the

Bollingbroke family in 1964, and we still publish her work now. Although, as you are probably aware, there is very limited interest in it. I have checked in our archives and there is a box relating to Turner Everett. I looked inside myself to make sure I wasn't wasting your time. All it contains is a contract, seemingly signed by the author, some notes written, I assume by the publisher and a few letters. You are welcome to drop by and look at it whenever you like. Our office is in Camberwell. Just ask for me at the desk, and I'll show you the file.

Best,

Tim Vincent

(Archivist)

22

JOSIE

MARCH 2018, DEVON

THE MORNING DAWNED BRIGHT AND CLEAR OVER ASHBURTON and the twins woke with it. Josie set about her morning rituals, getting the girls up and dressed. They sat on the floor of the bathroom playing with toy trains as she had a shower and stuck foam bath letters to her legs as she brushed her teeth whilst chanting 'Oh-sie' and giggling. With one twin on each hip, she took them down the dimly lit back staircase to the kitchen and set about making toast and filling beakers with water. She had thought that James was still in bed and so was surprised when he breezed through the kitchen door in faded jeans with his shirt sleeves rolled up.

"Morning, girls. Josie, I've found a bike for you, but I'm going to need to bring the saddle and handlebars down. Can you come and stand next to it in the yard?"

Josie followed him out as the twins sat in the highchairs, observing through the kitchen window. In the yard, was an ancient, cornflower blue ladies' bike, built, seemingly for a giant. If Josie were able to sit on the saddle, she doubted that she could reach the pedals, never mind the floor.

"Sorry. This is the best one. The others are all men's or racing bikes. This was my sister's. She's a bit taller than you."

Josie stood next to the frame, as commanded, the saddle coming well up to her ribs. This cycle into the wild wood was looking more and more like a dance with certain injury.

"I'll bring it down and give it an oil. It'll be fine. That's mine over there." He nodded towards the equally ancient men's bike, propped against the barn with a metal trailer attached. "The girls go in the chariot."

A grey cloud stole across the leaden sky.

"Lovely."

"You do like cycling, right?"

"Yes, of course. Love it."

And so, it was sometime later, armed with waterproofs and water bottles and packets of biscuits, they bounded forth into the wild wood. It turned out, fortunately for Josie, not to be that wild. She had plenty to contend with perched atop James's sister's rickety bicycle, which, with adjustment, was only just manageable. Josie teetered about, bumping uncertainly over tree roots, straining to keep her toes on the pedals, and keeping up with the father and babies team ahead of her. From nowhere, a muddy ditch appeared and, a moment too late to go around, Josie juddered straight into it, shrieking as the wheels slowed in the sludge. The enormous size of the bike frame seemed to taunt her. Try as she might, her legs weren't long enough to get traction on the pedals at such a slow speed and gradually, inexorably, she fell off. The sound of her splatting into the mud and squealing 'shit,' combined with the shuddering thud of her body hitting earth. The ancient bicycle then crashed down on her leg. She looked up to see James striding towards her, mud splattered jeans casting long shadows on the woodland floor.

"Don't move."

He shifted around her and pulled the bike up, flinging it, like a rag doll, against a nearby tree before kneeling down beside her. Josie reached up to take his offered hands, but he took her around the waist, and in one movement, eased her up, first to the knees and then to her feet. Her whole side was caked in mud. With his hand, he swept a collection of soggy oak leaves off her face. He was hot, but the wind against her wet body was chilling. She wiped more mud off her face and through her hair.

"Shit."

"Dramatic. You should have gone round it."

He was smiling, maybe suppressing a laugh. Spotting the two little heads in the chariot just beside them, she felt suddenly awful.

"I'm sorry for swearing in front of the girls."

She steadied herself on his arms, and, as their eyes met, he broke into the first completely natural, spontaneous laugh she had heard from his lips.

"Don't worry about it. If all you say is 'shit' when you fall into a lake of mud and rainwater, then you have nothing to worry about. Your Mary Poppins credentials are intact. You need a wash though." He reached for the baby supplies bag in the chariot and pulled out a packet of Wet Wipes. Without hesitation, he took one out and began running it over her face. Josie closed her eyes, unwilling to imagine how ridiculous she was looking or face the reality of the tingle that she felt under his fingers.

"You are also going to get cold." He swept his fleece over his head, leaving only a worn blue shirt and popped it over her wet head. As she put her arms in the oversized sleeves, the warmth from his body permeated hers. She shivered, and her tummy felt wavy.

From the chariot came a chorus of 'Oh-sie,' and she walked towards them.

"I'm a silly Josie. Hello, girls. Are you enjoying your ride? We haven't found the witch's house yet, though, have we? Have you been looking? It's a good job Daddy knows where it is..."

She looked around at him. He was stock still, just looking at her. Then, without speaking, he picked up his sister's colossal bike and walked it over.

"We will see the house another day. You are wet and need to go home. It's too big for you. I shouldn't have let you try to ride it. Your legs aren't long enough." Josie looked down at said legs and smarted. She wasn't a supermodel, but she wasn't in the habit of finding her body wanting. Josie wasn't too small. The bike was too big.

"If you can manage the ride back, you'll be home quicker. But if you can't, we'll walk the bikes back. Whatever you like."

"Up to you really."

"Josie, I'm giving *you* the choice. Make a decision."

The look he gave her was stinging. Unnecessarily so, she thought.

"Okay. Let's walk to start with, and when we're out of the wood, maybe I can cycle the rest of the way."

And so, it was that they wandered back to the house, through the glade, back across the fields and along the winding, pot-holed lane that ultimately led to the village beyond. Josie was far more comfortable wheeling the bike beside her than trying to ride it. At the apex of the hill, Ashburton just visible in the distance, they stopped to let the twins out of the chariot for a scramble around in the heather and a mid-morning snack. They each leaned against Josie, eating their bananas as, gradually, the sun broke through the clouds and the air warmed around them. After a time, Josie wiped the girls' faces and strapped them back into the trailer. The cold of the water had somehow sunk into her, and despite James's fleece, she began to feel teeth-chattering cold. Her hands shook slightly as she picked up the bike. As if from nowhere, he took it, and wheeled it together with his own, one on each side back to the house as Josie walked beside, hugging herself for warmth.

When they reached the house, James took care of the twins while Josie headed straight for the bathroom. She stripped off the layers of wet, muddy clothes and stood under the hot shower, knowing nothing for a few minutes but its thrilling, rushing heat. After washing her hair, she stepped out on to the thick pile of the bathroom carpet and wiped the steamed mirror. She dressed in leggings and a long, warm top that Santa loved to snuggle against, and leaving her hair loose, she bounced down the stairs.

It was a surprise to open the kitchen door and see, not only James and the girls, but a number of others as well. Four blond-haired children, two boys and two girls, all of school age, had joined the party. And sitting at the head of the kitchen table, nursing a large mug of coffee, was a blonde lady in a bright purple body warmer, drumming her manicured nails against the wooden edge and laughing.

"And this must be Josie. Fenella Stokes! James's sister."

She stood and held out her hand, which Josie took.

"Hello, Fenella. I recognise you. You're the lady in the painting." Josie recalled the full-size canvas with the long-limbed, casually dressed blonde staring self-consciously out of it, hanging opposite the fireplace in the snug. She was older, but it was unmistakably her.

"Oh god, I wish my parents would take that thing down. It's a ghastly object. These are my progeny. Peter, Edward, Mary, and Alice."

She pointed at each of them as she said this, and they all, dutifully stopped their activities to say hello to Josie.

"We live about twenty miles away and Mummy told me that you were all down here this week, seeking refuge from this ghastly body in the garden nonsense. So, I thought I'd look in. I didn't warn my brother, as I knew that he'd take you all out for the day if I did..."

James said nothing but handed Josie a cup of coffee that she gladly accepted.

"Well, we did try to go out for the day, but it turned out to be a bit ill-fated. Would you like to stay for lunch? I was going to make shepherd's pie."

"Gorgeous. Yes, please. What luck. We love shepherd's pie, don't we children?"

They each returned a chirpy 'yes' and James raised his eyebrows at Josie.

"Well, that's settled then."

Josie began assembling ingredients and sat at the kitchen table, beside Fenella, to chop. Peter, who Josie took to be about ten, sat down beside her.

"Can I help? I'm very good at cooking."

"Are you? Well, in that case, yes. I'll get you a peeler and a chopping board. How about you get going on the carrots? Think you're up to it?"

He nodded vigorously and began applying himself to the task with enormous effort. Fenella leaned back in her chair and drank the last of her coffee.

"So where do you all live, Fenella?"

"Charwelton. Back of beyond really. And you must call me, Fenny. Everyone calls me Fenny, even James, and he's allergic to showing affection, especially when it comes to family."

Her brother, who had been crouching on the floor beside the twins and their cousin Mary, who was about five, stood. He smiled a resigned smile of acknowledgement to his sister and spoke to Josie.

"I have to go and make a call. You okay?"

"Fine." She smiled her brightest smile, feeling Fenny's observation rather keenly. "I won't let the kids disturb you."

He turned and sauntered out of the room, ruffling young Edward's hair as he went.

"You finding him all right? I must say, I haven't seen him this relaxed in years. Maybe they should've dug a body up in his garden before! James is such a high-octane person. Is that what they call it? It's all work, work, work, money, money, money. Nothing's ever good enough for him. And then with that bitch of a wife buggering off and leaving him holding baby twins, well! He was the last man you would ever think that would happen to. Always thought she was a ridiculous article. Mother informs me that her latest trick is sending great quantities of presents for the poor little dears for no apparent reason. Guilt, that's what I call it."

Josie glanced to the twins playing on the floor with their cousin. She had always had a strong belief that children understood a lot more language than they appeared to and, although she wanted to hear what Fenny had to say, a lot actually, she was anxious to change the subject.

"Fenny, would you like a coffee top up?"

"Oh, lovely, yes, don't mind if I do."

The coffee gurgled out of the pot, and Peter announced that he had finished peeling the carrots. Josie showed him how she would like him to cut them, and then supervising his own commission of the same, she threw away the peelings.

"Anyway, you seem to be doing terribly well with him. James is an old stiff and it's not every girl who could handle him, know what I mean?"

Josie smiled and sat back down in her seat.

"He's fine. You get used to it in my job. You know, dealing with all sorts."

"I bet you do."

Sometime later, when the shepherd's pie had been assembled, placed ceremoniously in the Aga, and then removed, piping hot and golden brown, Josie left the children with Fenny while she went in search of James. From outside the study, she heard his voice on the phone. She tapped lightly before entering and finding him swinging back and forth on an ancient office chair, feet up on a leather topped desk. Seeing her, he placed his hand over the speaker end of the phone and raised his eyebrows.

"Lunch is ready. Are you nearly done, or do you want me to bring some up?"

He shook his head, and she knew that was all the answer she'd get.

"Okay." Josie closed the door quietly behind her.

As it turned out, they ate without him. Josie and Peter set places for four children and three adults and put up the twins' highchairs around the vast kitchen table. Josie played mother, doling out liberal servings of the delicious pie and pouring beakers of orange juice out for the children. Josie sat between the twins, administering their meals as best she could with some forthright assistance from their cousin Mary. Fenny lamented the fact that she no longer had a nanny to help at home and complimented Josie's hair in between mouthfuls.

James's place at the table remained empty.

Josie observed Santa growing fractious in her highchair and Maggie drooping against the padded back.

"I think the girls might be getting tired. Would you like your afternoon nap, poppets?"

They willingly put their hands up to grasp her as she lifted them out and rested one on each hip.

"I'll just take the girls up, Fenny. I usually get them down in about fifteen minutes."

"Of course, of course. In fact, Josie, would you mind if I left my brood here for an hour or so? I need to run a few errands. They won't be any trouble."

"No, of course not. That's fine. Will they be okay down here while I'm putting the girls down for their naps?"

"Oh, my word, yes. They have been staying in this house all their lives. I'll leave you to it, Josie. Thanks for lunch. It was delicious."

With that, she stood, zipped up her purple body warmer, kissed each of the kids and then Josie, and was gone. There was an empty space and a strange calm silence in her place after she had left. For a moment, Josie paused.

"Right, kids. I'm going to leave you down here for fifteen minutes while I get the twins off to sleep, is that okay?"

When Josie returned from upstairs, she found Fenny's children in the snug, trying to light the fire.

"Erm, kids, I think a grown-up ought to do that job. Shall we ask Uncle James when he comes down?"

Edward, who was clearly the ringleader, looked rather abashed and was saved by his sister, Alice whose sing-song voice piped up: "Josie, are you good at reading stories?"

Before long, all five were curled up on the sofa, *The Magician's Nephew* open on Josie's lap as she read, complete with voices. They seemed to find Josie's voice for Digory particularly hilarious, and the girls laughed themselves silly. Right at the end of chapter two, the door opened and in walked James. He paused in the doorway and regarded them all, a crossness about his face. Josie looked up from the book in acknowledgement. Mary stopped laughing and her expression grew stern. Her little lips pinched together, and she leaned back against the cushion of the sofa.

"Mary, is everything okay, sweetheart?"

"I've wet my knickers," said the little girl and immediately started crying.

"Don't worry, poppet, everyone has accidents sometimes." Josie picked her up and kissed her cheek. "Too much giggling."

They exchanged smiles and Mary buried her face in Josie's neck as they left the room and headed for the bathroom. In the doorway, Josie looked back.

"Do you know where there might be some spare girl's clothes?"

"Where's Fenny?" asked James, his tone sharp.

"She had to pop out."

"Have a look in the nursery drawers. There might be some in there."

"Thank you. Come on, sweetheart. Let's get you sorted."

Josie easily found a fresh pair of knickers and a rather ancient looking ra-ra skirt tucked away in one of the drawers for Mary to wear and as she was helping her on with them, the twins awoke from their nap. All four returned to the snug to find the boys watching James light the fire and Alice asleep on the sofa. It was decided that a film was in order and after a bit of searching, *The Jungle Book* was found and put on. James picked up the sleeping Alice and placed her on an armchair with a blanket, while everyone else curled up on the sofa to watch, even the twins. The afternoon drifted on in contented inaction and shortly after five, Fenny's four-by-four crunched onto the gravel outside and she sprang through the door.

"S'me! Sorry. I was a bit longer than advertised! Bloody traffic."

Josie glanced out of the front door as she held it open for Fenny. Shopping bags were piled up in the back of her car.

"Don't worry, Fenny. Everyone has been fine. Mary had an accident, but I've found her spare knickers and a skirt, although it's a bit eccentric."

"Oh, you are a treasure," she said as she swept past.

Everyone kissed everyone and goodbyes were exchanged. As Fenny shepherded the children into her car, Edward was heard to ask if they could come again tomorrow. And as they drove away, out of the dust-coated back windscreen, could be seen eight tiny hands in the air, waving. James, Josie, and the twins waved back from the rarely used front door and the chill of the early evening crept about their faces.

A silence had fallen over James like a shroud, and he busied himself with catching up on emails while Josie fed the twins and took them upstairs for bath, story time, and eventually, bed. She laid down their warm pyjama'd bodies on clean sheets, carefully removing her hand from behind each of their heads and watched them for a few moments.

In the kitchen, she found James pacing. He greeted her with an inscrutable look, but his body spoke volumes. Arms crossed, shoulders tense. He was taut as a drum. Josie paused in the doorway.

"Everything okay?"

"Fine."

He opened the fridge with more force than was needed and took out a bottle of white wine.

"Did you get all your work done?"

"Yep."

He placed the bottle down on the marked table, with more force than was necessary.

Josie had been here before, in other ways. Pussy footing about big houses that didn't belong to her. Gently treading around the rich, grumpy, and spoilt. All her experience told her to play the avoidance card. After all these years, she knew what worked. A yawn, a stretch, an exclamation of fatigue. And then she could withdraw, retreat. Sit in bed, reading her Kindle and leave him to his moods. Josie knew the drill, and she told herself again and again that he was no different to the others. But in her heart, she knew he was. Something she could not name, kept her there, like a target on a board.

"Lunch was fun."

"Was it?"

James looked doubtful. He poured two glasses and handed one to her. She drank immediately, too quickly.

"Yes, it was. The kids were sweet. Peter helped me with the food."

"Well, that is a consolation, I guess. For having to cook a hot lunch for five uninvited guests at the drop of a hat. And then babysit six kids all afternoon with even less warning."

He took a slug of his wine and leaned back against the side. There was a mirthless humour in his face, and challenge too. She saw it, but she wasn't cowed by it.

"It's no problem. I'm cool with it."

"You're cool with everything, it would seem."

"No, not everything."

Their eyes met for a moment and it was James who looked away. He stretched and held his hands behind his head.

"My sister is insufferable. She's spoilt, indulged, unreasonable."

"I don't know her. I only met her today."

"And she's bone fucking idle."

The word sent a shock through Josie. Some families were swearers, and some were not, she was used to that. She wasn't offended by cursing. But he had never sworn in front of her before.

"She turns up because she knows you are here. Never met you. Doesn't know you from Adam. But she can spot a bit of free labour at twenty paces."

Annoyance stirred in her and she exhaled sharply. She might be his employee, but she wasn't his commodity. It seemed like such a tawdry end to a nice day. There was no need for this bitterness of spirit, and she would not be a part of it. A ball of rebellion gathered inside her. Suddenly, she wanted to spar with him, argue it out, have her say.

"Are you cross that I helped her? Is that it? You're paying me, so I should only look after your children. Is that what this is about?"

He dropped his hands.

"Of course not."

She knew that wasn't the reason, but she said it to rile him.

"That's ridiculous. I don't even notice the mo—"

He stopped himself, but it was too late. The ball inside her burst, flamed. She felt her face redden.

"I know you don't notice the money. You're lucky."

He slammed his wine down on the table, and it sloshed in the glass.

"That isn't what I meant. The cost is irrelevant, Josie. What I mean to say is it has nothing to do with you looking after the twins. I trust you with them whether or not Fenny is here. It isn't sharing you that is the issue—"

His face tightened, and he grimaced. Josie had the impression that he had said more than he intended. She moved closer.

"Then what's the problem?"

"The problem is how you are. How you react." He turned and moved towards the table, fixing her with a disbelieving stare. For a moment, she was lost in it. Trapped, spinning down a vortex. He placed his hands flat on the table and leaned towards her.

"It's as though you like being exploited. You need to learn to say no. You let people walk all over you."

The outrage of it brought her up sharp.

"I do not."

"Come on. I get it, Josie. You've learned to survive by being like this. By being a pushover."

"I'm not a pushover."

She said it confidently, but she was trembling.

"Not in my house. You don't have to do it here. You don't have to bow and scrape and take any fucking thing that comes your way."

Something inside her shattered and tears pricked her eyes. She couldn't let him see. Turning away, she felt his eyes on her back.

"Shit. I'm saying this all wrong."

"Yes, you are."

She heard him move closer, and felt him too, like an animal knows when one of its kind is near.

"Why don't you experiment with saying what you damned well think for a change?"

"Really?" Josie looked up and straightened her shoulders. She turned around to face him. "You might not like it."

"Try me. It would be good to think you weren't just playing a role for a change."

"What role? I'm not playing anything. I'm just not as angry as you. I didn't mind Fenny being here or leaving me with the kids. I helped out because it's kind. It's normal. And I didn't complain about it for the same reasons. I was having a nice day, until..."

"Until when?"

Josie was breathless, panting.

"Until now! It was fine. She's a bit selfish but I don't care. I saw all the bags piled up in her car. She just went shopping, didn't she? There weren't any errands. She just wanted to get some time to herself and spend some money. I might be a nanny, James, but I'm not completely stupid. If that's what rocks her world, I don't care. I didn't mind looking after her kids. They were fun and sweet. And Fenny's not that bad. At least she's kind. She's quite funny. I can see that she's spoilt but so are you."

It was no more than the truth, but it made her gasp to say it. In all her years as a nanny, she'd never spoken to an employer like that, never raised her voice, never showed herself. The feeling of it winded her.

"Josie—"

But she couldn't stop.

"You think you're so superior to everyone. You look down on your family, but you're just like them! You're rude. When I met Diana, I thought she was the most condescending person I'd ever met, but she hasn't got anything on you."

She knew it was unreasonable, but a ball inside her was rolling.

"You harangue me the whole time. I'm not allowed to enjoy reading without being an expert. I should be demanding this and demanding that. You won't let me just be myself. It's like you hate me."

"I definitely do not hate you."

"You don't listen."

"*You* don't listen. But maybe actions speak louder than words."

And with that, he moved swiftly towards her and, circling her waist with his large hands, he silenced her lips with a kiss.

✿ 23 ✿

The Evening Standard, March 19, 2018

A SPOKESMAN FOR THE METROPOLITAN POLICE HAS
confirmed that unidentified human remains have been discovered
in the garden of a home in central London. Specialist officers were
called to an address in Veronica Gardens near Hyde Park on
Tuesday morning and neighbours report that the area has been
cordoned off to make way for forensic teams. The property, which
is one of London's most exclusive areas, is the home of wealthy
financier James Cavendish.

The Times, March 27, 2018

THE INVESTIGATION CONTINUES TO ESTABLISH THE IDENTITY
of human remains discovered in the garden of an exclusive
London home last week. The exhumation in Veronica Gardens
has attracted considerable public interest, and it is believed that
the residents of the home in question are no longer at the house. A
statement released by the Metropolitan Police confirmed that the
remains are of a young woman, believed to have been in her twen-

ties at the time of her death. Carbon dating suggests that the remains have been in the ground for some time, having been buried between 1855 and 1865. Police forensic teams have confirmed that the deceased suffered a heavy blow to the head, and the death is believed to have been unnatural. Members of the public are asked to refrain from loitering in the street and in the churchyard opposite the house and are reminded that this is a residential area.

The Times, April 15, 2018

POLICE HAVE CONFIRMED THAT THEY ARE INVESTIGATING possible links between the remains discovered last month in the Veronica Gardens 'Body-in-the-Garden' case with the disappearance of a society heiress from the same address in 1859. Records show that Miss Catherine Cathcart, a wealthy young heiress with a reputation for high living, disappeared from the address in 1859, never to be seen again. Victorian police conducted a lengthy hunt for Miss Cathcart and drew a blank. A likeness of Miss Cathcart's face and an unusual brooch, which she was believed to be wearing, were printed in newspapers in the hope that she may be found by a member of the public. However, despite a number of false alarms, no sighting was ever confirmed. It was believed by many that she had run away with a lover, possibly to the United States. However, the discovery of bones belonging to a young woman in her twenties and dating from the period, now suggest that the unfortunate Miss Cathcart may never have left home at all. Whoever the body belongs to, they are believed to have been murdered, police having confirmed the likely cause of death being a heavy blow to the skull. The investigation continues.

✤ 24 ✤

JAMES

MARCH 2018, DEVON

THE RISING SUN CREPT INTO THE ROOM LIKE A SCENT, AND James watched her sleeping face, framed by chestnut brown curls, beside him. He could lay here for the rest of his life and watch her breathe, watch the light graduating over her skin. She shifted, and he moved slightly to accommodate her soft, naked body. Being with her like this was like being caught in a world between worlds, in an uncharted landscape. There was no clock in this room, and he had left his phone downstairs, but from the light outside, it was about five, maybe later. He looked about the room, at the trail of clothes cast down on the carpet, at the plate of buttery crumbs on the floor, the product of the realisation, sometime after midnight, that they hadn't eaten since lunchtime. The door to the corridor was open, at Josie's insistence, so that she would hear the twins when they woke. The windowless hall cast a shadow into the room, and he closed his eyes.

Memories of the previous night flitted about. How she kissed him back. How they pushed each other around the kitchen for a time, jostling for dominance, ranging around the possibilities. The thudding of her heart next to his chest, the warmth of her flesh under his hand. How he had picked her up and ascended the stairs with her in his arms. How she had clung to him as though a storm were raging around her. Much of the night was a kaleidoscope of her body on his, of the music of her laugh, and the sight of her unruly head of hair snaking down his torso. Something, long simmering, had exploded. It had taken them both.

She shifted around and threw a slim arm over his chest, lightly sun tanned to the elbow, and alabaster white above. From the room next door came a tentative 'Oh-sie,' followed by another, and in a moment, her face looked up from the pillow, eyes wide, and she began scrabbling out of the bed. He stroked her thigh as it passed across his lap and watched her bound around the room, looking for something to put on.

"There's a dressing gown on the back of the door."

He realised when she put it on, pink floral patterned and floor sweeping, that it belonged to his mother. Half horrified, half wanting to laugh, he leaned back against the pillows as Josie trailed into the adjacent room saying, "Coming, Maggie. Coming, Santa."

Before long, the sound of her caring for them, moving unknown things about, talking to them and herself began. In his mind, he could see the sway of her hips, the curve of her arm sweeping back covers, offering embraces. The tender, seductive moan of her presence had been singing in his ear for hours, days, weeks beyond number. She hadn't looked at him on her way out of the room, and his stomach clenched with the uncertainty of it. If she was embarrassed and regretful, he couldn't bear it. Pushing the sheets back, he sat up as her chitter-chatter continued in the adjacent room. It occurred to him, like a meteorite from another paradigm, that there was something not quite right about lying in bed while Josie tended to both children on her own. They were, after all, his kids. Pulling on his jeans and a t-shirt, he strode next door to find her trying to carry twins and walk in a too-long dressing gown.

"Let me." He took both girls, who looked mildly confused, and they all headed for the kitchen together, Josie holding up the trailing dressing gown as she pattered down the stairs ahead of them in her bare feet. She poured milk into their bottles and warmed them briefly in the microwave before placing them in eager hands. Sat in their father's lap, the girls began gulping it down, little dribbles escaping here and there. James and Josie faced one another in the harsh light of the morning.

"So—"

"What's your favourite thing in the world?"

Josie grinned and glanced at the twins before replying. "Can't say..."

"Second favourite then."

"Erm, well—"

"Not reading. It can't be something you do on your own."

She closed her eyes and tilted her head back. He had the impression that she was considering this question for the first time, and he wanted, very badly, to kiss her.

"Swimming. In the sea."

"In the sea?" He wondered whether, by repetition, she may reconsider. "Are we talking the English variety?"

"Yep. The colder the better. Love it."

"WHERE ARE WE GOING?" JOSIE ASKED AS SHE CLICKED THE seat belt into place.

James turned the ignition and steered around the turning circle in the direction of the road without looking at her.

The topiary trees of his parents' driveway folded behind them like cards. Gravel crunched surreptitiously beneath the wide wheels. The radio played, too low to hear. In the back, the twins gurgled and squealed.

Turning on to the narrow, undulating lane, hemmed in by hedges, watched by cows, they sped through the Devon country-side. The fields flew by them like flags, villages appeared and receded. Church bells tolled and at some point, he glanced in the rearview mirror to see that the twins had fallen asleep. He turned the radio off and reached for Josie's hand that he had to uncurl from a knot between her crossed legs.

"Girls are asleep."

Collectively, they exhaled and, unexpectedly, she grasped his hand with hers. She was wearing tight faded jeans and a white t-shirt with a navy cardigan that came halfway up her arms. If he didn't think it would wake the children, he would have stopped the car and kissed her there and then. He remembered the holdall in the boot, filled with clothes he thought she may need, raided from her room while she was playing with the girls.

"Do you not have to work today?"

"No. Not today. I've called Helen and told her to re-arrange my calls and have Marcia and Charles cover everything else. This is a real holiday, and we're doing what you want."

He squeezed her thigh, realising that he had never done this before. Never sat with a woman and thought of nothing but her. Even on his honeymoon, he had spent an hour a day answering emails and joining conference calls. He felt himself moving into unknown waters, but he didn't mind.

"Lovely. Better turn back then."

She didn't move her head and her eyes fixed on the road ahead, on the curve and twist of the car worn grey tarmac, the white lines, the endless leaden sky. He smiled in response, knowing full well that if it weren't for the kids, they would never have left the house.

"You don't know where we're going."

Before long, they parked and beheld the tiny sandy cove, bathed in gentle sunlight, speckled with running dogs and welly-booted walkers. A black clad teenager sat against the breakwater reading a book, and a young man running, shorts flapping in the wind, dashed past them. To their right, a row of coloured beach huts sat like a string of beads. Josie zipped up her coat and smiled at him as he unstrapped the twins. Taking one each, and James shouldering the leather holdall he had brought from the house, they made towards the beach. Without saying where they were going, James led the way across the damp sand with Josie beside him. As they approached the huts, he reached in his pocket for the key. At the yellow door, he paused and let the bag slip from his shoulder before unlocking it. He recalled standing in this very place with his brother and sister in their inherited swimming suits, sandy buckets in hand, hair flat with salt water. An unexpected feeling of wellbeing washed over him. As he opened the door, he turned to see her open-mouthed smile.

"Wow. This is gorgeous. How did you book it with so little notice?"

"I didn't book it. It belongs to my family. The key is kept on the hook above the washing machine, if you are ever staying at Ashburton without me."

For a moment, he imagined that eventuality, and he did not recoil from it as he had with other women. Josie slotted in at Ashburton, like a book in his father's library, and in a way that he never had. She knew how *to be* when she was there.

She moved into the pale painted space within and considered the pile of multicoloured buckets and spades, the row of ancient wet suits and misshapen towels hanging on the wooden wall. They placed the twins on the swept floor, and they began helping themselves to plastic moulds of fish and crabs and palm trees. They gurgled gently to discover these new toys. Josie looked back at him by the door.

"Is this where you came for holidays when you were little?"

"Yes. Every summer and other times too." He nodded at the wet suits. "Fenny brings her kids here quite a lot, I think."

"But you hate borrowing things from your family. And you like everything to be shiny and new and bought with money you made yourself."

"I know. But this is a special occasion."

"Thank you." She blushed as she said this, and he thought of the previous night.

"So," he said, opening the holdall, "I don't think you packed a swimsuit, so I brought all the ones I could find in the house. If Laura Ashley of the 1980s isn't your thing, there's a beach shop up the lane, and I'll buy you a costume. If you're not quite as mad as you make out, you can always wear one of the wet suits."

"I am just as mad as I seem." She reached out her hand and gently touched his arm.

He moved towards her in one swift movement and whispered 'good' in her ear.

"I brought your fleece for after and decent towels."

Josie picked through the motley collection of ancient swimming costumes and alighted upon a faded red strappy number.

She held it up against herself, pronounced that it would be fine and began taking off her shoes and socks. Unsure whether to look away, he knelt beside the twins while she changed, goose pimpled white legs emerging from jeans, bra snapping off with shivery speed. The costume, once on, was only a little baggy. Josie looked perfectly at ease and having changed, wrapped a big towel about herself and sat on the bench. Santa leaned against her leg and looked questioningly.

"I'm going into the sea for a swim, girls. Will you watch me go in?"

They sang a chorus in the affirmative and each donated buckets and old sand dusted spades to her lap. After a bit of chatter, they gathered themselves and made their way out onto the beach, the girls carrying a bucket each. Not far from the shore, James sat them down with their beach toys. He watched Josie as she dropped the big, fluffy towel and jogged towards the lapping water. A tiny shriek as she splashed in, arms out, chaotic hair billowing in the wind. Her sleek body jerked into the waves, and she began to move like a fish through the surf. She was a good swimmer; her red clad body turned and swept before him. After a while, her curly head bobbed and rose from the horizon, and she ran towards him, soaked through and clutching her own arms. Her face beamed a pure joy that amazed him. At speed and breathing loudly, she thumped into his arms and the waiting towel he held out for her. He wrapped it around her small, shaking frame and kissed the top of her head. His arms clamped around her like a vice.

The rest of the day worked out much as he had planned on the hoof that morning. He missed a couple of calls from Inspector Grange, but the saga of the body in the garden was the last thing on his mind. Once he knew that the remains were over a century old, as he had been told they were before leaving London, the whole drama seemed laughably ancient. He was determined to focus on Josie. After she had dried off and dressed in the beach hut, they de-camped to the cafe on the hill for hot chocolate and cups of warm milk for the children. Warmed, they bundled back into the car and drove to the Cadogan Place Hotel where James had booked a table for lunch. He had reasoned that after the rigours of freezing cold sea swimming, Old World glamour and comfort were the order of the day. As they made their way into the wide, portrait lined, deep-carpeted entry hall, a suited man from behind the desk emerged and held out his hand. James began to wonder whether this place had been quite the right choice.

"Mr Cavendish, it is a pleasure to welcome you. Your parents are regular visitors when they are in the country. We also see Mrs Stokes from time to time."

James, who was holding Santa, while Josie helped Maggie to walk, falteringly along the deep pile of the carpet recoiled slightly at the immediate mention of his parents and his sister. He nodded by way of polite dismissal, if such a thing could exist. Silently, they headed for the beautifully laid round table, complete with two highchairs in the bay window overlooking the sea, just as he had requested. As the waiter pulled out Josie's chair and handed her the menu, he tilted his head in welcome.

"It is a pleasure to welcome you to the Cadogan Place, Mrs Cavendish. I recommend the salmon to start and the guinea fowl is excellent."

He bowed in the manner of another century and moved away from the table, where Josie had coloured deeply and begun talking unnecessarily to the children. One hundred things ran through James's mind. He thought of Rosaria, and how she would not have been seen dead wearing an old saggy swimsuit of Fenny's or wading into the icy sea on a sunless day in March. He thought of his parents who expected people they met to make assumptions about them and didn't care. Most of all, he thought of the woman in front of him and the affectionate, giving quality of her personality. He didn't believe in embarrassment, but here he was, wanting to take hers away.

Later, when they returned to Ashburton, dusk had already begun to settle down on the familiar shapes of the house and garden. Josie's long hair hung over her shoulder and she twirled it around her fingers for a while before turning to him, leaning over, and whispering, "I've had a lovely day."

"Good. You deserve more of them. It's about time someone started looking after you."

In the slight chill of the early evening, they hauled the children inside and Josie fed them a simple nursery supper before officiating at bath and bedtime. Left alone with himself, James roamed the house. He got dinner in the oven and put a bottle of white wine in the fridge. Restlessness took him up the stairs. In his own bedroom, the perfectly made bed announced the fact that Carol had been there. She would have found Josie's bed undisturbed and probably other things besides. Had she managed to wait until she got home, or did she call his mother from the house before leaving? Either was possible. It was certain, however, that his entire family now knew. Through the wall, he heard Josie's gentle voice reading *The Owl Who Was Afraid of the Dark*, and he didn't care if every man on earth knew that she had spent the night in his bed. With that thought, he took himself downstairs to make a few phone calls before dinner.

"Did you speak to that policeman?" asked Josie as she appeared in the kitchen doorway, smiling and brushing some fluff from her jumper. They had been in the car on the way back from lunch when James missed another call on his mobile from Inspector Grange.

"Yeah. I called him back while you were bathing the twins."

"Any news?"

She looked up expectedly from where she had sat at the kitchen table and begun to chop salad. If he could get her to stop working and relax for longer than a minute, he would declare victory. He looked down at the notes he had taken during his call with Slack.

"Well, if you can call any of it news after one hundred and fifty-odd years. They still don't really know who the girl was, but they've got an idea. Apparently, some Victorian it-girl called Kitty Cathcart disappeared from the house in 1859, never to be seen again. At the time, people thought she'd run away, likely with a guy. Grange says that the newspapers and police records suggest she was a bit of a good-time-girl, and she was engaged to some aristocratic old bloke. That's how it was spun at the time anyway."

"Hmm. I wonder what the truth is?"

"Who knows. Anyway, the police think that our resident corpse is her. Apparently, she was a well-known character. Beautiful, outspoken, brave, charitable."

He sat at the table, opposite her, and trained his eyes on the soft curve of her smile.

"You make her sound like super woman."

"Well that's what Grange said. He told me he'd been sitting up in bed reading the history of the thing. Funny, he sounded so much more human than he did at the house. From talking to him, you'd think he'd fallen in love with this girl."

He let those words settle, and Josie continued to chop the tomatoes.

"And this Kitty was wealthy too, apparently. She was the only daughter of some Victorian industrialist who made pots of money out of steam engines and married into the aristocracy. Kitty was his only child, and so was a rich heiress in her own right. Apparently, it was the story of the decade when she upped and disappeared."

She stopped the chopping and rested her hands flat on the gnarled wooden table. Tentatively, he reached out and took one of them.

"Josie, I—"

"What happened after she disappeared? Kitty, I mean."

"Nothing from what Grange was saying. There was a massive search, but they never found her. The case was closed and that was that. Apparently, she had a cousin who went pretty much to the ends of the earth looking for her, but he never found her. The father had a rough time. A couple of years after his daughter disappeared, he lost all his money in some huge legal dispute. He died bankrupt not long after, so he was pretty much forgotten."

She stood to toss the salad in an ancient plastic bowl, a relic that James recalled from childhood, which, like so many things in this house, had never been updated. Her hands and arms moving away dazzled him for a moment, and his thoughts were elsewhere, to the motion of those hands in other circumstances.

"What about the cousin?"

"Cousin?"

"You said that there was a cousin who went looking for the lost Kitty."

"Well, from what Grange said, he drew a bit of a blank. He did a thorough job but got nowhere. Name was George Christie and he had a sister in on it as well. Philomena, I think Grange said. That is an absurdly Victorian name, isn't it? Anyway, between the two of them, they travelled everywhere looking for her. Doorstepped every politician they could think of, hounded newspaper editors, followed up every lead they thought the police had neglected. Nothing came of it. The scandal had a pretty big impact on them. Apparently, they were ostracised by the whole of respectable London society because of it."

"That sounds terrible. Poor people. Did Grange know what became of them?"

"Not a lot. A good few years later, George Christie married and had a family. The police are trying to trace his descendants for DNA testing of the remains."

"And Philomena?"

"Never married. She was completely cut off from society by the scandal for years. But she was independently wealthy and set up home in Mayfair. She and her brother founded a charity dedicated to searching for missing people. It was called 'The Friendly Society for the Discovery and Recovery of Missing Persons.' Have you ever heard of anything that sounded more nineteenth century-worthy? They set it up with a vicar from the East End who'd had a parishioner disappear without a word, and a Mrs Leadbetter, some woman living in Brighton. Philomena Christie apparently threw herself into charitable work. She subscribed to campaigns and wrote earnest articles about the condition of the poor. You know the sort of thing. When she died, she left everything to the charity, with a few gifts to her nephews and nieces. She sounds like a bit of a bluestocking. And all the while, her cousin was buried in the garden of the house she was believed to have run away from."

"Well, *might* have been. I mean, it isn't certain, is it?"

"No, it isn't certain."

What was certain? he wondered to himself. And how long would they fill the silence between them with speculation about this strange mystery? It couldn't go on forever. At some point, she would have to give in and talk about *them*. But for the moment, James reflected that it was the invasion into their lives of this grisly and peculiar tale that had pushed them together. He had been expecting the arrival into his life of a long forgotten Victorian murder about as much as he had expected Josie herself. She moved about the kitchen lightly, doing jobs and busying herself, curls tumbling about as she worked. Suddenly, she spun around to face him and spoke hurriedly, as though she had been thinking about it for a while.

"I want you to know that I don't normally do this."

"Normally do what?"

"You know. Well..." She slugged her shoulders up and raised her eyebrows. "Hop into bed with my employer at the first opportunity."

"It wasn't the first opportunity. You could have had me a dozen times."

"When?"

"The night of the dinner party, definitely. The night you came back from visiting your sister. The night after they found the body. Probably every night after I met you, Josie. Tonight, as well, if I haven't put you off. Which is not to say that I hop into bed a lot either. Because I don't."

"Really?"

She looked at him enquiringly, like she didn't quite believe it. It was true though. James knew how women saw him, and he tried not to be an idiot about it. He knew that if he wanted a woman, he could usually have her. But it was a power he used sparingly, as though he knew it would diminish if over employed. He had never wanted sex for the sake of conquest; it just wasn't him.

"Yes, really. I've never been like that. I have been married once, and I've had a few serious girlfriends over the years. I'm too old for casual sex."

"So am I."

Her shoulders relaxed and she studied him. "Only thing is, what about if this is all a bit of a dream? Being here is so lovely. The house is amazing. I love the colours and the smells, the way the whole place sits on the land like it belongs. Being here just us and the girls. It's like a magical exile. When we go back to London, it might be different."

"It won't be different. It has nothing to do with the setting. It is about you and me. I should know. I have not been in love a number of times. Trust me."

She blinked, and an unspoken 'yes' sat on her lips as he kissed them.

❦ 25 ❦

PHILOMENA

NOVEMBER 1859

PHILOMENA LEANED FORWARD IN HER CARRIAGE AND WAITED. It was early November and the air was bone-gnawing cold. Smithers shifted in her seat on the other bench, muffled up in her warmest clothes, growing restless. The two had been in position for over an hour, their eyes trained on the same sight. The back entrance of a grand house in which Philomena was no longer welcome.

"Are you sure there is only one door?"

"Yes, miss, quite sure. Apart from the front door, of course. And she would never use that. When I was in service to Miss Arbuthnot, I came to a ball here because they was short-handed. It was years ago, but I remember the house as if it were yesterday. Servants only have one door, and we is looking at it."

Philomena groaned inwardly. She was in a tangle, body and mind. Famished but unable to eat. Bone tired but full of an endless, burning energy. Hopeful but desolate.

"Well, let us pray that my brother was not mistaken."

"I can't imagine that, miss. Mr Christie knows up from down. He's seen her enough times. I reckon all we got to do is wait."

"Pray that is the truth."

For a time, they sat in silence, time eddying about them. Pedestrians clicked past the closed door of the carriage and when other vehicles passed, it shook gently. Philomena's knuckles whitened as she gripped the reticule in her lap. The door opened a number of times, but one unknown face after another appeared.

"He called out to her. George, I mean. But he was too late. She was already disappearing back inside."

"Probably didn't hear him, miss. She was always hard of hearing if you ask me."

Philomena was silent, but her countenance was grave.

"I know you is worried, miss. But I knew that girl. And I reckon if she heard Mr Christie, she would have spoke to him. She's a talker, if ever there was one. There's no reason to think she won't want to speak to you, miss."

Smithers reached out and her finger touched Philomena's hand. It was a slight hint of a touch. Others might have looked askance, might have wondered. Or taken it as evidence, were evidence required that Philomena did not know the form of things, the proper way to be. But the loss of Kitty had bred much. It had been the cause of shock and grief and fear. Heartache beyond measure. But it had taught Philomena to hold those who were loyal to her near, to treasure them.

"I hope not."

"And if she does take fright a bit, well...I am here to help."

Smithers smiled brightly, and Philomena knew that she was attempting to jolly her along.

"I know. Let us hope that she is willing to speak. We have had such poor luck in finding the others. George has been around half the country seeking information. He found Coachman John's parents. They believed he had a new position but no address for him. So, we have left a note. Who knows whether we shall ever hear anything?"

"Well done, Mr Christie."

"And, he found Violet's brother. He is in service to Lord Castleborough. But he has no idea where she is. Told George that the two of them never got along. It is all so frustrating."

"You'll get there, miss. You and Mr Christie couldn't be working any harder."

"Sometimes, I feel that the whole world is against us. My mother, my uncle. Every friend we've ever had. Lady Fairfax herself—"

"Miss, look!"

Philomena's eyes darted up to the black door to see that it had opened. A brown skirt, a sturdy cloak, a bonnet holding against a gust of wind. Philomena held her breath. The girl turned and showed her face before trotting towards the carriage. Philomena exchanged a look with Smithers before releasing the door and slipping down onto the frosted street.

"Molly? It is Molly, isn't it?"

"Miss Christie!" After a moment, a smile broke through the surprise. "Oh, Miss Christie." She curtseyed, belatedly and begun to look embarrassed. "It's a pleasure to see you, ma'am. I'm at Lady Fairfax's now." She indicated the great broad house behind her.

"I know. Molly, would you mind awfully if I walked with you a while?"

Molly flushed, confusion wandering across her face.

"Course not, miss. I'm just going to the post office." She smiled nervously. "Is there any news of Miss Cathcart?"

"I am afraid not. I wish that there were."

"Me too, miss."

Molly said no more, but she looked sick to her belly, like a wire of anxiety was sprung inside her, tight, ready to rip.

"Would you mind awfully if we spoke about it a little? I am not here to embarrass you, Molly. But Mr Christie and I are desperate. We are trying to discover what can possibly have happened to Miss Cathcart. I've wanted to see you for some time, but I didn't know where you'd gone. Then Mr Christie saw you one day, and we guessed that you were in service to Lady Fairfax."

Molly looked thoughtful.

"Course, miss."

They walked along some more.

"How have you been?"

"Oh, all right, miss. I'm lucky in my new place. The housekeeper is a bit fierce. But her bark's worse than her bite. The butler's nice. He's better than that Havers!" Her voice was suddenly louder than before, and then she shrank back.

Philomena smiled.

"You do not need to mind what you say with me, Molly. I shan't breathe a word. In any case, I never had any affection for Mr Havers. I believe he was no friend to my cousin."

"No, miss. He never liked Miss Cathcart. She was always getting one over on him, and he didn't like it much. He was a right old stick! I shall never forget his face when he dismissed me that morning. I reckon he was enjoying himself right proper."

"How awful for you. You must have been so distressed."

"Well, I was that worried, miss. And he didn't say what I'd done wrong. Just said the house didn't need me anymore. 'Pack your things and sling your hook,' he said. If Mrs Cooper hadn't given me a reference on the sly, I should never have found a place."

"Well, bravo for her. Were you dismissed the morning after Miss Cathcart disappeared, or was it later?"

"No, it was that very morning."

Molly looked to Philomena, the crease on her brow deepened.

"Miss Cathcart had been confined to the house for days, ever since her engagement was announced like. We had strict instructions that she was not to go out without M—"

She stopped herself, as though the words had hit a wall.

"Yes?"

"Pardon me, ma'am. Without Mrs Christie. Mr Havers said that if Mrs Christie was with her, she could go out of the house. But as it was, she didn't seem to want to. Just sat about in the drawing room, reading that book of hers. That young man what she liked so much was gone. It was a funny time."

They both slowed, fell into step with one another.

"Go on. You are being so helpful, Molly."

"I remember it like it was yesterday. The master didn't come home for dinner, and Miss Cathcart ate alone. I saw her just before she retired. I'd done my hair in a new way, see. Cook said I was a silly piece, but I like to try things. Anyway, Miss Cathcart give me that twinkly smile of hers and said, 'It suits you, Molly.' She did! She always had a nice word, she did."

Her voice crackled, wobbled, but then she rallied.

"Anyway. I finished my duties in the kitchen, polished the breakfast table, and dragged me weary self to bed."

"Hmm?"

"I shared with Mavis, one of the other housemaids. She was already asleep, lazy devil! Anyway, I'd been in bed a while when I heard something queer. I says it was a scream. But Mavis woke up and she reckoned it was a bang. It fair give me the quivers. But Mavis said it could have been anything. 'Go to sleep,' she says. And I did."

Tears were flowing freely now, and Molly trembled in the cold wind. Philomena handed her a handkerchief.

"My dear girl. Dry your eyes. You shall catch a chill."

"Thank you, miss."

She blew her nose, noisily and looked up through glassy eyes.

"Next morning, before I'd even finished the fireplaces, I was in with Mr Havers. Dismissed. Booted out like I'd been caught thieving. But I hadn't done nothing, miss. I went back to my room to get me things. Mavis said that Coachman John had been sent packing and another one of the maids, Gertrude. Springer too. Now that was a shock because everyone knew Violet was the best servant in the house. What was more, Mavis said that Miss Cathcart was vanished from her room, and everyone was saying she'd scarpered off!"

They turned a corner and were assailed by the wind once more. Molly's cloak billowed about.

"They must have thought that we'd helped her, miss. That me and John, Gerty, and Violet had helped her clear off. But we didn't, Miss Christie. I didn't know nothing about it. Can't say as I do blame her though."

"No. I know. Nobody who knew could blame her."

"I hope she is all right, wherever she is. She's a rare, old spirit is Miss Cathcart. And then sometimes, I think of that sound in the night, and I'm frightened, like."

"I am sure you are, Molly. But Mavis was right. It might have been anything."

A knot of fear formed in Philomena's belly. It strained and locked, and she thought she may never make it loose.

"I am so pleased that you were able to find another position. I am going to give you my card." She fumbled in her reticule and pulled out the square of cream. "I've written my address on the back in case you should forget. If ever you hear anything, Molly, from anyone at Veronica Gardens, would you mind awfully letting me know?"

"Course not, miss."

"And if you don't want to put it in writing, please visit me. I shall always receive you."

Molly blinked, visibly shocked.

"I would like to find John and Springer and even Gerty. Anyone who might be able to help me find my cousin. If you hear from them, or see them, maybe you can let me know?"

She nodded. They had reached the post office and stopped. Smartly dressed strangers milled around them.

"I'd also like you to accept this, Molly."

Philomena fumbled in her purse and her hand shook as she handed over the guineas. It was a spur of the moment decision, and she wished that she had more upon her person.

"Oh no, miss. I couldn't."

"Please, Molly. I know that Kitty was fond of you. And it was not proper, turning you out of the house in a flash for no reason. Please, no arguments."

Molly opened her hand and took the coins. Philomena thanked her and made for the carriage. Every step, she thought that her legs might buckle under her, but they did not.

229

❧ 26 ❧

JOSIE

APRIL 2018

THE OFFICES OF BOLLINGBROKE & COMPANY BORE DOWN ON Josie in a blaze of mid-morning sunshine, and she paused on the pavement to check the time on her phone before announcing her arrival by pressing the buzzer.

"Bollingbroke."

"Good morning. I have an appointment with Tim Vincent. My name is Josie Minton."

"Second floor" came the disembodied voice in response, followed by the whirring of the electronic door being remotely unlocked.

Josie moved into the building as commanded and smiled at the unresponsive girl on the other side before entering the lift. She wasn't quite sure what she expected from the publishers of Ethel Turner Everett, but it wasn't this. In her imagination, the hallowed halls of her favourite novelist's publisher had been lined by leather-bound books and elderly top hatted men, sporting monocles and unnecessary walking sticks. She imagined great lined curtains, thick with dust, that she would throw back, letting in the light, before curling up on an ageing chaise to read a treasured first edition. Josie laughed inwardly and reminded herself of the reality of the situation. Currently, she was alone in a lift moving towards the second floor of a five-story glass fronted modern office block in the centre of London. This was a modern business, with modern writers and concerns. It was a miracle that they even kept any of the information. The idea that Ethel Turner Everett was an inconvenient legacy, a footnote in somebody's business plan, not even that, offended her in a silent way.

She recalled the time, a few years ago, when she had gone to the British Library to try to do some research. It had turned out that you couldn't just walk in and read as she had hoped. You had to enrol and persuade a grey haired, elasticated waisted librarian that you had a viable project to work on. Josie had found herself, on her hard-won day off, knowing that Annie was at home looking after the kids alone and counting the minutes until her return, unexpectedly having to pretend that she was a credible researcher, rather than just a girl with an interest. She recalled the feeling of exposure as though it were yesterday. This time had been different. Something inside her had calmed and hardened, and she knew what she was about.

On the last day at Ashburton, she had replied to Tim Vincent's email, arranging an appointment, making plans to be taken seriously. In bed that night, in the dark, they had planned her pitch, as James called it. His hand had stroked her body as he spoke, she could still feel it now. A life-long love of the prose of Ethel Turner Everett, an academic and teaching career cut short by practicality, an eye for history, an instinct for words, thwarted until now. James had said it, and she agreed dozily, cocooned in his bed. It was only on the Tube this morning, whistling through tunnels, clutching her handbag, she had realised those things were true.

Tim Vincent had suggested the morning after their return to London, and for a dazzling, unexpected moment, she had burned with energy, and said yes. James, who had not been fazed at all, just picked up the phone to Diana and asked her to look after the kids that day. And so, it was, like a pavement had been laid for her. Diana had turned up at eight and, after some pleasantries and chatter about the girls' routine, Josie had left for the throng of the Tube station. Now, here she was, alighting on the second floor of the building, onto an asymmetric, multicoloured carpet and looking about expectedly. Signing herself in at the reception desk, she was ushered beyond the garish foyer, into the world of corridors and disorderly offices beyond. The sight of various heavy, spectacled faces peeping over computer screens greeted her as she followed the girl from reception around a file-lined bend in the corridor before knocking on a white door marked 'archivist' and opening it.

A rickety office chair on wheels spun around to face her and a young, thin man in jeans sprang from it, holding out his hand to shake.

"You must be Josephine. Welcome to Bollingbroke!"

"Hi. Josie, please."

He bounced about the room, waving his arms as he talked, and Josie could feel his enthusiasm. Tim chattered away while he made her coffee in the small side kitchen.

"It's quite exciting for me, of course. I don't get many visitors. It's a lonely life being an archivist. Usually, people ask to see the same old stuff over and over again. There were so many requests for Graham Greene's files that we gave them to the British Library to save the carpet!"

He beamed a great smile at Josie and, gathering that it was a joke, she laughed quietly.

"There's quite a lot of interest in the between-the-wars period, you know rackety, old smokers who turned out to be Soviet spies and their glamorous writerly girlfriends. Quite a few students want to come in and see our Bloomsbury files."

He bounded back into the room with a dribbling coffee mug and a plate of biscuits that Josie gratefully accepted.

"But I've never, in ten years, had a request for Ethel Turner Everett. I'd noticed the name in the index before but didn't know a thing about her. So, I did two things, Josie. Firstly, I checked the records of the archive."

"Are you saying that the archive has an archive?"

"Yes, it's a bit circular, isn't it? It does. There is a logbook of who has looked at what and when going back to 1920 when the current system of filing was put in place. I think it's accurate. So, I checked it. And you are the first person, in the history of *ever* to look at the files relating to Ethel Turner Everett. Well, that's a bit dramatic. Someone must have put them in the box, but nobody's ever looked inside. How about that?"

His eyes sparked as he asked this, and he seemed to hover above his chair in excitement.

"Amazing."

Inwardly, Josie was smarting. Someone had written that entry in the *Dictionary of National Biography*, but they hadn't bothered to come here, to look at the only source known to exist on its subject. It was exasperating, but Josie smiled broadly as Tim continued.

"And the second thing I did was to get hold of her books. We keep a copy of everything on our books, so it was easy. I read *Thomasina* and then *Mariah* in two days. They're wonderful. Just wonderful. And they've been sitting, unread in the room next door to my office for ten years, and I didn't even know. Her poems were a bit dodgy though, don't you think? They are so Victorian, it's not true!"

Josie laughed.

They talked for a while about their favourite passages and how Josie had found and then re-read a hundred times the stories Tim had only just discovered. After another cup of coffee and a few more biscuits, he ushered her into another room, chocker block with aging filing cabinets. In the centre was a narrow desk, and on top of it, two shabby box files, laying side by side like sleeping ducks.

"So, this is it. Everything we have on good old ETE," said Tim standing in the doorway and gesturing towards the desk. "I haven't disturbed them. Story's yours."

He left the door open as he left and through the wall, she could hear him moving about in his own office. Josie approached the desk and sat, just looking. The files were thick with dust on one side and unmarked. Opening the first one, she felt as though she were taking a breath for the first time. It creaked slightly as it opened, and Josie gingerly began removing its contents. The brittle, yellowing paper announced the age of the documents. There were a number of loose, closely typed sheets on the top, and beneath them what looked like a cheque, but it was a funny size and shape, being large and square. Below that, some letters, and below those, three one-page contracts. A musty smell emerged from the box, and Josie gently levered the documents out, focussing on the signatures at the bottom of the contracts. She didn't read the words, that would come later. For the moment, her eyes luxuriated over the sure stroke of Ethel Turner Everett's signature. Suddenly, the author of *Thomasina* wasn't so far away. Josie stroked the page with her index finger and inhaled the scent of over a century of neglect. Was she fanciful to imagine Ethel in the room with her? Probably, but she didn't care. A sense that she had been preparing for this moment for many years, and unknowingly, took shape.

Having made out roughly what was there, Josie began to go through it more systematically. There were three contracts, one for each of the novels and one for the poems, each signed by the author and Edward Hepworth, his own signature as unwavering as hers. Josie had thought that she might need a lawyer to look at any contracts, but these were easy to understand. Ethel wrote the stories, and Hepworth printed them. Oddly, the contract provided for all communications to be through a third party who was known to the parties but not identified in the contract itself. How strange, thought Josie. Later, there were some letters, all typed on decaying paper but still clearly legible. On each one had been scrawled 'file copy' in ink, now greying and indistinct.

Thank you for the most recent instalment in *Mariah*. It was received at these offices and devoured immediately.

Josie turned the page.

I was grateful for your remarks on chapter ten which our friend delivered mostly promptly.

And another, and more.

I enclose a cheque for the sum of £10. 9s. 10d made payable as you requested.

More:

I enclose a copy of a review which has appeared in the *Manchester Guardian*. You may have already seen it, but for completeness, here it is. I trust that you are gratified by this, as I surely am, although I deserve no portion of the praise therein contained.

Josie turned again, wondering where the other part of the correspondence was. Hepworth referred to hearing from Ethel, but her letters weren't there.

You have always declined to meet me, and I respect that preference, but might I ask you to reconsider it in view of the success of *Thomasina*? You have my unbending assurance that I should respect your wish for secrecy, madam.

Why should she not? Where was her response?

I read your words, Miss Turner Everett, and accept them as they are. I shall not raise it again, but should you change your mind, the door to my acquaintance is always open to you.

Later:

Thank you for the first chapters of *Eppingworth Abbey*. It is excellent.

Josie's eyes widened. There was no *Eppingworth Abbey*. It didn't exist. Her mind danced around this new information like an excited puppy, but as she turned the pages, anguish grew.

Our friend delivered your comments, which I thank you. I am anxiously awaiting the next chapters.

Pages turned like a Catherine wheel on fire.

I regret to write but it has been many months since I heard from you. I trust you are well?

The next:

Still, I have heard nothing, and I fear that you are gone away. If this letter should ever reach your hand, pray write to me here, or at my home address which I also send.

Beneath this last, declaration of despair lay a stamped, addressed envelope, opened long ago. Josie gently eased the letter out and unfolded it to see the signed original of the letter she had just read. She turned it over and a silent shriek broke out inside her. Beside the haphazardly scrawled message 'Gone Away' was something altogether remarkable. The letter was addressed to a Miss Violet Springer at 50 Veronica Gardens, London. Josie's heart thumped and her vision blurred. A series of facts crashed down on her like waves, and she wished she hadn't had so much coffee. It is the same address. It is James's home. Her home. The words felt strange in her head, but that was how she saw it, even after so short a time. More than that, who was Violet Springer? Was she the friend Hepworth refers to? Was she the real identity of Ethel Turner Everett and, in any event, where did she go?

With these questions tumbling about in her head, Josie turned to the final document in the file, the loose pages on the top. It was dated 1875.

Dear Rupert,
Of all the notes I must write for you upon my retirement, this is by far the least satisfactory and gives me the greatest pause. I am passing you, and your successors, one of the great literary stories, never fully realised, of our lifetimes. Herein you find the collected papers, such as they are, of the published works of Ethel Turner Everett.

Some history may be useful to you. In the spring of 1856, I received a manuscript attributed to Miss Turner Everett,

delivered by hand to this office with a note inviting correspondence care of a Miss Springer in Veronica Gardens.
[The address, you may or may not know yourself. It is one
of those awfully brash streets of the last score years or so.
Full of the sort of persons who rarely trouble a quality
publishing house. Many a rich man lives there but it is not
at all known for literary associations. I recall that it was
mentioned during the Cathcart Affair but cannot now
recall why. In any case, I drift far from the point.]

I knew from the first line of the manuscript that I should
accept it, and so indeed I did, I could do no other. I corresponded with the mysterious Miss Springer for a time and,
shortly thereafter, she assisted in delivering a signed
contract between this firm and the author. Thereafter,
there came, as you know, two novels and a collection of
poems. Such correspondence as we had, be it letters or
submissions, great or small, was always delivered by hand
by Miss Springer, and I in turn, wrote to her at Veronica
Gardens, by way of reaching the author. It was made plain
to me that Miss Turner Everett was unwilling to reveal
herself and would act exclusively through the auspices of
Miss Springer. We came to know Miss Springer in a
manner of speaking, despite her best efforts.

She was a slightly built young woman, respectably but by
no means lavishly dressed. She only ever appeared on a
Tuesday and only ever during the social season. About her,
there was a watchfulness and a keen eye. Not a thing got
past her, and one felt that every word she spoke and action
she took had been measured out beforehand. On more than
one occasion, she was offered refreshment, or to rest her
legs. When she appeared in the rain, she was offered an
umbrella, in the heat, a cold drink.

She declined each and every one with a firm courtesy, and
I rather had the notion that she was unused to voluntary

acts of kindness in her daily life. Having tied the pieces together, there is no doubt in my mind that she is or was a domestic servant. Whether Miss Springer was the real identity of Miss Turner Everett or whether she was acting on behalf of another, I know not.

Whoever she may be, Miss Turner Everett has long vanished. I regret that I did not realise as quickly as I ought. The first chapters of what was to be her third novel, *Eppingworth Abbey* were delivered here in 1859. I waited for too long before writing to her to enquire for the rest. Neither she, nor any person acting on her behalf, has ever responded to me. My last letter to Miss Spinger was, as you shall see from the file, returned unopened. My own secretary opened it to ensure it was the same one, and we were, all of us, at a complete, desolate loss.

Since that time, we have heard nothing, and I have been forced to conclude that either Miss Turner Everett does not wish to communicate with me, or she is unable to do so. I hope that she is married, and well settled in some shire paradise of domesticity. But needless to say, I fear it may be otherwise. By reason of the sudden stopping of her work, interest in this great lady novelist has dwindled and her royalties with it. Such royalties, as there were, we paid by cheque made out to Miss Springer directly into an account at Coutts.

I only add, in case you should ever require to know, that my assumption has always been that Ethel Turner Everett is in the way of a pen name. I was never told this specifically, but it was my supposition formed over several years and cemented by the banking arrangements set out above. There were various female writers of the period who chose to present themselves as men, but I know of no other who hid so industriously her identity but not her sex. As to the reasons, I cannot comment.

With that, I leave you. Should you ever discover anything of this mystery or hear from either lady, I shall of course be on hand to assist.

Yours etc.
Hepworth

Josie closed the file and took a deep breath. Her palms were sweaty and worrying for the delicate paper, she laced it back in the file and shut it, sitting for a moment in perfect, chaotic silence. She was still in something of a daze when Tim looked around the doorframe and asked her if she needed lunch.

"That's kind, but no thanks. I'm not feeling hungry."

He disappeared as quickly as he came, and she moved onto the second file. On sight, she knew what it was. Her eyes danced over the yellows and blacks of the closely handwritten page before her and something inside her sang. Here, alone in a room with Josie Minton, sat the original words of Ethel Turner Everett.

It felt like only a few minutes that she sat there, turning the pages by the edges, reading what there was of *Eppingworth Abbey*, the novel that never saw the light of day and had rested here, incomplete, for so many years. When Tim appeared in the doorway for the second time that afternoon, he had his coat on and was jangling a set of keys.

"Oh my God, is it closing time! I'm sorry. I got lost in it."

"No worries. That's what a good archive does to you." He raised his eyebrows. Josie didn't realise before that day that there was a genre of archivist jokes, but there seemed to be.

"I've been reading her unfinished novel. It's all in here, handwritten. How amazing is that?"

"You can come back whenever you like, Josie. I didn't expect you to get through it in one day. Come back tomorrow, next week. Any time. Whenever's good."

"Thanks." She folded the file back together and stood jerkily, anxious not to delay him.

"Josie, do you have a boyfriend?"

"Umm, yes," she replied, not knowing whether that was the right answer. They made their way out into the street and parted.

"WE SHOULD TELL GRANGE."

"Hmm."

Josie stretched her arm across James's chest and looked to his face in the mellow lamp light. It was nearly midnight, and they were squashed into her queen-sized bed for the second night on the trot, crisp cotton sheets pooling about them.

"It's the same date. It's an obvious connexion. I'll call him in the morning."

She squeezed him gently to indicate agreement and kissed his body as she snuggled closer. This room, so anodyne only a few weeks before, was now their castle, and the bed, their keep. It was a fortress, marked into the landscape. They hadn't spoken about it, but both nights since they had returned to London, he had just come to bed with her, like they'd been together all their lives. It was just something that happened and was perfectly, blindingly, right.

"When are you going back to the archive?"

"I've been thinking about how it can be done. I can't be away every day, and I don't think Diana is cut out for a whole day with the twins. She looked done in when I got back."

"Okay, well do it in half days? Or I can get someone from the agency in."

"Are you trying to get rid of me?"

"No." She felt a light kiss on the top of her head. "Definitely not."

"Anyway. I might be able to cut down the time I need. There is a photocopier there, one of those great big things that looks like it came out of the arc. But the paper is too old to photocopy so I thought I'd ask Tim if I can photograph. That way I'd have a complete copy I could work on at home. But there'd still be a few trips. I don't think it's fair on the girls to have someone new. I was thinking... When it is school term time, how about Fenny?"

Laughter burst from his chest, and they both jerked upwards

from it. Josie, who was worried about waking the twins in the next room, quietened him with a kiss that he returned.

"It's not that funny. She could get the train. She'd love a trip to town."

"You bet she would. You'd never get her out of the shops."

"You're mean to Fenny. She's not that bad. Does she get on with Diana?"

"Yes." He sounded wary, but she persisted. It was a new sensation for Josie to see a plan for herself through, to look at obstacles and find ways around them, rather than simply turn back. New possibilities were opening in front of her like flowers.

"So how about this. I plan a few half days in the archive, stretched over a few weeks. Let's say eleven to three."

"Lunch?"

"I'll take sandwiches. Fenny and Diana can look after the twins together while I'm gone. How about it?"

"That works. I'll call them in the morning. We'll set it up."

"Diana will wonder what's going on."

"*Diana* is always wondering what's going on. Her favourite subject is other people's business. But in this case, I've already told her that you have a research project you need to do. Don't worry. She'll be first in the queue at your book signing, believe me. Mother drives me mad but, deep down, she is not the kind of person who holds people back. Everyone has something in life that they are made to do. She gets that, and so do I. It's one of the few things we have in common."

Josie smiled. Diana hadn't said a word about James. But when Josie had left that morning, she had taken the unusual step of kissing her cheek as she said, "Have a good day, Josie dear." Then and now, the question of how much Diana knew rolled about in Josie's mind like a lonely marble. James yawned and tightened his grip on her. He had been home early, at seven o'clock, but the quid pro quo was, no doubt an early start, his car pulling up outside at the crack of dawn. Josie stretched across him and turned out the bedside light, his strong hands touched her breasts as though they were jewels.

Her eyes got used to the dark, the orange sodium glow of the streetlight beyond the curtain throwing strange grey shapes about the room. She had found a thing for her brain to feast on, and for the first time in a long time, did not feel alone.

"James?"

"Hmm?"

"Are you my boyfriend?"

She felt, rather than saw, him smile beside her.

"Yes. I hope so. Are you my girlfriend?"

"I'd like to be. But I'm also your children's nanny, your employee. I'm a kind of servant. If we were in a Jane Austen novel, people would say I was a new acquaintance, of poor connexions, and no fortune."

He shifted onto his side and a gap opened up between them, a rivulet of air between their naked bodies.

"You are not anyone's servant. Never were and certainly aren't now. You're beautiful. You're unusual. You're important. You are the best thing to ever walk through that door, and that includes Ethel Turner Everett or whatever her bloody name was. I don't care how new you are. I've been in love with you almost from the moment you arrived here. It isn't a random gratuity. It isn't a bit of luck that might slip out from under you one day when your dice falls the wrong way. It's for real. And you deserve it. You, Josie, deserve to be loved."

It was a couple of weeks later, on a Saturday morning, that Inspector Grange sat at one of the stools in the kitchen, sipping his coffee in jeans and a t-shirt. He was like a new creature, in a new skin and had gratefully tucked into a piece of Josie's cake, as well as had Santa on his lap for a story. Later, the girls sat on the floor and played with their bricks while the grown-ups talked about the case, or multiple cases, as Josie thought of it. The missing heiress and the lost novelist and the body in the garden... and the serving girl who said no to an umbrella in the rain. Who was who and which was which? One thing she was sure of, was that James had been right about Grange. The officious Inspector was half in love with Kitty Cathcart. He had talked about her at indulgent lengths and produced pictures of her. Grainy black and white images from newspapers past and photographs of a couple of oil paintings in some stately home in the North. Languid eyes peeping out from another century, a fine full mouth, seemingly on the cusp of speech, a gleam of blonde hair arranged in that way the Victorians liked.

Josie had been back to the archive twice, and Tim had hovered about her, talking about his PhD while she photographed every page. At home, on her side of the bed, a steady collection of books on Victorian history had begun to pile up, although it is fair to say that she hadn't had much time to read them. Tim had surprised her by asking whether she was writing a biography or a work of literary criticism. Josie hadn't thought she was writing anything, nor had she said so. But the idea bedded down in her mind and began to take shape. Chapters started to form, headings, ideas, floating about each other like planets. She had started a notebook and a folder and didn't feel like a fraud. When James had called Grange to tell him what Josie had discovered, he had come around to the house immediately. It turned out that the police had powers enabling them to get information on the bank account at Coutts. There followed a period of radio silence, but yesterday he'd called and asked if they minded him popping over on a Saturday, said that Mrs Grange wanted to go shopping up west, and he could drop by to give them a ten-minute update. Currently, he was on his third cup of coffee and showed no signs of leaving.

"So, in a nutshell, we're waiting for the DNA tests to come in, but I'd be surprised if our lady doesn't match. The remains are the right age and period and there is no record of anyone actually seeing Kitty Cathcart leaving the house. It was simply reported that she was missing. I reckon the poor girl never went anywhere."

"When do you expect the DNA results?"

"Few days. It took forever to track the blighters down. The sample has been taken from George Christie's great grandson. Chap's in his seventies, and he was on a cruise with his wife when we first tried to contact him, so it took a while. If it matches the remains, that will be enough to identify them as the tragic Miss Cathcart."

"What about the cameo?"

"What about it?"

"Well, it's just the newspapers all seem to make a thing of it. They say that she had the cameo with her. It disappeared too. They even printed pictures of it in the newspapers to help people identify her. So, why wasn't it in the ground with her?"

"I can tell you don't work among the criminal classes... Saying that the cameo disappeared and saying that she had it with her aren't quite the same thing, are they? If you ask me, someone nicked it. Nice piece of jewellery, everyone in the house knows it's a family heirloom. They probably thought it was worth more than it really was. Mark my words, it fell into the pocket of some servant or other."

"Maybe you're right. More coffee?"

Josie smiled as she poured, but she had her doubts. That cameo wasn't just any old bauble. It was a rare and valuable piece. It was synonymous with her, that much was obvious. If Kitty was running away, which everyone seemed to think she was, she would certainly have taken it, so why wasn't it in the grave with her?

"Then of course, there's the business of this bloody bank account."

"Hmm?"

Josie wiped Santa's nose and gave Maggie a toy.

"I've been on to Coutts. Turns out that it was declared dormant and given over to the government a few years back. Last activity was in 1859. So that's as good as useless when it comes to clues, isn't it?"

Josie smiled at him and picked up Maggie who had begun to grumble.

"Course, technically it was the property of Violet Springer. But can we get a trace on Violet Springer? Not for love nor money! It seems as though she just vanished as well, but there was never a man hunt for Violet. I've checked the police records for mentions myself. Not a dicky bird. The boys are trying to find her family. They have a right to claim the money back, apparently."

"Hmm. Well that might be good news for some unsuspecting person. I hope you find them."

Grange smiled.

"It isn't often that I get to bring good news. But there you are. A case like this stirs up unexpected things, if you know what I mean."

Josie caught James's eye as he glanced at her, laughingly. She could not be sure if Grange noticed, but he didn't show it.

"I wonder what happened to her young man?"

"You mean Alexander Faraday? Not a trace. We've looked. No record of him ever marrying or dying or anything else. He could have gone abroad. Anything might have happened. He could have killed her for all we know. The only thing we know is he's not lying in the ground with her."

"We've read so much about Kitty. But I wonder what he was like?"

"Don't think we'll ever know, love. Papers had him down as a black-hearted villain. But maybe he was no more a trickster than your average man in love, eh?"

He smiled, finished his coffee, and said he had to get away. James and Josie, each holding a twin, crowded into the hall behind him and waved as he trotted down the stone steps and into the street. James closed the door after him with a certain clunk.

"Sounds like he's got that sorted out then."

Josie looked sceptical and plucked a piece of discarded rice cake from Santa's cardigan.

"What do you want to do tonight?" he asked unexpectedly.

They ambled down the hall towards the kitchen. The garden had been restored at lightning speed by a crack team of gardeners who Diana had employed when James wasn't paying attention, and it bore little trace of recent events.

"Don't mind," said Josie, gazing contentedly at the new flowers. "Girls' tea at five. And they need an early night. Maggie is banjaxed as she hasn't napped at all today."

At this mention of her name, Maggie nuzzled into his chest and drew her hands together at the back of his neck. Josie smiled to herself. Both of the girls had always adored him and been so excited whenever he was round. But this warmth, this comfort, was new.

"How about a film after they are in bed?"

Josie laughed, and Santa joined in, as children of that age do.

"What are you laughing at?"

"Nothing." She opened the door and cool scented air flew in. "Film sounds great."

27

PHILOMENA

1869

It was a Tuesday afternoon in early spring and the carriage of Philomena Christie clattered down the Commercial Road in a cloud of dust. Its black exterior, cleaned daily, gleamed jet in the pale sunshine and passing eyes paused to observe its motion through the dirty streets, a red coated boy hung on the back as if suspended by a thread. It was by no means a commonplace thing for so fine a conveyance to be seen thereabouts. For these streets were not smart and their residents not wealthy. A girl washing a shop front stopped her efforts for a moment and stared as the horses slowed, and the whole assemblage turned west, jostling into the chaos of the city. Did she imagine that its passenger was a great gentleman, a peer about some business? Or a grand beauty? A titled lady with lands as far as the eye can see and a skirt as wide as a sail? A young woman with a wealthy patron keeping her face hidden, as well she might? For what possible reason would a person of standing, a person of means, be in such a place as this, and so conspicuously concealing their identity.

Within, Philomena kept the curtains of her carriage closed, as was her custom. Her maid, Smithers, sat on the opposite bench, slim fingers folded neatly in her lap, head of flattened red hair, now flecked with grey, nodding forward, lost in some private wonder. Philomena had overheard Smithers making all manner of excuses to others for her mistress's foible: What dreadful poisons are in the city air, and how the delicate Miss Christie likes to stay cool in the summer and warm in the winter. She had spoken of Philomena as though she were a young flower in a sharp breeze. In fact, she was not afraid of the humours of the city, for it was her home of many years. She and its poisons were old friends. The truth was that Philomena had been observed by those whom she did not favour for too long. She had walked through crowds that silenced at her coming. She had seen the backs of lifelong acquaintances turn upon her approach, like sunflowers bobbing down in the evening. For many years, she had been attended in public by the whispers of passersby and the curious eyes of the unknown. Her name spoken but not to her face. She had had her fill of it.

Instead, she kept herself busy with good works. Rejection and heartbreak had given birth to purpose, and Philomena sought to occupy herself with matters more significant than her own self. Tasks piled up in her mind like bricks, and she laid each one in its proper place. She had attended a charitable meeting that very morning and was already thinking of the next one. What was this life for if not making a contribution to one's own world?

This rationale, she also gave to her brother when, some weeks before, he enquired after her health, and suggested that she may be taking on too much, spreading herself too thin.

"Nonsense, George."

She had responded immediately. A certain sharpness of expression, which had once seemed a necessary defence, was now habitual. Part of her regretted it, and she smiled, adding sugar to the salt. It had been just the two of them, in his garden in Surrey, the sunlight dappling through the leaves of a weeping willow, birdsong in the air. Her dear sister-in-law and nieces and nephews played at a slight distance, like puppets on a stage. When, some years before, the maidenly Miss Mary Pottinger had entered George's life, and shortly thereafter, a succession of children, Philomena had considered the change a blessing. She thought it still, despite the distance and the upheaval they had all engendered. Mary was a vicar's daughter, brought up far from town, and when she met George, she had not even heard of the Cathcart Affair.

Upon his marriage, George had set up home in the leafy countryside, in a village with a green and a church with a spire. He had offered Philomena a place in his house, and Mary had entreated her to take it, assuring her of independence and a position, equal but different, at their hearth. There was no call for her to remain in London, where she could find no peace, with the ghosts of the past about on the streets like bats.

Philomena had not doubted their assurances, but she did not wish to leave. Her home, which she had purchased with her own fortune, and whose visitors were few and far between, was perfectly calculated to suit her. It was furnished sparsely, expensively, to exactly her taste. It was close to Veronica Gardens but not too close. Its staff were a tightly bonded group, and absolutely trustworthy. It was hers and hers alone. She looked at the neat stucco front and the black front door on the day that George's engagement was announced and knew that she would never depart. At the time, he had accepted the decision, but now, some years later, seemed to take up arms again.

"Philomena?" he had mumbled after a period of silence.

"Hmm?" She did not open her eyes, sensing that some challenge was afoot.

"Are you still taking your students of the piano?"

"Ha! Yes, indeed. I now have two young people. A young girl of fifteen who is the sister of an acquaintance from the Enfranchisement Society. And the rector's son, of course. My original pupil. I see them each once a se'nnight and they practice in between"—she paused and turned her head, smiling at her brother —"if they've any sense, that is."

"I've no doubt you are a redoubtable tutor, Sister. I shudder to think of the force of your musical directives. Although, it is probably good for them. Maybe you should open a school?"

It was a deliberately provocative suggestion, and Philomena had no intention of rising to it. George knew as well as she that the legacy of scandal hanging over their name would be enough to scupper any such project.

"You know I am not sociable enough for that. I like my own company and the closed space of my own home. But a handful of young people to play and sing with give me great pleasure."

He shifted in his garden chair. The afternoon sun bounced off his pipe.

"Are you sure that you don't need something more?"

When she spoke not, he coughed and continued.

"I know you keep yourself busy, Philomena, and it is to your great credit. Don't think that I do not recognise the diligence with which you apply yourself, for I do. But life moves on, does it not?"

"Does it?"

"Yes. It most definitely does. Please, I beg of you, listen to me. These are the words of one who loves you."

Philomena closed her eyes tight. Light bright green spasmed into black.

"We all of us, need to feel that we juggle with another, Philomena. You have nobody in your keeping anymore. With Mary and I down here, and Mother gone. And—"

"I have Smithers."

George threw his head back suddenly, blinking, and then wiping his forehead with the back of his hand.

"Smithers would go with you wherever you went. If you came to live here, for example, she would too. So that is no argument."

"And all of my charitable friends."

"Nonsense. There are charities in Surrey, Philomena. And London, in these days of the railways, is only a short distance away. There are worthy causes everywhere, and I have no doubt that you would find them wherever you were."

He leaned forward and changed his tone.

"If you were to live with us here, you would be part of a household again. You could watch your nieces and nephews grow up. You could breathe the clean air of the countryside. Think on it."

"Oh George—"

A gale of laughter came through the trees, and they both

looked to see the children rolling on the grass; Mary throwing a ball.

"Think on it. You have a family who hold you dear, you have resources and good sense. There is no need for you to remain living alone in a society that has treated you shamefully—"

"Only we see it as shameful—"

"Where virtually every respectable door is closed to you, every back turned on you. Even now. Where the very worst masquerade as the very best."

"I do not care what people think."

"That is part of the problem—"

"And if I move away, and she comes back"—Philomena's voice shook—"she may not be able to find me."

"Oh, Philomena. Is that really the nub of the thing? My dear..." He stretched out his hand and took hers, feeling the weight of their mother's rings on her fingers. "It has been ten years and my heart is broken too. But you cannot truly believe that Kitty is coming back."

THE CARRIAGE JOLTED AT A CROSSROADS AND PHILOMENA came back to the present. Smithers was also brought out of a daydream.

"Good gracious, madam. Are you comfortable?"

"Thank you, yes."

Philomena smiled at the lady benevolently. She took such care of her, more than her manner sometimes deserved. There was a pause before the conveyance started off again.

"I do hope that we are not late home, Smithers. I have my new pupil, young Master Leadbetter."

Smithers nodded, and smiled. She had been a great champion of Miss Christie teaching the piano to a select number of young people. It had the effect of imposing society on her mistress. The pupils themselves and, of course, their parents, who came and went and sometimes stayed for tea. It increased the amount of music in the house, which must be a thing of merit. Smithers could not have encouraged it more.

"Yes, we are expecting him at three o'clock, miss. I wonder how his skills shall compare to Miss Fairclough and Master Oliver?"

"I wonder. He is but eight years of age, so I anticipate he is a little below their standards. But maybe I shall be wrong. One reads of child geniuses and the like. I know nothing of his parents."

"Really? But how did they hear of your lessons?"

Smithers leaned forward, looking alarmed.

"I believe that Reverend Lynch recommended me to Mr Leadbetter, although I do not know how they are acquainted. The family are lately returned to the country from abroad, but they are English. The boy is shy, and his previous piano master died. That is what his mother said in her letter at any rate."

"Well, let us hope he doesn't have any odd habits," pronounced Smithers, leaning back against the soft board of the moving carriage, clasping her hands in her lap.

They arrived home a little over twenty minutes later. The great door was opened to Philomena, who swept in, Smithers in her shadow. With a clicking of heels upon the tiled floor of the hall, and the removal of bonnets and cloaks, Mattravers announced that a Mrs Leadbetter and her young son were in the music room.

"They are early."

"Indeed, miss. I put them in the music room in order that you may sit in the drawing room at your leisure before meeting them if you wish."

"Thank you, Mattravers, but that won't be necessary."

Philomena walked alone down the familiar corridor. Later, she recalled a sense of rushing through the air, of noise mounting in her ear, an excited nausea stirring in her stomach. But she may, with the benefit of hindsight, have imagined it. It may have been that what came after had so changed her, that she could never hope to piece together the moments before. Reaching the door, which was ajar, she took a breath, pressed one hand flat to the front panel of her dress and entered. The first thing she saw was a young boy, laughing. He was a tall, slim, presentable sort of a child. His laugh ceased, and his eyes sought his mother beside him.

Upon Philomena appearing, the lady, who wore a blue dress and clutched a bonnet in one hand, stood. At first her head was bowed slightly, but then she looked up. Blonde hair, plastered to her head as was the fashion, gave way to so familiar a visage, that Philomena could have cried, and did. Faint, new lines; features just the same.

"Kitty!" The word came out breathy and oddly quiet, less than the sum of its meaning, and the two women clasped one another, hands on waists, eyes disbelieving.

Kitty's voice trembled. "I am sorry to be early, but I could not wait in the street when I could come in and be near you."

"I always knew you would come. I always knew."

The boy looked on. Kitty gestured to him.

"This is our son, William," she said.

LATER, THE LADIES SAT ALONE IN THE PARLOUR. TEARS HAD been shed and powerful embraces exchanged. Incredulity had given way to elation, to a sense of joy, to burgeoning celebration. And eventually, there had been calm. An express had been sent off to George, written in Philomena's shaky hand and dispatched by Smithers. A tea had been served, but only the boy ate, delving into sandwiches and cakes as though he were half-starved while his mother and her cousin looked on.

An hour evaporated and Alex, announced as a Mr Leadbetter, appeared. To Philomena, he looked not a day older for having been absent a decade. Their eyes met without rancour. So often Philomena had wondered if she should hate him. But in the end, she could not. For the love that he bore her cousin was writ plain. He made swift pleasantries before taking William home. Philomena had imagined the sight of her cousin so many times in the ten years that had passed since last seeing her, but she found her imaginings were unequal to the reality. The truth was altogether more golden.

Relief suffused her. But then questions tumbled out. Where had she been? How had they lived with no money and no connexions? How had she evaded detection for so many years? Philomena thought of the months of ceaseless searching, of George and herself travelling the country in hope but without reward. All the times she had nearly despaired.

Philomena was parched. She drank her tea swiftly, although it was cool. What was this? Nerves? Fear, maybe. Kitty reached across the table, and taking her hand, continued to talk.

"Do you recall how you were called away to your aunt?"

"Yes, I do. She was not really unwell, you know. George and I arrived. And found her with a slight cold, nothing more. We were a trifle confused, but having travelled so far, and not having seen her for some time, we felt duty bound to stay. It was the first of many tricks, but I did not see it at the time."

Kitty nodded, almost imperceptibly.

"With you absent, my father imprisoned me in the house. He used Aunt Margaret as his jailer, and she was most assiduous. I thought there was no way out."

"But there must have been. How did you do it, Kitty?"

"The only way possible."

"Meaning?"

"Disguised as another."

Philomena's very eyes were a question mark. Kitty sighed.

"I had been wearing Violet's clothes, that had been going on for some time. It was how I had been able to meet Alex outside of Veronica Gardens. It was a secret, but I never intended to keep it from you forever. As it was, only Violet and Coachman John knew. The dresses fitted me well, even the shoes. And I am a good player, as I believe you know. Violet, too, had hidden resources, unexpected gifts. I had come to realise that slowly, part by part over the years we had been together. She was clever and a good mimic. More than anything, she was loyal."

KITTY'S EYES RESTED ON HER TEA, BUT SHE HAD NO WISH TO drink it. How long had she waited to speak this truth? And now the time was come, she seemed to shake out the words like so many pennies from an old bag. Unsatisfactorily. Philomena gazed at her, questioning.

"One night, Alex gained his way into the house. Nobody could have been more surprised than me, but there it was. He is my soul's match, Philomena. No person could know me better. And he came when I needed him most. We decided how it would be. How I would make away, and the world would be well lost for love."

Here, she paused, and a heaviness stole down upon her pretty face.

"Go on."

"We, or rather I, included dear Violet. I could not have achieved one thing without her. We planned it all with such perfection, or so we believed. The day came. It was after supper. Violet emptied her room of her meagre belongings. No suitcase, no Sunday best, no bonnet, no cloak. She came to my chamber, and there, we swapped clothes. We really were very alike, you know. In body, in stature, in mannerism. Although nobody would ever have said so, for so many eyes only see the fashion and not the core. It was getting dark. The household was fatigued from the day. And most people are easy to deceive. They see what they expect to see. So it was. I exchanged nervous words with Violet and, scuttling down the stairs, was gone out of the servants' door.

"Violet's role had been settled between us. She should wait and, when the night had bedded down, slip out herself. The household would be abed. 'Take nothing,' I had said to her, 'and remove yourself as soon as you may. The longer you linger, the greater the risk.' I cannot, to my great shame, recall the last words that she spoke to me."

Kitty's eyes filled, but they did not spill. She continued.

It had been her belief that the swiftest possible escape was the only one that would be successful. She had thrust money into Alex's palm, and he had arranged a carriage to convey them to Dover and another to pick up Violet from an appointed place after midnight. More men who asked no questions. The boat was waiting, the captain expecting a Mr and Mrs Leadbetter and a Miss Dickens. It all came off remarkably well. For Kitty and Alex, the journey was an easy one. They slipped aboard the vessel without a single question being raised. But the time for departure drew near, and Violet had not come. Kitty began to stride about, to gnaw on her nails. She told herself that there had been a delay, poor weather maybe. Dear Violet was simply on the road, making her way. But would she arrive on time? And if not, what then? Panic had threaded through Kitty. She approached the captain, but he said the sailing could not be delayed. He took down the name of Miss Dickens, furrowing his brow. She could travel on the next boat. Kitty breathed but not easily. They set sail.

"AND? WHEN DID VIOLET REACH YOU?"

Kitty looked up and her eyes spilled.

"Oh, Philomena." She sobbed. "Never. I have not seen Violet from that day to this."

"Good god." Philomena shifted in her chair. "The household servants at Veronica Gardens were told that Violet had been dismissed. There was much speculation at the time, that you had taken her with you. But now you say that all this time, she has been missing? Really missing?"

"Really missing. Eventually, we heard from the man who was supposed to collect her and convey her to Dover. He wrote that he had waited and waited, but she did not appear."

Silence clumped down on the floor between them. Old worries grew large in Philomena's mind, took on colour and light, moved about. Worse, she turned up old resentments, stale fears.

"Why did you not write to me, Kitty? Not one line?"

Kitty blinked as she looked up, sharply.

"I did write. I wrote again and again. Not at first. There was so much to do in the early days, so much worry about Violet, finding a home, getting settled. And before long, I grew large with William. But I did write, Philomena, I sent so many letters."

Philomena's mind flew back to the days after the disappearance. The stomach-turning anxiety, the brittle conversations with her mother, then arguments, then worse. The realisation that her mother would support their uncle in all things, all weathers, that she was for him and not for them. Certainly not for Kitty. And Philomena would never understand why. The hours spent from home seeking Kitty. The look upon her mother's face as they had parted for the final time. No doubt any letters arriving in Kitty's hand had been discretely removed, destroyed probably. Unbidden, tears came to Philomena's eyes. Kitty moved to her side and embraced her with familiar arms.

Between them, they resolved never to be separated again.

28

MR AND MRS LEADBETTER

1876

IT WAS A SHARP CLEAR DAY IN SPRING AND HYDE PARK glowed green, spangled with trees of pink and white blossom, blessed with golden sunshine. The clatter of the road seemed far off, and the exquisite luxury of the surrounding houses, even farther. Altogether, there were many personages coming and going, cloaks and top hats and tasseled parasols jostling about like rafts on a great unchanging stretch of water. One hundred concurrent strolls, very few of which would ever meet, or even properly observe one another.

The lady and the gentleman who entered by the statue of Achilles at eleven o'clock did not draw special attention. They were a fine-looking couple in their middle years, the gentleman tall, the lady well attired in a navy cloak with a velvet trim. Her gloved hand perched on his arm and they walked along perfectly in step. The shape of the lady's skirt was a bell, finely dusted by the city at the hem. The gentleman carried a cane with which he tapped the path. Almost imperceptibly, he glanced towards her before he spoke.

"You are certain?"

She blinked but did not look up.

"Yes, quite certain. Once round."

His other hand briefly touched her hand on his arm and the cane brushed her voluminous skirts. It was only a moment, a snatch. No observer would ever have guessed the hours she had ruminated upon this walk before finally undertaking it.

And so, they joined the path and advanced. The trees threw shadows upon their passage, and others passed by. A light breeze played the ribbons on the lady's bonnet which, in common with the fashion, was deep. She squeezed her husband's arm. They spoke of many things and none. They studiously avoided any mention of the history that made this part of town a place to be avoided. So, they ambled happily on.

Ahead of them, a man in a brown coat stopped on the path and facing the pair, called out:

"I say!"

He smiled broadly and shaded his eyes from the sun with a hand. He seemed to squint, peering.

"I say! Well, bless my soul, it is..."

The lady tensed and dug her fingers into her husband's arm. He did not react to the provocation and his face looked a perfect blank at the increasingly excitable gentleman before them.

"It is. Well, my word. What a happening. Mr Faraday, sir. Well, it's been fifteen years if it's been a day. More, even. Do you recall me, sir? Archer, that's the name."

He seemed to bellow his words. The gentleman with the lady beside him appeared perplexed, but the man did not heed it.

"Charles Archer, at your service. Charles Archer, previous of Mrs Patting's boarding house. Well, my word that was another life, was it not? Another life. I have prospered since then. I should wager you have too from the look of you."

The gentleman bowed slightly; his brow furrowed. He did not try to hide his face.

"My good, sir, I believe you may have taken me for another." He smiled at the man, his appearance friendly, open. "My name is Leadbetter."

"No, surely not. Why I never saw such a likeness. I never forget a face. Never."

He stood stock in front of them, examining the gentleman as

though he were a railway timetable. The lady, he did not observe to twitch and grow anxious.

"I am sorry to disappoint you Mister, erm, Archer. But I am not your acquaintance. My face must be a deceiving one." He smiled and lifted his hat. "I bid you good day."

Mrs Leadbetter summoned a fleeting smile and the pair were gone, trotting into the distance as the man in the brown coat watched them. By inclination, she sought to move at a great pace, to quicken her step and, so, be gone sooner. However, her husband held her back, walking leisurely as before, his cane tap-tapping the ground like a metronome. After a time, she allowed herself to speak.

"Did you recall him?"

"Yes, of course. He was an inoffensive man. A little forward, maybe."

She exhaled and lifted her face to see his. The bonnet obscured her a great deal. Beneath it, she was still beautiful. Age had weathered her but slightly, and the hair that framed her face remained a stark sort of blonde, glinting, throwing light to anyone who looked. She possessed a vivacity that survived the years, a beauty that need have no fear of age.

"You admire forwardness, do you not?"

"In you, I admire it."

They walked on some way, and she began to feel herself restoring. Just beyond the green frame of the park, a world stood, that she had once called her own. In all the years that had passed since the lady had left Veronica Gardens, she had never returned to any place so proximate as this, save to visit Philomena. She avoided it. One did not know who one would meet or be observed by. In any event, it held for her no attraction, save mawkish interest. In all the great stucco-lined streets and the pleasure parks of the rich, there was nothing but anguished memories.

"I suppose you think it ironic, Mr Leadbetter?"

They had developed the habit, originally a means of remembering, and latterly, a joke, addressing one another thus. As the years progressed, the need receded but the habit remained.

"In what way?"

"Well, how many years have you and I acted this part together? Is it seventeen?"

"Almost to the day."

"Seventeen years. And in all that time, we have never been recognised. My face, which I once thought well known, has never been seen for whose it is. No finger has ever pointed to me in accusation."

"You are a fine actress."

"And you, an unknown clerk, are accosted on the public path in Hyde Park!"

"An unknown clerk?"

"I am sure that is one of many ways you were described once. Lowly lawyer. Ink-stained charlatan. A man with no public role whatever."

"Now, steady on. I am a respectable man of business. An esteemed importer of French wines to London. A man of significant property and comfortable situation."

"You are now."

He looked down towards her. With barely an appearance of doing so, he drew her closer to him.

"Is it not the *now* that really matters, Kitty?"

She looked straight ahead and answered his pull with a tightening of her hand.

"Of course. But we would not be human if we came to this place and did not mention the *then*. Our history is part of our present. One cannot forget it, still less, erase it."

"I have forgotten none of it."

The path they took meandered on, and for a period, they paused to admire a great bank of flowers. A gentle breeze rustled them about: red, pink, purple, yellow.

"I hope you do not regret coming here? You deserve to be able to be out in society, to walk freely in public spaces. It was pure coincidence bumping into that fellow, Archer."

"I know. And it was a sight better than bumping into Lady Fairfax or Lord Trefeusis or any number of others."

He brought his hand to hers and absently stroked it. The blue of his eyes warmed her heart.

"Do not think on such people. They are not worthy of your consideration. And as happy chance would have it, they are all of them, too stupid to recognise you."

"I do endeavour to remain away from their society, to be quite fair. It is far from a fashionable life that which we have lived. And all the better for it."

They moved away from the swaying flower bed in happy companionship. The sun continued to shine upon their progress as it had for many years.

"Do you also intend to live far away from the other life you had, the life of a writer?"

He peered down at her, but they neither of them, broke step.

"I cannot believe that it was your intended purpose to stop your writing. It simply happened as a consequence of events."

She did not reply immediately and appeared deep in anxious thought.

"You are right, of course. I did not think that I would never write again when we left London. I did not plan it. And although, one occasionally thinks of a tale, or has characters in one's head that begin to take on colours and stories, I cannot say that anything shall ever come of it. The odd thing is that I do not really wish to."

Kitty paused. Her eyes surveyed the park of pleasure seekers, but she did not *see* them. Their edges seemed to blur and weep into the back cloth of the landscape. Only the man beside her had a clear outline.

"Violet was such a part of my writing. It started out as a mechanical arrangement. But something in the friendship between us, the secret history of it, made way for the writing I did then. It was a sort of alchemy, and now it is gone. I could not even attempt it without her."

"Really? Is the romantic in you not troubled by an unfinished story? By promise, left to sequester?"

"Do you call me a romantic, sir?"

"Of course. We are both of us romantic. Sorely so."

"I do not have any notion of what you mean."

"Yes, you do. You cannot be pleased at the idea of a narrative about love being cut short."

"Oh, you mean the novel! Yes, it was rather a shame about that. But it was nothing to the other matters at stake during that time. What is an unfinished fiction as against the unfinished happiness of a person's life? There is more to life than art. I should always value reality more, my love."

And so, with those words spoken, they turned away from the flowers bobbing in the wind and finished their walk. The day was moving on and the time for departure nearing. A long carriage ride was ahead of them both. A bumpy, blustery road out of the capital to the coast at Brighton, where stood their own home, elegant, capacious, respectable. A picture of it formed in Kitty's head and she began to long for its comforts. The great white façade glinting in the sun, framed by blue skies, the sound of sea gulls, the wind against one's parasol. The South Coast had started as an expedient choice—far from London and well placed for Alex's business. But Kitty had grown to love it. William was home from school. Alex's business, which he had taken up in preference to seeking out a career in the law, was prospering. Kitty owed a letter to Philomena on the subject of her new charity. Life had moved on, as it surely must. And it would not stop now. The future was a landscape they could not know but should not fear. Nor had they ever done so.

As they approached the gate, Alex motioned to their driver, who kicked his heels against the carriage wheel. The door was opened for Kitty, who gathered her skirts and stepped up. As she entered, she glanced back. Almost imperceptibly, Alex kissed her wrist.

"I retract my earlier comment. You are a remarkably romantic gentleman."

They smiled upon one another for a moment too long, and then laughed. As the carriage pulled away, Kitty felt light and joyful. She squeezed his hand and watched the park recede, knowing that soon, the spring would bloom into summer.

EPILOGUE

A POSTSCRIPT FROM THE PRESENT: THE GUARDIAN, AUGUST 2019

A SERVICE TOOK PLACE TODAY TO COMMEMORATE THE LIFE OF murdered Victorian maid, Violet Springer. The service took place at St. Mary's Church, Kensington and was attended by Miss Springer's living relations and a number of members of the public who have become interested in the infamous Veronica Gardens 'Body-in-the-Garden' case. Human remains were discovered buried in the grounds of the central London home of wealthy financier James Cavendish over twelve months ago. A lengthy enquiry into the identity of the deceased and the cause of death followed and was the subject of extensive press and public speculation. It was thought for several months that the remains belonged to a Miss Catherine 'Kitty' Cathcart, a flamboyant heiress who disappeared from the property in 1859, and whom, it was later discovered, was the real identity of Victorian novelist Ethel Turner Everett. That hypothesis was later excluded through DNA testing. It is now believed that Miss Cathcart had absconded from the property in order to marry in secret and that Miss Springer, who was her maid, died in an attack by an unidentified assailant in her absence. The disappearance of Miss Springer, at around the same time as her mistress, appears to have been largely ignored by her contemporaries. At the inquest into Miss Springer's death last year, a verdict of murder by person or persons unknown was returned, however popular suspicion has focussed on her employer, the wealthy industrialist, Sir Roland Cathcart, who died in 1867. A book on the affair, and celebrating the neglected work of Turner Everett, is due out in December. It is also rumoured that the final unfinished manuscript of Turner Everett is being completed by the same author, whose name has not yet been revealed. Mr Cavendish (who is the younger son of Lord and Lady Ashburton) continues to live at the property with his family. He was contacted for a comment, however, his secretary reported he left for his delayed honeymoon directly after the service was over.

Finis

AFTERWORD

Ethel Turner Everett is a creation of the author; likewise her poem, *The Door*, was composed by Jenetta James.

ACKNOWLEDGMENTS

I have been writing this story since 2014 and a lot of thanks are due. Huge gratitude to Amy and Jan and all the team at Quills & Quartos for taking it on and for all the effort required to get it to this stage. Thank you to all of those who have read the story at various stages and provided thoughtful critical comments: Beau, Karen, Lona, Debbie, Sarah. My editor Christina - who has lived with this book almost as long as I have, and given it her trademark all. I could not have asked for more dedication and care and thank her very much.

Certain others deserve a call out: Claudine, Ana, Rita, Meredith, Lory, Ellen.

To friends who show an interest in my writing: Esther, Emily, Nicky, Lauren, Emma, Astrid.

To family who do likewise: Daddy, Liz, Laura, Susan, Adam, and Sophie.

To my poor household who have to put up with me in real life: Mummy, Marc, Harry, Charlie, Nina. Particularly Marc, who was the first person to read parts of this story and was generous enough to say I should keep writing it. Love you.

Lastly—thank you to all of those who have read my other

books and who I hope will read this one. You are what it is all about: thank you.

ABOUT THE AUTHOR

Jenetta James is a mother, lawyer, writer, and taker-on of too much. She grew up in Cambridge and read history at Oxford University where she was a scholar and president of the Oxford University History Society.

After graduating, she took to the law and now practises full-time as a barrister. Over the years, she has lived in France, Hungary, and Trinidad as well as her native England.

Jenetta currently lives in London with her husband and children where she enjoys reading, laughing and playing with Lego. She is the author of *Suddenly Mrs. Darcy*, *The Elizabeth Papers* and *Lover's Knot* as well as a contributing author to *The Darcy Monologues*, *Dangerous to Know*, *Rational Creatures* and *Elizabeth: Obstinate Headstrong Girl*.

Please follow her on facebook @jenettajameswriter and Instagram @jenettajames, she'd love to hear from you.

To learn more about new releases and promotions for Jenetta James and other great authors please join our mailing list at www.QuillsandQuartos.com

The Elizabeth Papers

"There are men, who if they knew the full truth, would say I have been a fool"

It is 1817 and Elizabeth Darcy is mistress of Pemberley, adored by her husband and splendidly happy. She does not know what adversity awaits her family: mistrust, scandal, tragedy, and a secret that must be kept at all costs.

Almost two hundred years later, Evie Martin does not even know that she is descended from the Darcys of Pemberley when their history disrupts her life. Who is Charlie Hayward, the charming, cynical private detective and why has he contrived to meet her? What are the elusive 'Elizabeth Papers,' and why did Elizabeth Darcy herself want them destroyed?

The full story—both truth and lies—unravels in *The Elizabeth Papers*, an era-spanning tale of mystery, deception, and love triumphant.

"If we live it then it shall become the truth"

Lover's Knot

A great love. A perplexing murder. Netherfield Park — a house of secrets. Fitzwilliam Darcy is in a tangle. Captivated by Miss Elizabeth Bennet, a girl of no fortune and few connexions. Embroiled in an infamous murder in the home of his friend, Charles Bingley. He is being tested in every way. Fearing for Elizabeth's safety, Darcy moves to protect her in the only way he knows but is thwarted. Thus, he is forced to turn detective. Can he overcome his pride for the sake of Elizabeth? Can he, with a broken heart, fathom the villainy that has invaded their lives? Is there even a chance for romance born of such strife? *Lover's Knot* is a romantic *Pride & Prejudice* variation story, with a bit of mystery thrown in.

Suddenly Mrs Darcy

Elizabeth Bennet never imagined her own parents would force her to marry a virtual stranger. But when Mrs Bennet accuses Fitzwilliam Darcy of compromising her daughter, that is exactly the outcome. Trapped in a seemingly loveless marriage and far from home, she grows suspicious of her new husband's heart and further, suspects he is hiding a great secret. Is there even a chance at love given the happenstance of their hasty marriage?

www.ingramcontent.com/pod-product-compliance
Lightning Source LLC
Chambersburg PA
CBHW011507170626
46812CB00009B/3012

* 9 7 8 1 9 5 1 0 3 3 9 9 6 *